Children of Hope

Children of Hope

Michael C. Fine

For my children, who light up my life with a brilliance that still boggles my mind.

Many thanks to my early readers, Fern, Zach, Vicki, Wendy, Lindsay, Jeremy, Lisa, and Vivien. Your feedback made the book far better than it would have been without your help. Thank you to my editor, Kurt Lipschutz, who helped flesh out my characters and added a healthy dose of humanity and artistry.

Writing can be a solitary slog and I can't thank Vivien and Jeremy enough for being "creative buddies" over the past few years. Thank you, too, to Joan and Adam, both of whom provided encouragement at the very early stages of this effort. I will never be able to fully express my gratitude for your warmth and generosity.

"The decision whether or not to bear a child is central to a woman's life, to her well-being and dignity. It is a decision she must make for herself.

When Government controls that decision for her, she is being treated as less than a fully adult human responsible for her own choices."

— *Ruth Bader Ginsburg*

Thanks for reading *Children of Hope*. I sincerely hope you enjoy reading it. Even more, I hope this book makes you think and—if at all possible—become active in defending women's reproductive rights, which remain under fierce attack by religious extremists, misogynists, control freaks, and misguided souls across the country.

And now, on to the show...

Foreword

In the United States, there is a reported rape every 6.2 minutes. One in five women will be raped in her lifetime.

Between 1815 and 1861, a complete structure of church and Christian faith-based organizations made up what came to be called the Benevolent Empire, an interlocking network of missionary and supporting organizations devoted to Christianizing America and the world.

Ten states— Arkansas, Idaho, Kentucky, Louisiana, Mississippi, North Dakota, Missouri, Tennessee, South Dakota, and Utah—have "trigger laws," statutes that will automatically ban all abortion if *Roe v. Wade* is overturned.

Chapter One

Thursday, July 4
Louisiana State Fair
Baton Rouge, Louisiana

Hope Hunter

It was supposed to have been such a nice day.

Angel and I finished our chores around the farm, showered, and put on our nicest dresses. I drove down the 19 and the 110 to Baton Rouge. I made sure to stay under the speed limit, like I'd been doing for years, making sure not to draw attention to myself. Technically, while I had my driver's permit, I still didn't have my license. Of course, I'd been doing a lot of stuff I'm really not supposed to do since Mom left almost three years ago. So we stay off the radar, literally. And I've gotten pretty good at forging her signature when I need to. In case you're wondering, Dad's been gone since the day after Angel was born and I turned two. That was over fourteen years ago.

We got down to the fairgrounds in about forty-five minutes, by about five o'clock. The fiery orange sun was low in a cloudless sky. I parked the truck under a massive cow oak, hoping the shade would help keep Dad's old truck cool.

Angel looked so cute in my old lavender-colored sundress. She'd curled her long strawberry blonde hair so her wavy locks spilled over her shoulders, and put on a bit of lip gloss, too. At fourteen, she's already developed sizable breasts, which overflowed a bit out of the top of the dress. Even though I'm two years older, I'm still waiting for my chest to develop; maybe if I had 'em, I'd flaunt 'em too. I don't know. In any event, I didn't say anything. I wore my yellow church dress with little white stars all over it. My shoulder-length blonde hair hung straight, like always; I don't like to spend time curling it.

The fair was enormous. There were dozens of rides and all the popular carnival games: ring toss, dime pitch, balloon darts, and so many more. It looked like there were cotton candy and candy apple stands every ten feet. I smelled buttery popcorn as soon as we approached the ticket booth.

"This place is—" I started to say.

"Enormbo," Angel said, completing my thought.

"Jumbnormous," I replied. Maybe it was because we were born on the exact same day two years apart or maybe it's because we've been on our own together for so long, but we complete each other's thoughts most of the time. This was one of our favorite games.

"Monstrossal."

"Collostrous."

"Garping."

"Whopgantuan," I said after a beat.

By this time, I was laughing so hard I couldn't see through the tears in my eyes. Angel, too.

I'd brought enough money to pay for a pack of ride tickets for each of us, and we each brought a small amount of spending money. As soon as we had our tickets, Angel asked, "Can I get some cotton candy?" She pointed to the nearest stand, just a few feet away.

"Up to you. It's your money," I said. "You can get it if you want but you only have, what, ten dollars?" Even though she's been gone all this time, Mom instilled the discipline that we spend our money wisely. Well, at least I'd learned that lesson; Angel was still trying to.

"You're right," Angel said. She frowned, but only for a split second. Her radiant smile came right back, bracketed by her cute dimples. "Let's go on the Tilt-a-Whirl!" She grabbed my hand and tugged me toward the ride.

We only had to wait a few minutes before we got on. Angel couldn't stop smiling the entire time we were spinning. I love seeing her smile. We kept our hands up in the air the whole time.

As we were getting off the ride, an older lady wearing a light blue windbreaker a few feet in front of us dropped to the ground just outside the ride's exit gate. I rushed forward and knelt down near her head. A young boy, maybe ten years old, was next to her crying, saying "Grandma! Grandma!" over and over.

"Are you okay?" I asked.

"Yes, I think so." the woman said. She smiled weakly. She turned her head and said "I'm okay, sweetheart" to her grandson, as she patted his hand.

"Can you feel your fingers and your toes?" I asked. She nodded. "Any head or neck pain?" She shook her head. "Okay then, let's get you up. Nice and slow." People were just walking right by, the jerks.

I turned to the boy and asked, "What's your name?" He answered, tears streaming down his cheeks. "Okay, Zach. Will you help me get her up? You take that side." The kid was shaking, but I could see resolve in his bright blue eyes.

I held her right elbow and wrapped my left arm around her waist while her grandson held her left elbow. Slowly, we helped her to her feet.

"How do you feel?" I asked the woman again.

"I'm okay. Really I am. Thank you very much young lady," she said. To her grandson she said, "I think that ride was a bit too much for me, Zachary. Let's go get some lemonade and sit for a while, okay?"

Zachary looked up at me. Tears still filled his eyes, but none dripped down his cheeks now. Then he did something that I'll always remember: he reached his little hand out to shake mine and said, "Thank you very much for helping my grandma."

I crouched down so our eyes were at the same level and said, "You're welcome. Maybe it's a good idea if you let your grandmother sit out the next few rides. What do you say?"

He smiled, bobbed his head up and down, grabbed his grandmother's hand and the two walked toward a nearby picnic table. I could see him wiping his tears away with his free hand.

Angel crushed me in a big hug. "Wow. You are so amazing, Hope!" Angel said as she let go. "You know exactly what to do when people need help. You're amazing."

"Thanks sis. Lucky I had that nursing class last year," I said, deflecting her praise. I hugged my little sister back.

"Come on," she said. "Let's go on that roller coaster that goes upside down."

After a few rides, I looked at my phone to check the time. It was about ten minutes before 6:00, which was when the boys were supposed to meet us just inside the entrance. I told Angel that we should start heading back to meet them.

"What do you know about Todd's cousin?" Angel asked. Todd was a boy from our school. He was going to be a senior in high school in the fall like me, but, at seventeen, he was a year older because I skipped the third grade. He was really nice and was pretty much the only boy at school that didn't gross me out. Derek, his second cousin from Texas, was also seventeen. I'd made sure to tell Todd to tell Derek that Angel was only fourteen. Todd said that Derek was cool with that.

"Not much, really," I answered. "I know he plays football and basketball at his high school." I turned to face her directly and added, "Be careful, Angel. He's three years older than you and—I don't know—he seems like a punk to me."

Angel nodded but I could tell she didn't really hear me. I knew that she'd looked up Derek on social media and pretty much every time I saw her on her phone she was looking at the pictures he'd posted of himself throwing a pass, shooting a basket, or staring into the camera with smoldering eyes. That's how I'd formed my opinion of him... all the pictures he posted were of himself, without teammates or friends.

On our way back to the entrance, we spotted a young girl sitting alone at a card table with a sign that said KITTENS $10 and a large cardboard box full of kittens climbing all over each other. I suspected her "booth" wasn't sanctioned by the people who ran the fair. Angel, who loves animals—she wants to be a veterinarian—made a beeline to the table.

"Can I hold one?" Angel asked the girl. Angela's hands were almost in the box by the time the girl said yes. She pulled out a little grey guy with white spots on each of his paws. He purred as Angel stroked him. "Does he have a name?"

"Nope. You get to name him if you buy him," the girl said. "Only ten dollars." She looked around, as if on lookout for someone official who might come by and shut her down.

Angel looked at me with her big blue eyes as wide as they'll go.

"Maybe you should wait until later, until after we're done with the guys?" I suggested to Angel.

I was about to ask the girl how late she was going to be there when she said, "I'm just about to close up for the night." I couldn't tell if she was being honest or not.

Angel kept looking at me with her wide eyes. "What do you say, Hope?"

"It's your money," I said. "If you get the kitten, it means no cotton candy." "And," I quickly added, "you have to take care of him; I've got too many AP classes next year."

"I'll take him!" Angel squealed. She quickly handed her ten-dollar bill to the girl, who gave

Angel a small brown cardboard box in which to carry the kitty. Angel put the little guy into the box and stroked him. "Hello, Xander," Angel cooed to the kitten, whom she'd apparently already named after one of the iconic characters played by one of her favorite actors, Vin Diesel. She stroked and prattled to the kitten the entire walk back to meet the guys.

Todd and Derek were standing just inside the entrance when we walked up. Todd was as cute as ever. His blonde hair is a bit unruly. Shaggy even. He beamed a bright smile and came toward me to give me a hug and a quick kiss. We've kissed a few times, but nothing more than that. Maybe someday. Someday soon. He really is a sweet guy.

Derek waited for Angel to walk up to him before he finally said, "You must be Angel." I swear I saw his eyes travel up and down her body a half a dozen times before he greeted her. "I'm Todd's cousin from Houston, Derek." Before Angel could say anything, Derek moved in and hugged her tightly, and for a beat longer than appropriate. Angel almost dropped the box when she had to swing it to her hip so her new kitten wouldn't be crushed. She backed away, a bit flustered, and said, "Nice to meet you." I could see she was blushing.

The boys treated us to a few games of dime pitch, the squirt gun race game, and balloon darts. Derek won every time except for one time when I won a squirt gun race. I could tell he was fuming that he'd lost. What a competitive jerk. I was quickly confirming my initial opinion of the guy: I didn't like him one bit.

For a while, we just walked around the carnival, taking in the sights and sounds. Angel and Derek walked together in front of Todd and me. At one point, she rested her head on his shoulder and wrapped both of her arms around one of his. Later, he put his arm over her shoulder. I suppose that would have been fine except he made a point of wrapping it all the way over, so his hand was pretty much hovering over her chest.

"Hey Derek," I called out.

I'm pretty sure he heard me, but he didn't acknowledge me or turn around.

"Hey douchebag," I barked. "Watch it." Since our mother's been gone, I'm the closest thing to a mom Angel's got. I get pretty protective of her, I guess.

He must've known what I meant, because he moved his arm back to where his hand rested on Angel's shoulder. Todd shot me a look, but I shot him one back and he backed off, wordlessly.

After walking around for ten or fifteen minutes, we all went on the Tilt-a-Whirl! ride and then a rickety old wooden roller coaster that wasn't scary but jostled your insides. I found myself hoping young Zachary hadn't asked his grandmother to go on that ride.

We stopped for cokes as the sun was setting—Todd treated, which was nice—and then Todd looked at me and said, "Let's go on the Ferris Wheel." I looked over at Angel, who had her fingers intertwined with Derek and was giggling at something he'd whispered into her ear.

"Let's do it," I said. "Angel, Derek? You guys ready?"

Angel didn't take her eyes off of Derek when she replied, "You guys go on ahead."

I was reluctant, but it seemed like Angel liked Derek and I figured at least they were out in public.

I left the table with Todd and we walked toward the Ferris wheel in the distance. I glanced back toward Angel and Derek, but there were too many people between us and the table for me to see them.

Todd put his arm around my shoulder as we walked to the Ferris wheel. "Having a good time?" he asked. I liked that he cared. My answer was to pull him closer and give him a squeeze. We walked like this past the strongman game, where a middle-aged guy was sweating and panting while his girlfriend or wife stood waiting for him to finally give up, and the rope ladder, where five kids tipped over and fell off within moments of each other. I still have no idea how to win at that stupid game.

We boarded the Ferris Wheel and slowly rose as other passengers were loaded into the other cars after us. At some point, we got high enough where I could see the table where we'd stopped for cokes and I could see Angel and Derek still sitting there. It seemed like Derek was sitting way closer to Angel than before, but I really couldn't tell for sure from so far away and so high up.

Finally, everyone was loaded and the Ferris Wheel started to go around without stopping. Todd turned to me, grabbed my hands in his, and leaned in to kiss me. The motion of the ride and the sounds and lights of the carnival and Todd's warm, soft lips were dizzying.

We were locked in the most glorious kiss for two full cycles of the ride when I felt my phone buzz. Without breaking lip contact, I shifted my hips forward a bit, pulled my phone out of my back pocket, and looked at the message. It was from Angel, and it was just one word, if you could call it that:

Hwlp

As soon as my brain registered that Angel was in trouble, I pulled away from Todd and called out to get the attention of the kid running the ride. As we swept by the bottom of the ride, I yelled as loudly as I could, but the idiot had his face buried in his phone. I kept screaming as we rose, knowing I was wasting my breath. As we swept past the bottom of the ride a second time, I kept yelling, but the kid still didn't hear me. I needed to do something!

I had no idea how many more times the ride was going to go around, and I didn't really know if I'd be able to get the attention of the kid running the ride. I examined the structure of the ride and realized there were radial struts from each bucket to the center of the wheel. Todd was shocked when I stood up and jumped onto the strut for our bucket.

I scampered down the strut, keeping my arms wrapped tightly around the metal and using the small holes in the metal as toe holds. Eventually I got to the center of the wheel. By this time, a bunch of people had noticed me and at least one of them got the attention of the kid, who hit the emergency stop button. As the ride slowed, I climbed down the center post. Before the wheel stopped spinning, I'd already hit the ground and was running toward the table where we'd left Angel and Derek. They weren't there.

In a panic, I ran around in the pea soup of dusk looking everywhere, calling out her name. I tried not to think about what it might mean that she wasn't answering.

I bumped into a bunch of people and knocked over a few of them. I tried to stop and apologize each time, but eventually I just started yelling "sorry" each time as I frantically ran by, looking for my sister.

At last, I heard whimpering around the back of one of the tents along the edge of the fair. I slowed as I came around the corner and there she was, laying crumpled on the ground behind an air conditioning unit. Her hair was full of straw and her legs were covered in dirt. She was curled in the fetal position, crying softly. Her new kitten, Xander, mewed in his box next to her.

Suddenly, fireworks went off in the distance and the sky lit up with a burst of red, white, and blue. That's when I looked down and saw a pair of Angel's white cotton underwear lying nearby on the patchy grass and a small spot of blood seeping through the pleats of her lavender dress.

Chapter Two

By eight o'clock, the men had made their way to Senator Carrington's home along the Long Island Sound on Long Island. Even in an affluent area, Carrington's home was spectacular. The Egyptian Revival style mansion sat on a ten-acre property that faced the Sound and was surrounded on all other sides by thick foliage, making the home almost invisible to anyone who didn't know it existed. Carrington's grandfather had bought the property and built a modest home for his growing family. Carrington's father, a successful real estate developer, razed that house and replaced it with the current 12,000-square-foot monster sixty years earlier. Carrington didn't really like the fact that John Gotti, Jr. had a home in the area, but he liked the privacy of the village and of his grand home.

"All right gentlemen, take your seats," Senator Carrington said. He didn't have to say it twice; within moments, Porter Brooks and Julian Kingsley sat as directed.

Senator Royce Carrington, the senior Senator from Mississippi, was seventy-three but looked like he could be in his late fifties. He had short, impish silver hair and a bushy silver mustache. Despite his age, he was trim and fit. As a young man, he had been devastatingly handsome. Now, in his seventies, he still was. He spoke with a southern drawl that stayed on the charming side of the charming-bumpkin drawl line. He owned a modest ranch in Mississippi and made sure to be seen there a few times a year for the sake of his constituents. Not many would appreciate that their "down home" Senator actually owned a mansion in upstate New York.

Reverend Porter Brooks was a conservative activist and the pastor of Christ's Fellowship Church, a mega church in Tennessee with an average weekly attendance of over fifty thousand. He was three years younger than Carrington but looked his age. Where people would call Carrington's hair and mustache silver, they would call Brooks' hair and beard gray. The man, while not obese, was a good forty pounds overweight and had taken to wearing overalls because none of his belts fit anymore. He was too lazy to shop for new ones.

Associate Justice of the United States Supreme Court Julian Kingsley, at fifty-two, was two decades younger than the other men. Where Carrington's unruly silver hair gave him an air of playfulness, Kingsley's shaggy, unkempt brown hair just made him look messy. A lifetime of beer drinking had made his cheeks blotchy and had made him soft around the belly. His less than imposing physical stature belied a keen legal mind, however, and he had risen to his position on the highest court in the land, the reason Carrington had approached him a few months earlier.

The three men were in Carrington's richly appointed study, which was in the far northeast corner of the house. As private as the house was, Carrington had made a few modifications to the home after his father died. Obsessed with privacy, he had contractors replace the large bay windows on the north and east walls with walls that had no windows, and which were specially constructed out of three-foot-thick stone slabs. He also sound-proofed the interior walls so that the room was a soundproof fortress. Thankfully, he had the forethought to ensure the room had air conditioning, although it was late enough in the evening that he'd actually started a small fire in the study's fireplace.

Carrington sat, as always, in the Dragon Chair, the most expensive chair in the world, designed by Eileen Gray, first owned by Suzanne Talbot, and later sold to Yves Saint Laurent by Christie's auction house. Carrington had paid over thirty million dollars for the upholstered brown leather chair framed in sculptured, lacquered wood with two models of intertwined serpentine dragons. Brooks and Kingsley sat in luxurious brown leather chairs that paled in comparison. All three had cigars in hand or nearby.

A skilled orator, Carrington had been a Senator for most of his adult life. His professional experience and his family wealth made him well suited to the pomp and seriousness of the duty he had accepted many years earlier.

"Almighty God," he began, as all eleven men who had held his position had done before him, and precisely as he had been trained, "we bow before you, and recognize you as our great Savior. We lift our hearts in praise to you, and as your beloved children and your redeemed servants, we lay our lives before you in worship. We ask for your strength that we may be bold proclaimers of your Word. Amen."

"Amen," said the other two men in unison.

Reverend Brooks preferred the full verse of Luke 2:8-20, but he understood that here, in this group, they obeyed a different set of rituals. Judge Kingsley, despite attending church dutifully for decades, had no idea that the prayer was at all similar to a traditional Christian prayer; he rarely paid much attention during services.

Carrington stood solemnly, lit a match and used it to light one of the top corners of a thick one-inch square piece of cardstock with a single number on it. He held onto the opposite corner for as long as he could before gently tossing the card into the small fire frolicking in the fireplace. He walked over to his desk, opened his desk drawer, and removed another one-inch square piece of cardstock, this one blank. He lifted his Aurora Diamante fountain pen out of its holder and deftly wrote the number 2035 onto the card. After putting the pen back into its holder, he gently waved the card through the air, helping the ink dry. The card would be the only physical record of their meeting, as had been true for the previous 2034 consecutive monthly meetings of the ultra-secret Benevolent Overlords Society over the past 169 years.

Carrington set the small card down on his desk and walked to the small wet bar in the corner of the room. He lifted a bottle of champagne out of an ice bucket and turned to his colleagues.

"Nothing official today, friends," the Senator said. "This," he said, lifting the bottle solemnly, "is our first and only order of business."

Reverend Brooks, while a man of the cloth, was not against a little bubbly. He rose and got three champagne flutes from the bar, handing one to Kingsley and one to Carrington, who had popped the cork on the bottle. Carrington filled the three glasses and set the bottle down.

"To the sanctity of life," Carrington said, raising his glass.

"To the sanctity of life," Reverend Porter repeated.

"To winning," Julian Kingsley said.

The three men sipped their champagne, savoring their quiet victory: Earlier in the day, Julian Kingsley and four other Supreme Court justices had overturned *Roe v. Wade*, the landmark 1973 Supreme Court decision in which the Court ruled 7–2 that the right to privacy under the Due Process Clause of the 14th Amendment included a woman's decision to have an abortion. They had finally done it, in large part thanks to Kingsley's swing vote.

Kingsley got up and walked over to the fully stocked wet bar in the corner of the study. He set his champagne glass, still full, on the cherry wood bar and reached into the refrigerator for a Stella Artois. He popped the top off and chugged it down. After setting the empty bottle down, he reached in to grab a second beer and opened it, too.

Carrington shook his head in distaste but said nothing.

Reverend Brooks opened the wood-paneled armoire, grabbed the remote control, and turned on the TV. It was, as always, tuned to Fox News. Porter turned the sound up and the three men watched the celebratory mood on screen. The commentators could not hide their glee.

The men watched the celebration on Fox for a half an hour. Carrington and Reverend Brooks nursed their champagne. Kingsley repeatedly went to the bar to get more bottles of beer.

"Seriously, how many is that already?" Carrington finally asked.

"What's your problem?" Kingsley responded. He poked his finger at the Senator. He was already drunk.

"*My* problem? I'm not the one with the problem. *You're* the one with the problem, buddy boy. I heard that you had a drinking problem, but I had no idea it was this serious."

"Oh, lighten up, Royce. I delivered. I delivered big time, didn't I?" Kingsley slurred. Immediately realizing he'd overstepped, he added, "What I mean is, we did it. So cut me some slack. I think I deserve to celebrate. We all do."

Carrington was about to explain how much work he, personally, had put into selecting and orchestrating just the right case with just the right plaintiff with just the right law firm and lawyers when Reverend Brooks stepped in to calm the waters.

Reverend Brooks said, "I know! Let's watch the libs' reaction to the decision." He picked up the remote control and tuned to MSNBC, the liberal-leaning news station that none of the men could normally tolerate. He turned up the sound.

"Today's decision is a travesty," said one guest, a liberal pundit who was a frequent guest on many of the station's shows.

"This will go down in history with *Dred Scott, Plessy, Korematsu, Bush v. Gore,* and *Citizens United* as one of the worst decisions in the Court's history," said a constitutional scholar from an elite law school.

The host interrupted and announced that protests were swelling all over the country. Footage was shown of a spontaneous gathering of a half a million people walking across the Golden Gate Bridge in San Francisco, California.

As the three men watched, mocking the protestors marching in the streets across America, the Greenwich, Connecticut fireworks began exploding in the sky across the bay. The men couldn't see or hear the fireworks because of Carrington's remodeling, but they could feel reverberations from the explosions in the distance.

"Greenwich does a nice job with their fireworks," Carrington said to his guests when he realized what was happening. "Let's go outside and enjoy the show."

Carrington and Reverend Brooks took their champagne flutes and headed out of the study, through the sliding French doors in the kitchen, and to the back yard. Kingsley quickly went to the refrigerator, grabbed two more beers, opened them both, and followed after the others.

The three men stood, heads raised, enjoying the fireworks in the sky to the north. As bursts of sparkles and light filled the sky and deep thuds boomed, celebrating America's freedom, millions of women now no longer had the freedom to control their own bodies.

Chapter Three

4:30 a.m. Friday, July 5 AFT
(8:00 p.m., Thursday, July 4 EDT)
Undisclosed location near the village of Deshu
Less than 100 miles from Pakistan border
Helmand Province, Afghanistan

About the time fireworks shows were wowing crowds along the east coast of the United States, Second Lieutenant Diamond sat on his pack and gazed out into the Afghan desert. The sun would be up in less than an hour, and he'd come to enjoy a few minutes of cool, and calm, before the start of another hundred-plus degree summer day—and the chaos it could easily bring. Behind him were his platoon sergeant and three squads totalling twenty-four men. The youngest, an Indian kid named Patel, was just barely eighteen. The oldest was only twenty-five. Such babies. At forty-five, Diamond was the oldest second lieutenant in the Army's history, having been commissioned just weeks before his thirty-sixth birthday, when he would have officially been too old for the position. He'd been on the front lines leading platoons of baby-faced soldiers in Afghanistan or Iraq for the past nine and a half years. He loved his country, the army, his men, and the good work they did every day.

"Hey L.T.," Private First Class Lancaster said as he walked up behind Diamond. Lancaster was a pain in Diamond's ass, always joking and laughing, but the man was also preternaturally gifted when it came to explosives work.

"Mornin'."

"What's the plan for today?" Lancaster asked. Not for the first time, Diamond found himself thinking that Lancaster would some day take his spot, or one even higher up the chain of command. The man was smart, dedicated, and oozed charisma.

"Air support is due at oh six hundred," Diamond said. His internal clock was so tuned he didn't have to look at his watch to know that this was less than ninety minutes away. "From there, it's a shit show. First to Bagram to pick up some CIA tool, then back to FOB Lagman, which reopened recently, then to KAF." KAF was the airport in Kandahar. The trip would take most of the day and take them across the country and nearly back. "HVT should be in Washington by early Saturday morning, local time. We done good here." The HVT—or High Value Target—was the twenty-year-old son of Mullah Akhtar Mansour, former leader of the Taliban, who himself was now a rising star in the Sunni Islamic fundamentalist political movement.

"Holy backtrack, Batman," Lancaster said, his disdain for the military's planning capabilities obvious. "Why don't they just fly the CIA guy to the airport?"

"Tell me about it. On second thought, don't. Go ahead and get everyone up and ready. That bird is not going to wait for us."

"You got it, L.T.," Lancaster said before he turned to walk back to the sandy trench where most of the guys were sleeping.

An hour before their expected pickup time, his men were packed and relaxed. Most were downing an MRE or sitting around and chatting. Lieutenant Diamond unhooked his radio and was about to radio command when his field artillery firefinder radar operator, who manned the platoon's AN/TPQ-36 counter artillery radar Firefinder Weapon Locating System, came rushing up.

"L.T.! We've got company. Approximately a hundred enemy combatants from the north and another forty from the west. All headed straight here. About five klicks out."

Diamond didn't have to say anything to the men, all of whom had seen the radar operator running to talk to their lieutenant. The squad leaders had their men ready and on alert within seconds.

Lieutenant Diamond held the radio's button down with his meaty thumb. "Blue Moon, this is Blue Six. We have inbound hostiles from the north and west of our position. Approximately a hundred and forty persons. They are five klicks out, which puts them here right about the time our bird is set to arrive. How copy?"

After a several second delay, a reluctant voice came over the radio. "Blue Six, this is Blue Moon. Copy. But, uh, we have a problem... Apparently little Mansour Junior made a deal with the local ISIS leadership before you took him into custody.

He told them that he'll give up control of Helmand Province to them if they come to his rescue."

"So? Send air support right now. Or get us the *fuck* outta here in the next thirty minutes."

"Well, uh, see... that's part of the problem. Brass says our peace deal with Russia is at risk if we unseat Mansour Junior. We already killed his father years ago. Bottom line is that your op is over, kaput."

Diamond had been in the service long enough to control his anger at the situation. It wasn't the first time the left hand didn't know what the right hand was doing, or that they put good men at risk to achieve a mission only to abort the mission later.

The desert wind whipped what felt like a million miniature bullets of sand into Diamond's face.

"Okay, fine. Whatever," he said as he wiped his eyes. "We'll cut junior loose. But I've got twenty-five men here that need air support, or exfil, and they need it right now." He glanced at the radar operator's screen and saw that the men approaching were now no more than twenty minutes from their position.

"Blue Six, I wish I had better news for you, but I don't. My recommendation is that you make your way southeast through Pakistan to India."

"Listen up, fellas," Diamond said to his men. "We are in deep shit. No air support is en route. I repeat, no air support is en route. Worse, our ride was cancelled. We're on our own. Sixty seconds until we move out. South, then east."

Lieutenant Diamond's men might have lived through the day if it weren't for a pair of Russian Sukhoi Su-34s, which each dropped a KAB-500S-E guided bomb on their position. The Taliban had air support that day, not the United States Army.

When the smoke cleared, all but Lieutenant Diamond, Private First Class Lancaster, and Private Patel were dead. Diamond had lacerations on his face and shrapnel embedded in his right pectoral muscle. Lancaster had a huge piece of metal in his left leg, lucky it had missed his femoral artery. Patel was unconscious. Mansour's son lay dead, face down on the ground. Diamond walked over to where his body lay and shot him twice in the back of what remained of his head.

Acting on years of military training, Diamond grabbed a first aid kit and tended to Lancaster. After telling the man to bite down on the strap of his helmet, Diamond ripped the metal shard from Lancaster's leg and immediately applied pressure, doused the wound in hydrogen peroxide, and wrapped the man's leg in a tight bandage. He knew the hydrogen peroxide would actually delay healing, but he didn't have a ready source of clean running water. Diamond tried to rouse Patel, but the man did not stir.

Checking his watch, Diamond realized the approaching Taliban forces were probably only a few minutes out. He didn't hesitate, and after hoisting Patel over his left shoulder and helping Lancaster to his feet, he had Lancaster lay over his right shoulder. He made his way south toward the Pakistan border.

Twenty-three days later, the men made their way into India and to the town of Jaisalmer. Nicknamed "the Golden City," Jaisalmer was a city in the northwest corner of the Indian state of Rajasthan. The city, in the heart of the Thar Desert, with

summer temperatures regularly over 110 degrees
Fahrenheit, stands on a ridge of yellow sandstone
and is home of the impressive, ancient Jaisalmer
Fort. To get there, they'd traveled over 1,400 klicks,
or almost 900 miles, mostly on foot.

The men would never speak of the twenty miles
Diamond carried his mates through the Afghan
desert and away from the Taliban threat, but a
bond was formed that day. Lancaster and Patel
would forever be indebted to their lieutenant and
friend, and the three men would forever hold a
grudge against the United States government.

Chapter Four

Friday, February 14
East Louisiana State Hospital
Jackson, Louisiana

Thirty-two weeks later

Three men in their mid-twenties stood with their faces pressed to the glass window of the nursery, where their newborn children—two sons and a daughter—were swaddled tightly in baby blankets. Each baby had a tiny little knit cap on its head. Two were dozing quietly. One, with a headful of hair peeking out from his cap, was twitching and moving about. The strangers shook hands and introduced themselves; today was a day full of peace and love and joy, to be shared even with complete strangers. They were all fathers now, the most important and most fulfilling role a man can play.

Down the hall, a husband gently lowered himself into his wife's bed, lying on his side and kissing her forehead and temple and gently rubbing her now-deflated belly. Their daughter lay sleeping nearby after two hours breastfeeding atop her mother's stomach.

Another woman slept after having a Cesarean. Her son was healthy; she would be again soon. Her husband sat on the floor of the bathroom in the birthing suite and wept from happiness and the release of the worry he'd been feeling for weeks.

Hope Hunter

Angel found out she was pregnant six weeks after the fair, on Friday, August sixteenth. I'll never forget that date. Her period was late, but she insisted on waiting two full weeks, hoping it would come. It didn't. She didn't even want to trust the at-home pregnancy test, so I drove her to the health clinic in Baton Rouge, where the doctor confirmed Angel's predicament. Angel was so distraught she stayed curled up in bed the entire weekend, her shades drawn, her lights out, her room dark and gloomy. She didn't eat or bathe until I finally shoved her into the shower Monday morning and forced her to eat a bowl of Cream of Wheat.

I spent that weekend researching Angel's options. Before those jackasses overturned *Roe*, she could have gotten an abortion, despite our horribly restrictive state laws. But Louisiana's trigger law fired when *Roe* was overturned and so now state law completely prohibits abortions, period. Even in the case of rape. Even when the rape victim is just fourteen years old.

Barbaric.

I looked online and saw that Mississippi also had a trigger law, like Louisiana, so even if I could afford the gas, which I couldn't, we couldn't get her one there. Ditto for Arkansas. Texas was a possibility, but it's even farther away—it's over one hundred and fifty miles to Beaumont— and, oh so conveniently, Texas law insists on two trips to an abortion provider. I was barely able to put food on our table and pay for enough gas to get us to school and back during the school year. And after I'd read some horrific articles about how badly botched many illegal abortions are, I simply refused to let Angel get an illegal abortion in some back alley somewhere.

After Angel was at least human-looking and out of her cave, I drove to the high school and withdrew. I got information on how to arrange to get my G.E.D. since I knew Angel would need me around over the coming months and especially for today, whenever today came. I enrolled in the local community college last fall. Luckily, I don't have any classes on Fridays this semester, so I won't have to miss class to help her through this abomination. I am so angry that a small group of old men took away her ability to decide for herself, to control her own reproductive choices.

I sat by Angel's hospital bed all day. We'd checked in around 8:00 a.m. when she first said her contractions were getting stronger and it was now just before midnight. The room was nice, with a couch and oversized faux-leather chair in the corner and bright flowers painted on the walls. Most of the time, we just talked about everything and nothing. Sometimes she dozed off.

When we first got situated in the room, Angel was in a talkative mood. I think she felt the need to talk about things now that her ordeal was about to be over.

"Did I ever tell you what happened at the winter dance at school?" Angel asked. The high school insists on holding this schoolwide rite of passage every December, despite the discomfort it causes to ninety-eight percent of students, whose attendance is mandatory and who stand—embarrassed, bored, or both—along the walls of the gymnasium until they're allowed to go home.

"No. What happened?" My blood pressure rose and my mind flashed to an image of me storming the high school and kicking the asses of whomever hurt my sister.

"Well, you know how those dances are. I was just hanging out in the bleachers and having a cup of punch, talking with Cindy and Tina, when a bunch of guys came over to where we were sitting." Her eyes started to well up, but she pushed through. "I was showing quite a bit by then. Some senior leered at me and said something about how, since I clearly put out, maybe he'd break his rule and date me even though I'm just a freshman. Then all his buddies piled on. Did I want to go out back? Or behind the bleachers? A couple of guys showed me that they had condoms. It was gross."

"Oh, Angel, I am so sorry."

"They were so mean. They called me 'slut' and 'whore' and made lewd gestures."

"Did they... touch you? Who was it? I can go to the school and get them suspended or expelled. Or—"

"No, luckily one of the teachers came over and broke things up. She could see I was upset, so she sat with me for a bit. I think she teaches A.P. Gov."

"Mrs. Miller?" I asked, pretty sure it was her. She was a great teacher and a really nice lady.

"Yeah, that's right. She was so kind to me. I made her a friendship bracelet, remember?"

"I do," I said. Angel had put so much work into it.

"Listen, Hope, I need you to promise me that you'll become a doctor or a researcher or something. You have to promise me that you'll try to help other girls like me. It's been so horrible. You have no idea. It's so unfair that I've had to live through this. I didn't do anything wrong! You've always been the smart one. I need you to promise me that you'll figure out a way so other girls don't have to go through what I went through, what I'm going through."

I had no idea what Angel expected of me and no idea what anyone could do, let alone me, but I promised. And I meant it.

Over lunch—a small piece of poached salmon for Angel and a tuna fish sandwich from the cafeteria for me—we talked about Mom, something we rarely did.

"Do you forgive her for leaving?" Angel asked at one point. Angel, who wasn't even twelve years old at the time, was furious with our mother when she left, but she says that she's forgiven her.

"I don't know," I said. "I'm not very good at forgiveness." I took a sip of my Diet Coke. "But I understand why she left, I think."

She was about to get angry with me just for saying that, so I said, "You know, Mom didn't date at all after Dad left. I mean, I don't think she did. She certainly never had anyone over, at least when we were around. I think she was really, really lonely. So when she met Norberto, it changed her life. She was happy for the first time in a really long time."

Angel took a bit of her salmon. For hospital food, it looked pretty good. "Do you think they would have gotten married?" she asked.

"I don't know. They loved each other, that's for sure, but Dad leaving kinda turned her off from marriage. We'll never know because President Spencer started his so-called 'Move to National Greatness' nonsense. I was only thirteen, I think, and I didn't watch the news then like I do now, but Spencer talked openly about ethnically cleansing the United States. Of course, he didn't use those words, but his intentions were clear. He constantly repeated his campaign promise to purge every illegal alien from the country if he got elected."

"And then he got elected," Angel said, heartache and resignation evident in her voice.

"Norberto was deported six months later, remember?" I finished off my sandwich and took another swig of my soda. "Mom loved him and she loved us, but she felt so strongly about how wrong Spencer was that she decided she had to do something about it, that she had to fight him and his hateful policies."

"So when Spencer was elected—"

"She left the very next day," I said. She'd always been into politics and I guess this was the straw that led her camel to Washington. "I was angry and sad back then, too, just like you, but Mom said something to me the day she left that I'll never forget. She said, 'Anyone not outraged is not paying attention. You need to start paying attention.' So I started watching the news every night, like she used to. Then I started reading news blogs and stuff like that. I don't understand everything, but I think I understand what she meant, and I think she was right. She got her job in Washington just three days after arriving there, did you know that? She wants to make a difference, and I've come to respect that."

"But why isn't she here, now? I mean, I'm only fourteen years old!" Angel was raising her voice now.

I gently smoothed her hair with my hand. "I don't like it any more than you do. But when she came last summer, she made it pretty clear she wasn't going to be able to come back out, that she could only take a limited amount of time away from work." I hated my mother for not being here to help us through this. Angel sure could use the help. Hell, so could I.

We paused our conversation when the nurse came in to take Angel's vital signs and another woman came in to clear her lunch dishes. I think we were both happy for the interruption.

At one point, the conversation turned to Derek.

"I can't believe they didn't believe me," Angel said, her voice quivering. "I said 'no.' So many times."

It was a classic "he said, she said" case; her word against his. He claimed that she flirted with him, kissed him, and let him touch her. That she wanted it to happen. His lawyer made a big deal out of the fact that her dress was so revealing. The jury, mostly antediluvian fossils, mostly men, didn't seem to understand that Angel's protestations needn't have started from the very beginning, that she was allowed to decide to say "no" at any point. Derek had walked, the fucker. Thankfully, Todd's family moved out of the area; I think they realized Angel and I would not be able to take seeing Todd around school. Todd's dad apologized, tears and snot flowing freely down his face, before getting in his car and driving his family and packed Ford F-250 truck out of town. Todd sat crying in the back seat, his fingertips pressed to the window.

"I don't think I'll ever forget his hand over my mouth," Angel whispered. Tears slid down her cheeks. "He was so strong. Then... It hurt so much. And then it was over, just like that. He just zipped up his pants and walked away, leaving me there. The whole thing took less than a minute and now here I am, forced to give birth to a baby that's part monster."

I smoothed her hair with my hand again to calm her. "Shh," I whispered repeatedly until she finally drifted off to sleep.

At midnight, the overnight labor and delivery nurse, a sweet heavyset woman with oversized scarlet glasses, declared that Angel wasn't producing enough oxytocin, perhaps because she was so young. She administered Pitocin and Angel went into labor almost immediately. Angel was in so much pain, but the nurse assured me that everything was fine. She paged the doctor so he could deliver the baby.

Angel crushed my hand in hers every time she had a contraction. Less than forty-five minutes later, she gave birth to a baby girl, Isabelle, who was technically Angel's daughter and my niece despite the fact that Angel was immediately giving the baby up for adoption. I recommended that she not give the baby a name, but she'd insisted. "She needs a beautiful name," she'd said.

As my hand recovered, the nurse administered the Apgar test to the baby. Within just a minute or two, I could tell something was wrong by the way the nurse and doctor whispered with seriousness in their tones.

"What's wrong?" I asked.

"Isabelle's Apgar score is low," the nurse said. "We're going to need to monitor—"

The doctor cut in, "Her skin is too pale and she's not breathing regularly. Her pulse rate is way too low." Before I could say anything, she added, "Stay here with your sister. We have to resuscitate the baby and get her into surgery." The doctor and nurse rushed out of the room with the baby.

"What? What's happening, Hope?" Angel said, barely coherent.

"I don't know, Angel. There's something wrong with the baby and they're going to help her. Right now, all you need to do is rest."

I ran my hand over Angel's forehead and the top of her head to soothe her. It took a while, but she eventually dozed off. I must have too because the next thing I knew I opened my eyes and Angel was shaking uncontrollably.

"Angel! Angel!" I screamed. Her eyes were wide open but she seemed to be staring out into nothingness; I couldn't get her attention. She started to shriek.

"Help! Doctor!" I yelled toward the door. "Something's wrong! Somebody help my sister!"

Angel was holding the right side of her stomach and screaming. Her hair was matted down from sweat and she looked so uncomfortable. Then she leaned away from me and vomited over the side of the bed. Finally a different nurse came in. A moment later a different doctor followed her into the room.

"Her blood pressure is through the roof," the doctor said after glancing at Angel's vitals. "Administer a quarter mic of sodium nitroprusside."

I sat and watched as the doctor and nurses tried to save Angel. I was terrified, but also mesmerized by their competence and composure. Less than an hour later I heard her heart monitor emit a constant high-pitched tone. My little sister was dead.

Later, the doctor came back and told me that Angel died from a particularly bad case of eclampsia, something that was extraordinarily rare. My diagnosis was simpler: My sister died because she was raped and then forced to give birth to a child while still just a child herself. Tears streamed from my cheeks. I wanted to scream but somehow I was unable.

As if to cheer me up, the doctor told me that despite complications from some kind of congenital malformation, baby Isabelle would survive.

I'm not sure how or when I got there, but I sat on the floor in the corner of the hospital room. I had my hands on the top of my head and my head between my knees, rocking. Tears dripped freely from my cheeks.

"Poor girls," I heard one nurse say to another. They looked to be cleaning up the table where the doctor first tried to help Isabelle.

"That horrible court ruling last summer is ruining so many young girl's lives. Children should be born of hope, not despair."

"These men don't seem to care at all," the first nurse replied. "Can you imagine how different it would be if men could get pregnant?"

"Ha! Either mankind would end because men are pussies and wouldn't be able to take it, or every anti-birth control and anti-abortion law would be overturned in a heartbeat."

"Amen, sister."

I rocked in the corner, in my own little world, a world that had just shrunk considerably. I looked over and saw Angel's overnight bag under a new, empty bed that had been wheeled into the room at some point after they transported Angel's body to the morgue. Peeking out the top of the bag was Xander, Angel's kitten. It looked like I was going to have to take care of him after all.

Chapter Five

Saturday, September 8
Hope's Apartment
Redwood City, California

Two years, seven months later

Just a block off busy El Camino Real, a boulevard that ran along the eastern side of the San Francisco peninsula, Hope's five-hundred square foot, one-bedroom apartment in a sketchy part of Redwood City was walking distance to a neighborhood grocery store, a Mexican food restaurant that reeked of lard, and an adult book store. She'd found the place on her very first full day in the Bay Area, motivated by a restless night in an awful motel up the street, and while she wished the run-down, three-story building was in a better part of town, she knew she needed to pinch her pennies. Now, after just two weeks and having to buy mountains of textbooks and supplies for her first year at Stanford Medical School, Hope realized that even with her scholarship and the research grant money she received from working at the neonatal research lab at the hospital, she'd need extra income.

While Hope finished getting dressed, her phone buzzed, and she saw that it was a message from the private detective she'd hired the day she received her scholarship. She'd made a promise to herself that she'd eat tuna fish for dinner every day if necessary in order to afford the man's services. The detective told her that his first order of business would be to figure out Derek's last name—Hope didn't know it—and that after that he could go about trying to find him. She wasn't even sure what she would do once she found Derek, but she felt compelled to confront him.

Now she knew his last name: Johnson. Derek Johnson. Rapist. Ruiner of lives.

Hope grabbed a light jacket, her keys, and the small slip of paper on which she'd written the addresses of some local businesses that were hiring. Before heading out the door, she walked over to her bookshelf in the corner of the living room.

"I'm going to find him, sis. I promise," she said to the urn that held Angel's remains. She kissed her fingertips and pressed them to the urn. "Oh, and wish me luck today," she said waving the piece of paper. "I need a j-o-b. Bad." She headed out the door.

A few minutes later, Hope parked in the small asphalt lot behind the Pancake Shack restaurant, which sat at the corner of El Camino Real and California Avenue in midtown Palo Alto, California. She'd seen the place while exploring the area a few mornings earlier, noticing that the line at the front door snaked around the corner of the building.

Now, at 5:30 a.m., the restaurant was a half an hour from opening; she figured it was a good time to apply for a job, before the crowds came and before she was due at the research lab.

She walked up to the entrance and pushed through the door. Bells above the door chimed.

"Hello? Anyone here?" Hope called out.

The restaurant was well-lit but quiet. After a moment, an attractive man in his late forties came out from the kitchen. He had short-cropped white hair on the sides and back of his head, a white beard and mustache, and a mischievous twinkle in his dark brown eyes. He wore jeans and a loose-fitting Stanford t-shirt, and had a makeshift bandage on his forearm.

"May I help you?" the man asked.

"I saw the Help Wanted sign in the window. I'd like to apply."

"You live in the area?"

"Redwood City, just a few miles up the road. I'm a med school student at Stanford."

"Congratulations. Not an easy school to get into."

"I work hard."

"And you have enough time for work?" He'd seen his share of students bail once their course load grew heavy. Still, he'd rather have to deal with turnover of smart, motivated students than to hire reliable idiots.

"Yes. I don't sleep much and I'm a hard worker. I also work at the Department of Pediatrics research lab fifteen or twenty hours a week, but if I say I'll be here, I'll be here."

The man crossed to the entrance of the restaurant, where Hope was still standing, and reached out his hand. "Name's Charlie."

"Pleased to meet you Charlie. I'm Hope. Hope Hunter." As she introduced herself, Hope motioned to the now-bloody bandage on Charlie's right forearm. "You okay?" she asked. "That looks pretty bad."

"Fine, fine," Charlie lied. In fact, he was in a good deal of pain and had been trying to clean out and tend to his wound when Hope had come through the door.

"Do you have any clean bandages? Maybe some antibacterial cream?" Hope asked. "I can help clean your wound and wrap it better for you."

Charlie assented and led Hope to the large industrial sink in the kitchen. Hope noticed that the entire kitchen was spotless, every surface practically shining. A large, mostly-used tube of Neosporin sat next to the sink.

Nodding over to the meat slicer on the counter and then looking down at his wounded arm, Charlie said, "Careful with that thing."

Charlie stood at the sink and let Hope unwrap his homemade bandage. As she ran lukewarm water over his injury, she furrowed her brow in concentration, not saying anything. She carefully ran soapy water over what she could now see were three deep gashes along his right ulna. Once the wounds were clean, she applied a generous layer of ointment and deftly wrapped his forearm tightly in a bandage.

"You should probably go to the hospital, Charlie. You likely need stitches in at least two of those lacerations."

"Okay, thanks. I'll think about it," Charlie said. Hope could tell from the tone of his voice and from his posture, this man was not going to go to the hospital.

"Well, at least clean your arm and apply antibacterial cream a few times a day."

Charlie smiled. "I will. Promise." He led her back out into the main area of the restaurant. "We're open Tuesday through Saturday, 6:00 a.m. to 10:00 p.m. Most of our customers are here from opening to about noon. I can probably give you ten hours a week. Does that work for you?"

Hope reached out her hand and shook Charlie's. "Definitely."

Charlie went behind the cash register and came back with a job application. "Fill this out. Bring it back with a W-4 on Tuesday, okay?"

"Consider it done."

"Well then," Charlie said, "get on outta here and enjoy your Saturday, kiddo. Unless you want to work right now?"

Hope had to be at the lab in ten minutes, so she said, "See you Tuesday morning. 5:30?"

"See you then. Oh, and Hope, thanks for the medical attention. Most appreciated." He lifted his arm in a kind of salute.

Chapter Six

Monday, September 10 (two days later)
Parking lot near the Indiana Department of Administration
Indianapolis, Indiana

In the three plus years that Diamond, Lancaster, and Patel had acted as a small band of avenging angels, it never ceased to amaze them how people figured out how to contact them and request their help. It hadn't been intentional, and it started slowly, but over time the men realized helping the powerless was their calling.

A few weeks earlier, they were approached by a man, Tyson Nathanson, who years earlier had sold three hundred dollars worth of heroin to undercover police here in Indianapolis, as a way to raise money to support his own drug habit. It was his third such offense and Nathanson was arrested and eventually sentenced to six months of home confinement and two years of probation, and assessed $1,300 in court costs and fees. The state of Indiana then seized his $48,000 Range Rover, which he'd purchased just months earlier, through civil forfeiture.

After the incident, the man had gotten clean and was trying to turn his life around. It seemed wrong to him that the government could seize his $48,000 car for a minor drug offense. After all, his lawyer had told him that the maximum criminal fine he faced at the time was only ten thousand dollars. He filed a lawsuit against the state of Indiana, saying that the state's seizure of his car was unconstitutional under the Excessive Fines Clause of the Eighth Amendment.

The ACLU funded the case. Both the trial court and an appeals court held for Nathanson, but the Indiana Supreme Court ruled that the U.S. Supreme Court had never explicitly held that this clause of this amendment applied to the states, only to the federal government. Nathanson appealed and the case went to the U.S. Supreme Court. When the case was finally heard, Nathanson lost, 5–4. Newly appointed Associate Justice Julian Kingsley, citing *Barron v. Baltimore* from 1833, wrote the opinion for the Court, overturning the many cases where the Court had since incorporated provisions of the Bill of Rights against state governments through the Due Process Clause of the Fourteenth Amendment. Nathanson was pissed, and when he saw that the State was going to auction off his Range Rover, he couldn't take the injustice of it all. Through a friend of a friend, Nathanson reached out to Diamond, asking if there was something Diamond and his team could do to help.

Now, a few minutes before nine in the morning, they were sitting in a rented white Ford Taurus in the parking lot across from the Indiana Department of Administration building on Washington Street in Indianapolis. They'd had a hearty breakfast of pancakes and eggs at a nearby diner, savoring a few cups of some of the best coffee they'd ever had, and were ready for the day's activities. The hard work had been accomplished the night before.

"New watch?" Lancaster asked Patel. He'd noticed yet another new watch on his friend's wrist, this one a garrish bright orange one, on which a cat's front paws and tail kept time.

"Like it?"

Lancaster shook his head and chuckled. Ever since they'd returned from Afghanistan, Patel seemed hell bent on being the poster child for American consumerism. "It's, uh, unique, that's for sure."

Diamond smiled in the driver's seat. He checked his own watch, turned to Lancaster and Patel and said, "We're all set, right?"

Lancaster appreciated the tight ship run by the Indiana Department of Administration, or at least that of their online auction operation. The auction website showed the precise times at which each item was to go up for its five-minute-long auction, and the site showed that Nathanson's Range Rover was scheduled to go up for auction as the third auction of the morning, at 9:10 a.m.

"All set," Lancaster said confidently. He'd been less than impressed with the organization's I.T. security practices.

At exactly 9:10:00.00 a.m., the small piece of software Patel had loaded onto the server computer sitting in a hot, dusty closet on the second floor of the building did its thing and submitted a bid from Tyson Nathanson for exactly one dollar.

Immediately after that, at 9:10:00.01, the infinitesimally tiny bit of explosives Lancaster had wired to the computer exploded, critically damaging the computer's motherboard. The auction site went down immediately.

At 9:15 a.m., Diamond turned to Nathanson, who was sitting in the passenger seat, and nodded toward the building.

"All set. You should be able to claim your truck now." He handed a crisp one dollar bill to the man and added, "Here you go."

"I can't thank you enough," Nathanson said.

"No need," Lancaster said from the back seat. "This one was fun."

As Tyson Nathanson walked toward the building to reclaim his truck, Diamond waited for Lancaster to hop in the front seat and then drove off. He had to be at work in California first thing in the morning.

Chapter Seven

Sitting in his royal throne, which, truth be told, was how he thought of his Dragon Chair, and smoking a custom King of Denmark cigar, Royce Carrington was in a reflective mood. His father had made a heap of money in the real estate business and he, personally, had turned that heap into ten heaps through shrewd investments across the globe. At seventy-six, it was time to give back a little, he decided. With no wife, no children, and no close family members, the decision was easy: he would pour some of his wealth into Christian charities and other organizations that spread Christianity and Christian values. He'd focus on America, unlike several recent high-profile philanthropists who gave their attention to the far corners of the world.

At exactly 8:00 p.m., his phone rang. His money manager, as scheduled.

"Good evening, Senator Carrington," the man said. "Your secretary asked me to call you? Is there a problem with your portfolio? I know last month's returns—"

"Relax. This isn't about my investments, at least not directly. Although I will say that I am disappointed in how poorly you've done over the past few months." He looked out the french doors from his kitchen table. "No, I am calling for a different reason. I'd like to set up a charitable foundation."

The money manager's stress receded. He'd never been comfortable with how much risk Carrington wanted him to take with his investments. The last few months were some of the handful where those risks were coming back to bite Carrington, to the tune of an eight percent drop in the man's fortunes.

"Okay, sure. What did you have in mind?"

"I'd like to start with a hundred million. Depending on results, I can do more."

"That's very generous, Senator."

Carrington didn't think of it as generosity, really, just promoting the Christian worldview he knew in his heart to be critical to helping the country.

Realizing that the Senator wasn't going to reply, the money manager continued. "It'll take a few days to settle your accounts and a few months for a 501(c)(3) to be set up. With the holidays coming up, it's possible it might be early next year by the time you're all set."

"Fine," Carrington said, annoyed. Why did he have to go through so many hoops? It was his money he wanted to give away, after all.

"What most donors do," the man went on, "is give approximately four or five percent of their funds each year. That way, with nominal returns on your endowment, your foundation can continue indefinitely and you can keep giving each year while keeping your fund balance intact. I can arrange for you to speak at a few of the various philanthropy conferences each year, introduce you to Bill and Melinda, the Vanderbilts, and other big-name givers, that sort of thing."

"You misunderstand. I would like to grant this money over the next year or two."

"I strongly advise you against that, Senator."

Carrington was peeved. "I'm not in this for prestige or to hobnob with the rich and famous." As much as he appreciated the man looking out for his money, he was not one who tolerated anything short of obedience. "I intend to make an impact, quickly."

"Certainly," the man said, backing off. "I can take care of everything. There will be some paperwork you'll have to sign. Do you want me to send it to your office in D.C. or to your home?"

"Here," Carrington said. This was his personal fortune he was giving away; it had nothing to do with Washington.

"Okay, I'll get to work on this first thing tomorrow morning."

"Please see that you do," Carrington said before hanging up.

Chapter Eight

Monday, November 6
Division of Neonatal and Developmental Medicine, Department of Pediatrics
NICHD Neonatal Research Network Laboratory
Stanford, California

Six years, two months later
The day before the Presidential election

Hope arrived at the lab by 5:00 a.m., as she always did on days when she had rounds in the main hospital at 9:00. At twenty-five, Hope was now in her third year of residency at Stanford University Medical School. She was at least three years younger than her colleagues, having skipped third grade, finished high school early, and graduated college in just three years. Given her passion for developmental biology and neonatal care, she also worked twenty hours a week at the research lab. To make rent, she continued to work as many hours as possible each week at the Pancake Shack with

Charlie, who'd become her favorite person on the planet. Somehow, she also made time each week to work out and keep her body lean and fit.

Mom would be so proud of how well I've channeled my grief about Angel into becoming such a hyper-driven overachiever. Her thought dripped with disdain.

Hope made her way to the small kitchen at the back of the lab. She needed coffee, bad. As she turned the corner, she found her mentor, Dr. Faye Young, sitting at the small round table in the corner of the kitchen. With her gentle smile and shocking white hair, Dr. Faye Young looked more like a stay-at-home mom who baked chocolate chip cookies for her kid's soccer team than the no-nonsense, hard-driving head of such a prestigious lab. In addition to running the lab and mentoring residents like Hope, Dr. Young also carried out her own research into how prolonged mechanical ventilation adversely impacts incompletely formed lungs.

"Morning, Hope," Dr. Young said without looking up from the research report she was reading. Hope Hunter was the only resident who arrived so early, so consistently. Sometimes Dr. Young worried about her young protegé. There is driven and there is obsessed, and Dr. Young could tell from the first moment she'd met Hope that the young woman was beyond driven. The question was whether Hope could control her obsession.

"Hi Faye," Hope said. Dr. Young had insisted that everyone at the lab call her Faye, saving the "Dr. Young" formality for when she presented at conferences or visited foundations when she was looking for grant money. Hope walked to the counter and poured herself a cup of coffee, choosing her favorite bright purple mug from the shelf above the sink. She plopped down on a chair next to her idol.

"What're you working on this morning?" Dr. Young asked.

"I'll finally be able to finish the write-up of my latest trial this morning. I just need to make sure the tables and diagrams are formatted correctly, and triple check all my citations. Thrilling work."

Dr. Young ignored the complaint. Writing up research findings, including making sure that all citations were correct, was a necessary part of the job. "That's great!" she said. "Send it to me when you're done; I look forward to reviewing it."

"Will do," Hope said. She took a gulp of her coffee and savored the bold, acidic flavor. She imagined the caffeine molecules rushing through her bloodstream, silently urging them to rush faster. Shifting to face Faye directly, she said, "Faye, as you know, the trial was a huge success. The lambs developed perfectly. They were developmentally equivalent in every way to lambs that develop naturally."

Dr. Young knew where the conversation was headed. It wasn't the first time she'd had one like it with an eager researcher and it wasn't the first time with Hope, who always seemed to be in such a hurry all the time.

"Hope—" Dr. Young began. Hope cut her off.

"Faye, my artificial womb works. It can gestate lambs that have been removed from their mothers at the equivalent of the twentieth week of a human pregnancy. When they are removed from the artificial womb, they live! They are normal at birth and they develop completely normally. We should push for grant money to try removing them even earlier. We should even try to get approval to start—"

This time it was Dr. Young's turn to interrupt Hope. "Human trials?" Dr. Young flicked her bangs out of her eyes and put a hand on Hope's knee. "Hope, listen to me, please. Please don't get ahead of yourself. You are doing amazing research and making amazing strides. But these things take time. You have to take one step at a time."

Dr. Young knew about the death of Hope's sister, Angel, almost ten years earlier and the circumstances around the poor girl's passing. Hope was channeling her anger into productivity, but Dr. Young knew that it was her job to keep her young colleague from stretching into recklessness. Faye, now sixty-three, had been a widow for over twenty years; she had been just forty-one when her husband died suddenly of a heart attack. Never remarrying, she had immersed herself in research. Her focus had helped her get to where she was in her career, but she would forever be grateful to her own mentor, years earlier, who had finally shown her there was more to life than work.

Dr. Young continued, "Yes, the autopsies revealed normal development. But the lambs are observed alive for just a few days and then euthanized and autopsied. We only test for what we test for. We don't know if they will live and thrive in the long-term."

Hope drew a deep breath. She was so tired of hearing that she had to take things slowly. What about the thousands of young girls being forced into unwanted pregnancies? There were so many more now since Roe had been overturned on the very night that Angel was raped and impregnated against her will. How many were raped, just like Angel? How many were adolescents, just like Angel?

"But the womb works," Hope said. She sounded lame even to herself.

"Yes. So far, so good. But there's a process. Yes, it's slow. Yes, it's painful. But it's necessary. What happens if you're wrong? Fast forward in your mind to human trials. What happens if the extraction procedure fails or if the artificial womb doesn't work and the fetuses die? Your trials would be stopped. Your reputation would likely be tarnished beyond repair. Funding for your research would dry up in a heartbeat."

Hope wanted to say, "I'm never wrong," but she knew better. She took another sip of coffee, hoping to regroup and form a persuasive argument. It didn't come because, in her heart, she knew Dr. Young was right.

Faye stood up, walked to the sink, poured the small amount of green tea in her cup down the drain, rinsed the cup, and put it in the small dishwasher. "Listen," she said, "Go finish your paper. I know you don't like it—hell, nobody does—but it's important work. Peer review is going to be critical, and you need to dot all your I's and cross all your T's so nobody has any reason to refute your findings." She put her hand gently on Hope's shoulder. "Okay?"

Hope looked up at her mentor, thankful for her wisdom and her kindness. She nodded.

"Okay, good," Dr. Young said. "I've got to go to a budget meeting later this afternoon and I need to prepare. You have citations, I have budgets. Frankly, I think you're getting the better end of the deal." She smiled kindly and walked out of the kitchen toward her office.

Hope got up and refilled her coffee. She put the pot back in the coffee maker, rested both of her palms on the counter, and took several deep, calming breaths. Then she picked up her cup of coffee and headed for her desk. She had work to do. Step number whatever of however many steps it took.

She silently asked herself, not for the first time, Will it make the boat go faster? It was something her Mom used to say, based on the story of the Great Britain Men's Rowing Eight team, which won Olympic Gold in Sydney, Australia in 2000 against all odds and after years of failure. The team's unrelenting focus, exemplified by critically asking the question, "will it make the boat go faster?" about every single decision and action they took, was one of Hope's guiding lights. She'd made a promise to Angel, and to herself, all those years ago, and her artificial womb would be the fulfillment of that promise. It might be a workaround for women's inability to get safe, legal abortions, but at least it would help millions of young girls and women legally shorten their ordeals.

Chapter Nine

Taking advantage of a rare break, Hope went to the small cafeteria on the main floor of the hospital and bought a can of Diet Coke. She walked out the side entrance nearest the cafeteria, hoping to sit in peace for a few minutes. She'd been up since 4:00 a.m., already worked four hours at the lab, and been on call since 9:00. Hope checked her phone and saw that it was only three o'clock. Her shift didn't for another three hours.

The normally blue northern California sky was an oppressive blanket of gray and Hope hoped the weather wasn't an omen for the election tomorrow. Thankfully, President Fred Spencer, the farcical, flamboyant jackass-pretending-to-be-President served just one term. Still, the damage he had done to the nation and the world was incalculable. In response to Spencer's ultra right-wing agenda, the nation jerked left and twice elected Gabriella Davenport. Davenport served eight distinguished years as the nation's first female president. Harvard-educated, serious and competent, she was—at least for people with Hope's political sensibilities—a breath of fresh air. Sadly, her Vice President for her second term, Zachary Grant, wasn't nearly the politician or person Davenport was. He was in a tight race.

Hope was happy that at least it wasn't raining. The chill in the air gave her goosebumps, but she'd never really be cold here given the Bay Area's mild weather. She cleared out her email inbox and checked her social media feeds. Lots of posts by people worried about the election.

Hope stood, chugged her Diet Coke, and threw the can into a trash bin next to the worn wooden bench on which she'd been sitting. She headed back into the hospital.

When she arrived on the pediatric wing, the residents in her cohort were already standing around together, waiting for their attending physician to take them on afternoon rounds. None of the other students acknowledged her arrival.

The beeps and buzzers of the floor filled the silence. A few of the residents spoke quietly to each other. Each was grateful that the antiseptic smell that was so powerful in the surgery wing was absent here. Finally, Dr. Vic Isaacs walked up and greeted the group.

"Good afternoon, everyone," he said. "Let's get going," he added, as if he had been waiting for the students to arrive rather than the other way around. "Try to keep up." Every student knew that he didn't just mean they should keep up with the pace of his walking; he was known as a brilliant doctor and an exacting teacher.

The group entered the room of a pregnant woman in her late forties who was suffering from kidney difficulties due to being pregnant at her advanced age.

"Statement of the case, anyone?"

"Mrs. Edwards is forty-seven years old," Pamela Westin said, beating other students into the spotlight, something she did regularly. "She is presenting with acute kidney pain, and blood and protein in her urine," "Mrs. Edwards is thirty-five weeks pregnant. This is her fourth pregnancy."

"Good morning, Kim," Dr. Isaacs said, turning on his best bedside manner. "How are we today?"

Kim Edwards snarled. "Well, I don't know how *you're* doing today, but *I'm* fucking miserable. The pain is unbearable." After a beat, she added, "God I hate my fucking husband."

A few of the residents laughed. Dr. Isaacs snapped his neck around and stared them back into silence.

"Sorry to hear that, Kim," Dr. Isaacs said. "What can we do to help make you more comfortable?" It was important that the residents came to understand that while their primary job was the physical well being of their patients, it was very much also their job to attempt to help the "whole patient." This sometimes meant silently absorbing abuse from patients.

"Can you keep my husband from jumping on me all the fucking time? Can you do that?" Mrs. Edwards smiled a wry smile.

Dr. Isaacs was momentarily at a loss for words.

"Yeah, I didn't think so," Mrs. Edwards said. "So how about a cup of ice chips instead?"

The nurse, who had been quietly taking Mrs. Edwards' vitals, said, "Comin' right up, hon." She packed up her cart and wheeled it out of the room. She was back before the Doctor and his residents finished talking with Mrs. Edwards.

After a few more minutes of small talk, the group left Mrs. Edwards to herself and gathered just outside of her room. Dr. Isaacs asked the group, "What can be done to keep Mrs. Edwards' kidneys from failing?"

This time, before Pamela Westin could answer, Hope said, "Transfuse Mrs. Edwards' umbilical cord blood into her bloodstream. Umbilical cord blood is ideal for treating immune-mediated diseases like kidney disease because it hasn't been exposed to disease or illness. Mesenchymal stem cells derived from umbilical cord blood have been shown to significantly aid patients' recuperation from kidney disease."

Dr. Isaacs was impressed. He smiled and said, "Excellent, Hope. A bit aggressive compared to what I was thinking, but excellent."

Most of the other residents once again found themselves in awe of Hope's seemingly bottomless reservoir of medical knowledge. Some found themselves defensive because of it, none more than Pamela Westin, who jumped in.

"We need to help her control her blood pressure."

Annette, one of the Pamela Pack, as Hope thought of it, raised her hand. "Maybe we should keep her husband away from her until after the birth," she joked.

Dr. Isaacs said, "That's enough, Annette. Pamela, you're correct. Keeping her blood pressure down will be helpful."

Pamela pouted, unhappy that Dr. Isaacs' praise of her wasn't as effusive as it was for Hope, that bitch.

"But how?" Dr. Isaacs asked the residents. "Are there medicines we can use to help treat Mrs. Edwards?"

"ACE inhibitors and ARBs would help," Hope said, aware of, but unconcerned by, the resentment her excellence caused in many of her classmates.

"Explain," Dr. Isaacs said to Hope. He could see the blank looks on the faces of some of the other residents.

Hope explained at length how ACE inhibitors and Angiotensin II receptor blockers, or ARBs, help relax blood vessels, which lowers blood pressure and makes it easier for the heart to pump blood.

Dr. Isaacs couldn't hide his smile. Hope Hunter was far and away the smartest, most focused resident he'd ever overseen. Pamela, Annette, and the others in the Pamela Pack couldn't help but notice Dr. Isaac's reaction. Pamela openly sneered at Hope.

Hope happened to look at Pamela just as the sneer formed on the woman's face. She knew what jealousy looked like; she'd been seeing it in the eyes of her fellow students her whole life. Hope smiled her biggest, most radiant smile at Pamela, who quickly dropped her gaze. It was a technique Hope learned years earlier, and used often.

"Okay everyone. Let's keep going," Dr. Isaacs said. He started walking down the hall and his gaggle of residents followed.

By 5:45 p.m., Dr. Isaacs told the residents that rounds would end fifteen minutes early. He had reports to write and wanted to leave the office early enough to have dinner with his wife before she fell asleep on the couch. Before he left the group, he walked toward Hope and pulled her aside.

"Hope, I just wanted to let you know that once again you impressed me today. It is a pleasure having you in my cohort."

"Thank you, Dr. Isaacs," Hope said. "As you know, I have a real passion for this rotation."

Out of the corner of her eye, she noticed Pamela, Annette, and friends clustered near the wall. That wasn't unusual; they were the very definition of a clique. They were looking at her, snickering and laughing. That wasn't all that unusual either, she thought.

Dr. Isaacs continued speaking to her, but she couldn't concentrate on what he was saying; she could hear Pamela and Annette talk about her.

Annette said, without a shred of self-awareness, "She never goes out with us to the bar." She crossed her arms. "Of course, she's such a loner, she probably doesn't have any friends. She probably never goes out with anyone."

One of the other residents said, "Well, I think she works at the research lab and also at that Pancake Shack place. So, she probably doesn't have much free time."

Hope made a mental note to thank the woman for trying to defend her.

"I heard she cleans toilets at that dump. A friend of mine found her on her hands and knees in the bathroom there once."

Hope finally snapped her attention back to Dr. Isaacs, who was winding down. She wished he had been able to concentrate on what he was saying.

"...See you tomorrow," Dr. Isaacs said.

"See you tomorrow. Thanks again, Dr. Isaacs," Hope said, hoping it was the right thing to say. She checked her phone and realized it was just a few minutes before six. She had thirty minutes to get ready and get over to the Watering Hole. Despite what Pamela and her pack said, Hope did go out on occasion.

Chapter Ten

Hope showered and changed into jeans, a black t-shirt, and her favorite oversized lavender-colored sweatshirt. She wore her tennis shoes, as always. She was exhausted, an all-too-common state for her, and starving. She drove to the restaurant, just a mile or so from Stanford's campus, and parked in the back.

She swung open the door to the famous burger joint and immediately smelled the grease. Her mouth watered. She hadn't eaten since she wolfed down a protein bar mid-morning. She spotted Billy sitting at one of the booths along the back row, and he waved as she walked toward the table.

"Hi Billy," Hope said. She forced herself to call him Billy, at his request, despite the fact that she much preferred his full legal name. Her relationship with Billy/William Valentine was complicated, she thought, not for the first time. She liked him; she just didn't have him high on her priority list. That and the fact that she knew she was more than a bit screwed up when it came to men.

Billy got up and gave Hope a hug. "Hi babe," he said, and Hope tried not to bristle at the pet name. He sensed she was in a foul mood, and asked, "Rough day?" He was enamored by her intelligence and strength, her sparkling blue eyes, long blonde hair, blemish-free skin, and lithe body, and wanted desperately to win her heart. If that meant listening while she vented, so be it.

"Not rough. Just long." *Like most days.*

"Come, sit," Billy said. He motioned to Hope to sit across from him in their booth. "What do you want? I'll go order for us."

Hope told Billy what she wanted and he made his way to the long line at the counter near the front of the restaurant. While she waited, she opened her purse and pulled out her phone, checked her email and immediately wished she hadn't. Buried within dozens of spam messages was a message from Faye at the lab. The subject read, "I found some citation errors. Let's discuss." She read the email over a few times, fretting. She hated citations. And she hated letting Faye down. For a brief moment, Hope thought about telling Billy that she had to go back to the lab, but she was starving and he was one of her few social outlets. She could work on fixing the citations when she got home.

Hope reached over and grabbed the basket of peanuts on the table. She cracked open a few and shot them into her mouth. As was tradition at the restaurant, she tossed the shells on the floor. The contrast between the floor here and the cleanliness of her lab and of the hospital always struck Hope as amusing. What would it be like if she could just chuck used instruments on the ground? She smiled at the idea. It was her first real smile of the day.

Billy returned and placed their burgers and a basket of fries on the table. He slid into the booth across from her and reached out with his palms up. She extended her arms and placed her slender fingers into his hands for a moment. He squeezed them gently, knowing how skittish she was about the possibility of injuring her hands.

Billy let her hands go and pulled his burger toward him. "What do you think is going to happen tomorrow?" Billy asked, referring to the election. "I think Grant can hold on." He took a bite and wiped his chin.

"From your lips to God's ears," Hope said, although Billy knew Hope definitely did not believe in God. She'd told him once that it was a saying she'd picked up from her childhood in the South, where it was easier to pretend she believed in God than to defend her atheism. She, too, dove into her burger, and sighed audibly after each of her first few bites.

"Even if Owens wins, he seems way more reasonable and committed to bipartisanship than Spencer was," Billy said. He popped a french fry in his mouth. "God, that guy was horrible," he said while chewing.

"Let's not talk about him," Hope snapped. "He's ancient history, thankfully."

Billy knew that Hope had strong feelings about former President Spencer. She blamed him, indirectly, for her sister's death. Spencer nominated Julian Kingsley, who was the swing vote to overturn

Roe, which set off Louisiana's trigger law, which outlawed all abortions in the state, including Angel's. Not to mention the fact that her mother left Hope and her sister in Louisiana and went to Washington to fight the man and his horrible policies. He let the subject drop.

Billy asked Hope about her work at the lab. He wordlessly absorbed her complaints about her distaste for citations and congratulated her on the success of her latest trial. When she told him about Pamela and Annette at the hospital, he *tsk tsk*ed and provided moral support. Hope, so preoccupied by her thoughts about her own day, didn't once ask Billy about his.

When they finished their burgers, Hope said, "Thanks, Billy. That really hit the spot. Thanks for making me come out tonight."

Billy smiled. "I didn't make you do anything. Nobody can make anyone do anything, least of all you."

It was Hope's turn to smile. "Well, thanks just the same. Listen, I have to do some work on my citations tonight and I have to get up early for work tomorrow morning."

Billy could tell just how "Type A" Hope was when he'd first seen her in the hospital cafeteria a few months earlier. He didn't care. He'd been instantly mesmerized by her drive and intensity. A week after the first time he saw her, he bumped into her again and had the courage to ask her out. With her schedule, they'd only had a few dates so he made a point of walking over from the I.T. Department, where he worked, to wherever she was doing rounds just so he could wave or say hello. He was in love. And he was willing to take things slowly.

Billy and Hope walked out of the restaurant and stopped just outside the door. Hope shivered from the cool evening, despite her sweatshirt. Billy reached out and rubbed his hands up and down her arms to warm her. She smiled.

Billy reached in to kiss her, but Hope pulled away.

"You know I don't like kissing," she snapped. She was actually shaking. She knew it was a subconscious reaction but she couldn't help it. She backed away from Billy.

Billy, who had patiently accepted Hope's busy schedule for many months and, as he often did, had patiently listened to Hope's complaints through dinner, temporarily lost his cool. "Christ. It feels like I'm with a prostitute who saves kisses for her boyfriend. Well, except for the part where we don't have sex either." As soon as the words came out of his mouth, he immediately regretted his outburst.

Before Billy could apologize, Hope said, "You know about what happened with my sister," as tears welled up in her eyes. "What I didn't tell you was that it was my fault. I was making out with a boy named Todd like some kind of slut while that asshole raped poor little Angel." Tears streamed down her cheeks.

Billy wanted to comfort Hope, wanted to wipe her tears away, but somehow knew it would be the wrong thing to do. "It wasn't your fault, Hope," was all he could think to say.

Hope took a deep breath and wiped her eyes. "I'm sorry, Billy. Really I am. I've been a pretty shitty date tonight, haven't I?" She laughed sadly. "Look, I'll text you tomorrow okay? I've gotta go."

"I get it. You have those citations to fix tonight and you have to get up early for work," Billy said, unable to keep the sadness from his voice.

Chapter Eleven

A keen observer of people, Diamond observed Camila García. It was a skill he'd honed in the army where being wrong about a person could cost lives. Despite tiny crow's feet forming in the corners of her eyes, the woman was absolutely stunning, he thought. She had short-cropped black hair, warm brown eyes, and wore little makeup. Even so late in the evening, her cream-colored tailored suit somehow looked to have no wrinkles. The deep purple satin blouse underneath was open just enough for him to see the two points of her collarbones. He admired the passion she had for her work; it beamed from her eyes and radiated whenever she eagerly gesticulated while making one point or another about the state of immigration in the country.

"He'll be here," Camila García, Executive Director of We Are the World Charities, said to the band of angels sitting across her IKEA conference room table. It was nearly 11:00 p.m., but the IRS agent knew that she often worked late and slept on the couch in her office. There were just too many immigrants who needed the legal advice and public health services her organization provided for her to spare the time for the commute home and back most nights.

Lancaster leaned forward and said, "When he arrives, we'll stay here, in the conference room. We'll be out of sight, but we will be able to see and hear everything." He wanted to reassure García, who, despite her obvious poise and confidence, was clearly scared of what they had planned. "I know it will be difficult, but you need to let him, uh, approach you on the couch."

"Got it," she said. She crossed her arms and rubbed her shoulders.

"We've got cameras and microphones everywhere," Patel said. "We'll get him," he assured her. García liked the man's kind face and warm eyes.

The buzzer for the front door sounded and Camila García jumped. She smiled nervously and stood up.

"Show time," she said with as much courage as she could muster.

Diamond stood and walked to where Camila was standing. He reached out and gently held her shoulders. "You've got this."

Camila García took a deep breath and walked to let IRS agent and all-around sleazebag Mr. Ike Reynolds into her office, and into their sting operation. Diamond closed the conference room door to the point where it almost touched the door frame. The blinds were already closed.

"Hello, Camilia," Reynolds said as he strutted past her into the office. "I hope I'm not disturbing you." He mindlessly picked up, fondled, and replaced family photographs, children's art projects, and other knick knacks from various desks. The casual intrusion into the lives of her employees sickened her.

"No, it's fine," García lied. "Come in." Taking a huge risk, she bluffed, "Should we go into the conference room to go through whatever paperwork you have?"

In the conference room, Diamond, Lancaster, and Patel understood exactly what Camila García was doing, but stiffened nevertheless.

"No, no. That's far too formal. I just want to chat."

García, relieved that her bluff had worked, motioned to the couch along the back wall. "Should we sit over there?"

"That'll be perfect." *Just perfect.*

García sat as far to one side of the couch as she could, keeping her knees locked together and placing her hands over her skirt. Her heart sank when Reynolds sat at the other end of the couch. Maybe he wasn't the creep she thought he was? Maybe they wouldn't be able to catch him doing something horrible in order to get him out of her life.

"Where do things stand?" she asked flatly.

"My calculations remain the same, Camila. Your organization owes the U.S. Government over two hundred thousand dollars."

They'd been through this before, but Diamond and his compatriots had encouraged her to get the IRS man talking.

"But how can we owe taxes? We Are the World is a 501(c)(3)."

"Well, yes. But you see, as I've told you, we did not receive your IRS Form 990 last year, and you can lose your tax-exempt status for that."

"I don't understand. I sent it in on time, like I've done every year since we've been up and running. I can make a copy of my copy right now." García started to stand up.

"I'm afraid it doesn't work that way. Giving me the form now doesn't qualify as having submitted it on time." Reynolds himself had received the charity's Form 990 six months earlier, but he'd seen a picture of Camila on the organization's website and was infatuated.

"So what can I do?" García asked as she sat back down on the couch. "Can we arrange a payment plan? We don't have that kind of money in the bank. Almost every penny goes into the services we provide to the people we help."

Ike Reynolds loved this part, when the women asked "what can I do?" with a sense of desperation in their voices. He patted the cushion of the couch near him and said, "You could perhaps repay your debt another way."

Even knowing it was coming, Camila García had a hard time not throwing up. She shivered but didn't move.

Impatient, Reynolds stood, smoothed his pant legs and walked to where García sat hugging herself. He stood directly in front of her, reached down and gently lifted her chin with his thumb and forefinger.

"For example, here's one way I can think of." He unzipped his pants and pulled out his flaccid penis.

Camila García was scared and horrified. She was paralyzed, unable to speak or move.

"You know what to do, don't you?" Reynolds leered at her.

Behind the conference room door, Lancaster was about to rush out and pummel the IRS agent, but Diamond pulled him back. They needed García to get the man to admit the quid pro quo he was looking for.

Ike Reynolds waggled himself in Camila's face.

Somehow, some way, Camila García regained some measure of composure and stammered, "You mean, if I, uh, have sex with you, you'll drop my fine?"

Reynolds, who was just hoping for a blowjob, tried hard to hide his glee. Sex with this beautiful creature? My God! "Yes, that's what I'm saying. Now come on... it's not going to suck itself."

Three seconds later, Ike Reynolds was face down on the ground, his arms held firmly behind his back and Lancaster's knee squarely between his shoulder blades. He was bleeding from a cut on his forehead, which had hit the edge of the glass coffee table.

"Sorry about the blood on the carpet," Patel said to Camila.

To Reynolds, the IRS man, Diamond said, "We thought this would be more efficient than having Ms. García contact an IRS tax attorney to lodge a complaint."

Reynolds squirmed, but to no avail.

"Settle down there, stud, or we may have to see if there's a pair of scissors around here somewhere," Lancaster said as he pressed even harder with his knee.

While Lancaster held Ike Reynolds to the ground, Diamond and Patel carefully removed the six cameras they'd set up around the office, including the three specifically aimed at the couch. Diamond knelt in front of Reynolds' forlorn face and replayed the key portion of one of the tapes.

"Will We Are the World Charities retain its 501(c)(3) status?"

Lancaster shifted his weight forward, and Reynolds moaned, "Yes."

"And does the charity owe any taxes?"

"No. No. All right? No."

"Good. That's good," Diamond said. "Now, I suspect Ms. Garcia is not the only woman you've pulled this kind of shit on, so here's how it's going to go. You have thirty days to return any blackmail payments you may have received. And you're going to email detailed apologies to every woman you've done this to, blind carbon copying this email address." He handed Reynolds a business card with nothing but an email address printed upon it. "If we're not satisfied with your emails, we'll be back. And we're going to keep our tapes to make sure you don't pull this kind of shit again. Understand?"

Before Reynolds could respond, Lancaster yanked the man to his feet. Reynolds eyed Diamond with rage in his eyes. He said, "yeah" casually, as if shrugging. Diamond punched him square in the nose.

"I'll ask again," Diamond said. "Understand?"

This time, Reynolds didn't hesitate or equivocate. "Yes. I understand."

"Good. One last thing... You can start with an apology to Ms. García here."

Ike Reynolds did not want to be punched in the face again, and his apology reflected his fear, if not genuine contrition.

Patel and Lancaster ushered Ike Reynolds to the door. Lancaster released his grip on Reynold's arm, and the man ran.

"You have a good night, now, you hear?" Patel called after him.

"I love how polite you are, Mr. Patel," Lancaster said as the men walked back into the offices of the charity. "Oh, by the way, I like the new watch. This one's classy."

Patel looked down at the Piaget Altiplano 18-karat white gold and alligator watch he'd purchased on an online auction site. He'd seen Camila's picture on her charity's website and wanted to impress her. *Just my luck*, he thought, *I impressed Lancaster instead.*

As Lancaster and Patel reentered the office, Camila García was still wrapping her body with her arms, but her stress had receded greatly.

"Is it really over?" she asked.

Her guardian angels said that it was, and she believed them.

Later, as the men drove back to the airport, they talked about how much they enjoyed helping Camila García. Patel admitted he was smitten by the woman, and Diamond and Lancaster needled him to call her and ask her out. Patel giggled and sheepishly agreed he would.

As he drove, Charlie Diamond thought that perhaps he and his team should find a way to locate Angel Hunter's rapist, who had gone unpunished all those years earlier. Hope had told him that she'd tried to locate Derek, but that she couldn't seem to find the guy. Charlie suggested the idea to his brothers in arms, and as the team was returning their rental car, the men decided they had a new mission: helping women and girls in need. And their first job was a personal one for Charlie.

Chapter Twelve

Tuesday, November 7 (the next day)
Pancake Shack
Palo Alto, California

Election day

After four and a half fitful hours of sleep, Hope was back at work. She'd started working at the Pancake Shack over six years earlier, when she first came out to Stanford for medical school. Even though she indeed had to clean toilets like Pamela had teased her about, she liked the feeling of mastering the chaos when the restaurant was busy. That, and she absolutely adored the owner, Charlie.

By 6:15 a.m., almost every table was full. Hope found herself wondering whether it was because people were getting an early breakfast before going to vote. It was election day.

"Good morning," Hope said to a table of three elderly women. "What can I get for you?"

"I'd like a short stack of pancakes," said the first woman. "No butter, please."

"The same for me," said the second woman.

The third woman, who seemed a few years older than the others said, "I'm hungry. I'd like a full stack and I'd like mine with extra butter."

The first two women simultaneously said, "Marge!" One continued, "You know the doctor told us not to eat so much butter and oil."

Marge smiled and replied, "I've been eating buttery, oily, fried food all my life, and I'm ninety-four and healthy, thank you Jesus." Clearly the three women had had this conversation many times before.

Hope tamped down a smile and recorded the orders on her pad. She'd learned long ago that even though her medical school training enabled her to memorize pretty much any order without writing it down at the table, many customers worried that she wouldn't get their order right if she didn't write anything down. "Anything to drink?"

"Just water," said the first two women. Marge ordered a Bloody Mary.

Hope didn't hide her smile this time and said, "Comin' right up." She picked up the women's menus and turned to take the order of a businessman sitting alone at the counter.

"Good morning. May I take your order?"

The man didn't look up from his paper as he said, "Two eggs, over easy. Wheat toast. Fruit instead of potatoes." He handed Hope his menu while he continued to read the front page.

Hope glanced down and saw the headline: "Grant's Lead Gone." Hope's medical school education also gave her the ability to speed read pretty well and the guy wasn't paying any attention to her anyway, so she skimmed the article. The piece described how Zachary Grant, the Democrat, had lost his once sizable advantage in the polls over Brock Owens, the Republican. Hope could feel the stress signals in her body: her heart rate was up, her breathing was shallow, and she could feel perspiration begin to form on her face and neck.

Hope placed both orders with Charlie, who helped José cook breakfast every morning as well as most lunches and dinners. She made Marge's Bloody Mary, purposely using a tad less Tabasco than normal, thinking no matter how vibrant the woman was, she was still ninety-four years old. She grabbed two ice waters and carried the three glasses to the women's table.

Hope thought about how she, along with millions of others, wished that Vice President Grant had even a quarter of the charisma of President Gabriella Davenport, who'd become the first female President eight years earlier, holding that jackass Fred Spencer to a single term. President Davenport was fiery and bold, and unapologetically liberal. She was the nation's counter to President Spencer, who was a mix of eighty percent incompetence and twenty percent radical white nationalism. Grant was an able politician, but was more of a technician than a leader, and he'd lost the big lead Davenport had bestowed upon him.

Hope was lost in these thoughts as she made her way to check in on a few tables in the far corner of the restaurant. She made her way through the maze of tables, past the three women who were still arguing about Marge's fat intake, the businessman with the newspaper, and past the guy eating alone who she'd mentally tagged as "the creep." The guy had finished eating almost an hour earlier and was just sitting around doing not much else but staring at her. She'd never seen him before.

As she walked past his table, time slowed. Hope felt his hand squeeze her right butt cheek, and her reaction, the result of years of self defense and martial arts training, was swift. She slowed her forward momentum, did a reverse pivot on her right foot and swung her left elbow backwards in an arc aimed directly for where she knew his head was. He must have seen her elbow coming and turned toward it because her elbow struck him directly in his nose.

"Ahh," he screamed. "My nose! You broke my fucking nose!"

Hope turned full circle to look at the guy. She rubbed her elbow as she looked at him. He was one of the creepiest guys she'd ever seen. He had thinning mousy brown hair, a cheesy mustache, a flabby face, and a smarmy 1980s "hey baby"-style aura.

"Do. Not. Touch. Me." Hope said slowly. She threw a stack of napkins on his table.

The guy picked up the napkins in a wad and held them to his nose. Blood was everywhere: his nose and mouth, his hands, the table, his shirt and pants, and the floor. He kept screaming and kept repeating, "You broke my fucking nose." His cousin, who paid him a thousand bucks to harass this chick, didn't say anything about the fact that she was violent.

By this time, Charlie made his way out from the kitchen and approached the table.

"You okay, kiddo?" he asked Hope. She loved him for asking about her well-being first.

She nodded. "He grabbed my ass."

"What's your name, asswipe?" Charlie asked the man.

After a few deep breaths, the guy calmed enough to answer. "Norman. Norman Underhill."

"And are you okay, Norman?" Condescension dripped from Charlie's voice.

"No, I'm not okay," Norman said. "She broke my fucking face." *I am out unless cuz pays me another grand.*

Charlie looked the man directly in the eyes and said, very slowly, "Well, you're lucky I don't break your fucking kneecaps. Do not ever touch a woman without her permission. Especially not this one."

Norman started to say something when Charlie added, "Your breakfast today is on the house. Leave now and do not ever come back."

Still pressing a wad of napkins to his nose, Norman Underhill slunk out of the restaurant, and once he was sure the man was gone, Charlie turned and made his way back to the kitchen. The women at the tables closest to what happened clapped and cheered. Most of the men did, too.

Soon after Underhill left, a group of middle-aged women came in wearing I VOTED! stickers. Hope motioned them to an open table with her left arm. She winced from the pain and turned to make herself a makeshift ice pack for her elbow.

Later, Hope picked up her tip from the table where Marge and her concerned friends sat. They'd left a twenty dollar tip on an twenty-eight dollar bill. She also picked up the businessman's tip: a crisp hundred dollar bill. She suspected, but would never know for sure, that the tips were a reaction to how she'd handled the creep who'd grabbed her.

Chapter Thirteen

Tuesday, November 7 (later that night)
24-Hour Fitness
Redwood City, California

Except for the high-school-aged girl who sat quietly doing her algebra homework at the front desk, the fitness center was empty. It was just a few minutes before midnight. The place was absolutely silent except for the thuds of the sporadic impacts Hope's boxing-gloved fists made on a punching bag along the mirrored back wall.

Hope was exhausted but kept pounding the bag. She was in a kind of daze, punching on autopilot, just like a story she'd read about a swimmer who kept stroking even after her head hit the side of the pool, causing her to become unconscious. Her arms were heavy. Her heart was heavier.

The TVs on the walls of the gym, whether tuned to CNN, MSNBC, Fox, or local stations, all showed the same thing: Brock Owens, the Republican, had narrowly defeated Zachary Grant, the Democrat.

For the third time in the past six elections, the winner of the popular vote did not win the electoral vote.

Hope couldn't bear to watch. She kept pounding the bag until she was resting her head against it and her punches were barely more than her arms flailing forward, barely making contact.

Finally, just past midnight, she sagged to the floor, utterly wrecked. She glanced at the TV airing CNN, which showed an earnest looking commentator yammering on. The chyron scrolling along the bottom of the screen stated "Owens commits to bipartisanship." As Hope removed her gloves and packed her gym bag, she muttered, "Let's hope."

Chapter Fourteen

Royce Carrington finished off his cup of Silver Tips Imperial tea from the Makaibari Tea Estate in Darjeeling, West Bengal, while sitting in one of the upholstered armchairs near the fireplace in his nine-hundred square-foot corner suite at the Greenwich Hotel. After putting his cup down, he folded the newspaper he'd read cover to cover, and crossed the suite to the spacious marble and glass bathroom. He brushed his teeth, combed his hair, straightened his tie, and then headed out. After two months looking for causes to which to donate his money, Carrington had identified his first beneficiary: The Friar Tuck Institute. They were doing impressive work fighting poverty.

After a mind-boggling number of legal I's that had to be dotted and legal T's that had to be crossed, Carrington's money manager had finally set up his charitable foundation. Now that the fund was ready, he was eager to get started. As the sun crowned on the horizon, Carrington walked a few blocks north through the northern part of Tribeca, which had become one of the hippest areas in New York City, full of residential lofts, trendy boutiques, and upscale restaurants.

Carrington introduced himself to the young man working at the front desk in the building's lobby. The place had exposed brick walls, which were covered with framed news articles about the good work the organization had done, and exposed HVAC ducts and Ethernet cabling in the ceiling.

"Mr. Moore is expecting you," the young man said cheerfully. "He'll be right down. Can I get you a water while you wait?"

Carrington declined and took a seat on one of the couches in a small sitting area. He'd barely sat down when his host exited the elevator and walked briskly toward him, right arm outstretched.

"It's a pleasure to meet you, Senator Carrington."

"Likewise," Carrington said, standing and shaking hands.

"Please, follow me," Moore said. He led Carrington to the elevator and up to the fifth floor.

Once the men were seated in Moore's cramped office, Carrington said, "I read from your website that you're the largest poverty-fighting organization in the city, is that right?"

"That's correct. We provide our partner nonprofits with whatever they need to be successful: financial support of course, but also assistance with real estate and management issues. And we optimize the impact of every grant we make.

We average over ten dollars in income and quality of life improvements for every dollar we invest."

Carrington liked the idea. Far too many charities, while well-meaning, didn't understand the power of leverage. Real change—systemic change—only comes through leverage.

Moore continued. "If you've read our materials, you know the data. One in six New Yorkers rely on soup kitchens and food pantries. One in five workers in the city earn less than twenty thousand dollars a year. One in three babies born in the city are born into poverty. The statistics go on and on."

"That's why I want to contribute to your efforts. The magnitude of the problem you're fighting is undeniable. That you're doing the best job of anyone out there combating it is too."

"Thank you. I appreciate the kind words. And I appreciate your offer to help. What did you have in mind?"

"Ten million."

"Over what kind of time frame?"

"Oh, no, you misunderstand. I'm going to write you a check. Here. Now. For ten million dollars."

In his many years as the organization's Executive Director, Moore had never experienced such largesse, at least not all at once. Still, he did not lose his composure in the moment.

"We will put it to good use," he said. "One hundred percent of your donation will go to our partners."

"I know," Carrington said. "It's one of the many reasons I chose your organization."

"Well, I can't thank you enough, Senator."

Carrington said, "Then he looked up at his disciples and said: 'Blessed are you who are poor, for yours is the kingdom of God. Blessed are you who are hungry now, for you will be filled. Blessed are you who weep now, for you will laugh.' Luke six, twenty through twenty-one."

The Senator's bible quote caught Moore by surprise, but he'd been down this road before.

"Senator Carrington, as much as we very much can use your donation, I feel the need to tell you that we are a secular organization. I just want to make sure you understand that."

"I do," Carrington said. *God works in mysterious ways, ways you may not understand.* "My motivations are based on my religious beliefs, but I don't mind if your motivations are different. On this, our interests are aligned."

Carrington took out his foundation checkbook and wrote his first check. He handed it to Moore.

"Again, I can't thank you enough."

"It is my pleasure to help those less fortunate," Carrington said, a little too haughtily for Moore's taste.

The check in hand, Moore asked, "May I ask why you're investing here in New York instead of Mississippi?"

Carrington's response was cold and calculated. "There isn't an organization in Mississippi that's as effective as you are here. I refuse to donate to organizations that will just end up wasting my money. And, besides, I don't think Jesus would insist that the hungry I help have to live in my state." After shaking hands with Moore, Carrington showed himself out. He said nothing about the fact that he had his house upstate or that he intended to retire in New York at some point.

Chapter Fifteen

Saturday, January 20
Hope's Apartment
Redwood City, California

Two and a half months later
Inauguration day

Hope slept late for the first time in months. Of course, sleeping late was a relative term for someone like Hope. By nine, she had made her bed, cleaned her apartment, read her email, and fed Xander. Her apartment might be small, but she liked to keep it tidy. She'd replaced most of her IKEA pieces after graduating medical school, figuring a comfortable couch and a decent desk would help get her through her internship and years of residency. Pictures of Angel filled the warm space, and her urn sat in its special place on her bookshelf.

For breakfast, Hope ate a toasted bagel with peanut butter and banana, and had a glass of orange juice. She rinsed the dishes and put them in the dishwasher.

Hope snatched her keychain and headed down to the mail slots on the first floor of her building. She grabbed the handful of mail in her mailbox and returned to her apartment. Sitting at her kitchen table, she went through the pile of mail. Most, as always, was junk: advertisements, flyers, and the like. There were a few bills and another envelope from her mom.

Hope tore open the envelope from her mother and looked inside. The contents were what they always were: nothing more than a check with a yellow sticky note stuck to it. "Hope you're well -Mom" was written on the note. When Angel died, their mom had written her a long letter that attempted to explain her decision to leave for Washington and stay there through Angel's pregnancy and death. Since then, each month it was just a crappy sticky note with a few trite words.

Hope crumpled the note and threw it in the pile of garbage mail. She stared at the check for a beat and then rose and walked to her bedroom closet. She reached up and pulled a shoebox down. After one last look at the check, Hope opened the box and dropped in the check, which would remain uncashed along with all the others. She returned the box to its place on the shelf.

Hope returned to her table and wrote checks for the few bills she'd received. Her apartment was in a pretty iffy part of town, which meant rent was affordable enough for her to have the one bedroom to herself. Rent wasn't due for another ten days.

Satisfied she was keeping on track financially—well, other than the fact she was racking up hundreds of thousands of dollars of debt in student loans—Hope put her checkbook away, cleared the table of the junk mail, and turned on the TV.

The inauguration of President Brock Owens was all over the airwaves. She left the TV tuned to CNN. Hope noticed how Owens, the poster child for exercise and watching one's diet, wore just his suit, while all the other dignitaries around him were bundled in their overcoats. Hope remembered seeing a TV special on the man, which showed him working out at a gym. The man could have been a Mr. Universe contestant, Hope thought. In fact, as a younger man Owens had considered competing, but was unwilling to take steroids like the other contestants. Rumors about his diet ran rampant. Some said he ate nothing but green vegetables and whey protein. Others said he ate red meat at every meal. Incredibly media savvy, the man was sure never to confirm or deny any of these rumors.

Hope watched as President Brock Owens took the oath of office. She looked over to Angel's urn on her bookshelf. "Oh, Angel. It's happening again. I can feel it." She got up, walked over to the urn and ran her fingers lightly over the precious ceramic vase. Within moments, tears slid down her cheeks as she silently grieved for her lost little sister.

Steeling herself, Hope turned and dropped to the floor in her living room. She did a hundred crunches while the network moved to a commercial break. She was doing pushups when a panel of pundits gave their analyses of the inauguration and pontificated about what they expected from Owens and his administration.

Hope moved to doing seal planks when she heard the news that President Owens—or one of his people—had just posted a controversial message on his social media feed. The screen showed the text of the post:

```
After   eight   years   of   Gabriella
Davenport's  extreme  liberal  agenda,
it  is  time  for  a  correction.  I  am
proud to lead that correction.
```

She pushed herself to move back and forth across her room until her abs burned. She let herself lay flat on the floor for a moment, then asked herself once again, *Will it make the boat go faster?* Looking at Angel's urn, she said, "I made you a promise, sis, and I intend to keep it." She got up, turned off the TV, and headed for the shower. It seemed clear that it was now more important than ever that she focus on her research. There were millions of young girls and women who might benefit from her artificial womb, who might need it more urgently now that Owens was President.

Chapter Sixteen

The day after the inauguration, Hope's shift at the hospital ended at 10:00 p.m. She changed into street clothes, packed her backpack, and spent a few minutes giving a status update on each of her patients to the nurses at the nursing station. By a quarter after, she was out the door, heading for her car.

As Hope walked past the fountain in front of the hospital's main entrance and toward the parking garage, she found herself amazed, as she always was, at the temperate Northern California weather. Just like back in Louisiana, her light jacket was more than enough. She thanked her lucky stars, again, that she lived in the Bay Area now.

Hope hadn't slept for over twenty-four hours. Despite this, she sensed more than saw that someone was behind one of the concrete pillars in the parking garage. She stopped a few feet from the post.

"Hello? Is there someone there?"

Nobody answered but her senses were still on high alert. She asked again. "Is someone there?"

She waited a full minute. Nothing. She wondered if it was just that she was so tired. She slowly began walking toward her car but veered away so she would be as far as possible from the pillar.

Just as she walked past it, a man jumped out at her. He was wearing a red baseball cap and was dressed in black pants and a black jacket. He wore a black bandana over most of his face. The man came at her, his hands raised like an extra in a B-rated zombie movie.

Hope's first thought was: *At least he doesn't have a weapon, at least not in his hands.* Her second thought was: *I don't know what it is, but this guy somehow seems familiar.* There was something about his bearing and about the fact that as menacing as he was trying to be, he somehow wasn't pulling it off. Still, she was scared.

Her training kicked in and she assumed a strong, defensive stance, with her left leg forward, her right leg back, and her knees slightly bent. She rocked on her toes.

The attacker reached out with his left hand and attempted to grab her throat and pin her to a pillar she'd accidentally backed into. As she was thinking, *stupid, stupid, stupid*, his hand closed around her throat. Hope thought, too late, that she should have screamed before the man had grabbed ahold of her windpipe. With his right hand, the man punched Hope squarely in her left eye.

Hope cried out, but before he could punch her again, her instincts kicked in. She raised both of her arms and brought them down with all her might on his outstretched arm. The force of her blow dislodged the assailant's hand from her neck. He cursed under his breath and reached to nurse his sore arm just as Hope reached for her tender left eye socket.

"You bitch!" the man said. Hope somehow recognized the tone of his voice as pain and fear, not aggression. Still he charged at her again. This time, Hope didn't wait for him; she stepped toward him at the same time and gave a jab with her left hand and then a right hook.

Her punch landed squarely on the man's cheekbone, and she heard a quiet crack. Probably a zygomatic maxillary fracture, she figured. He staggered away again, this time crying out in pain. She'd purposely hit him with the heel of her hand to prevent broken bones in her hand. She could do her work at the hospital and her research at the lab with a black eye, but not with a broken hand.

Hope didn't care if he was in pain. As often happened through the years, she flashed back to her sister's rape. Now she channeled that anger into intense retaliatory force. While the man was hunched over, nursing his cheek, Hope walked the few steps toward him and grabbed his balls. He looked up at her and winced.

With her left hand, which was free of testicular slaughter duty, she ripped the man's bandana off his face.

"You!" she said. She had been right; she did know the guy. It was the jerk who'd squeezed her butt at the restaurant. "Norman Underhill?"

"Please. Please stop squeezing. You're hurting me."

Hope squeezed harder. Underhill yelped.

"Are you stalking me? Why did you jump me?"

Norman Underhill made a quick calculation. Even with the extra thousand bucks, this gig wasn't worth it. His cousin could go fuck himself.

"My cousin asked me to harass you."

"Your cousin? Who the hell is your cousin?"

"Derek. Derek Johnson."

Hope felt like she'd been punched in the gut. It took all of her will to maintain her grip.

"He asked me to intimidate you. That was the original plan. I was just going to come to the restaurant and make you uncomfortable, stare at you, grab your butt, that kind of thing. Creep you out for a few days and then let you know that Derek knows you're looking for him and that you need to stop. But then you cracked me in the nose. I told Derek that I was out, but he agreed to pay me more if I escalated things."

"You tell Derek if he wants to scare me off, he better come do it himself." Hope was now more committed to confronting the bastard than ever. And she wasn't just going to yell at him, either. Adrenaline surged through her body.

"And if you ever—and I mean ever—come near me again, I will take my scalpel and cut these off," Hope said, squeezing the man's privates harder still. "Do I make myself perfectly clear?"

"Uh, uh..."

"Uh, uh, what?"

"Uh, yes. Yes. Clear. Clear. Totally clear. Yes, yes, yes. Just please, please let go."

"We understand each other, right?" Hope asked.

"I won't bother you again. I swear."

"And you won't bother *any other* woman either, right?"

"Right. Yes. Right. I promise."

Hope unclenched her fist. Norman Underhill dropped to the ground and crawled into the fetal position, with his hands holding his crotch. His red hat fell off and rolled to a stop a few inches away from where Hope stood. Hope finally noticed the hat had the word RESISTANCE printed on it. Republican zealots had been using the term for the past eight years while out of power, stealing the term from liberal zealots who'd used it the previous four years. As Hope made her way to her car, she thought, *Of course he's a maggot.*

Chapter Seventeen

Charlie stood at the back door of the International Center for Social Change in downtown Miami, enjoying the warm evening breeze and a few minutes of quiet. He'd been to the city many times, and always enjoyed the vibrant colors, Cuban-influenced food, and balmy weather. At 7:45 p.m., a limousine pulled up and a tiny woman with sepia-colored skin, a broad nose, short-cropped hair, and dancing eyes stepped out.

"Welcome to the United States," Charlie said warmly, giving her a hug.

"Not so welcome, actually, huh?" the woman replied wryly.

Nearly forty-two hours after leaving Lilongwe, Malawi, and flights that took her through Nairobi, Paris, and London, Roshin Dausi touched down in Miami, Florida a half an hour earlier. Despite the distance and difficult logistics, Dausi was upbeat and bursting with energy, partly because she'd taken the last leg of the journey aboard a patron's luxurious Gulfstream G550 and partly because she was in the United States against the U.S. Government's wishes.

Dausi, just twenty-two years old, ran an up-and-coming Malawan social and economic justice organization, Rise and Thrive, which promoted birth control and women's reproductive choice across Africa. She wanted to spread her message in the United States, which in her mind was now a third-world country when it came to women's issues. Gabriella Davenport had been a liberal president, but President Fred Spencer packed three extreme right-wing justices on the Supreme Court, including Julian Kingsley. For years now, the court regularly ruled 6-3 to slowly but surely reduce the rights of women, LGBTQ people, and immigrants.

Administrations since the 2001 Patriot Act have been using provisions in the law to engage in a kind of "censorship at the border." The idea is simple: keep scholars with undesirable political views out of the country. President Gabriella Davenport had not abused the law in this way, but President Brock Owens, in office for just one day, had, while on the campaign trail, publicly stated his intentions to renew the practice. In the months since the man was elected, his incoming administration had made it clear that Dausi was not welcome in the United States.

Dausi was unwilling to take "no" for an answer, even when that answer came from the great and powerful United States. Through her robust network of contacts, she reached out to the almost-mythical trio of Diamond, Lancaster, and Patel.

To avoid the normal scrutiny of U.S. Customs, Charlie arranged for Dausi to fly into Opa-Locka Executive Airport, ten miles north of Miami International Airport. The man had somehow arranged for the Gulfstream, too. If things went according to plan, she would have more to thank him for than just a ride in a nicely appointed airplane.

Charlie said, "Yeah, that's true. Uncle Sam would be pissed if he knew you were here. That's why we've arranged things the way we have."

"I understand," Dausi said. "I appreciate everything you've done. Oh, and thanks for the ride; that's one amazing plane."

"Don't thank me for that. That was all Sanam's doing. His parents are big fans of your work and are apparently richer than God." After a beat, Charlie asked, "You feeling okay?"

"I'm good. Slept a solid four hours on the plane from London."

"Okay, then. Let's do this. Follow me."

Charlie led Roshin Dausi to a comfortable "green room" in the back of the Center's offices. It was really just a well-appointed room with a comfortable couch, a makeup station, and a table full of fresh fruits and vegetables. A makeshift desk with a camera was set up in the corner. A green screen hung behind the chair.

A few minutes before 8:00 p.m., Dausi took her seat at the desk. A volunteer who worked at the Center brought her a pitcher of water and a glass. He poured some water into the glass and whispered, "Thank you for all you do." His twelve-year-old sister, still in Zambia, was still a virgin, and still healthy, in large part due to the efforts of this incredible woman and her organization.

"You're all set," another volunteer holding a clipboard said. "You'll have video calls for two hours tonight, until ten, then again from eight to eight Monday through Friday. You're booked on a nine o'clock flight immediately after your wrap on Friday. Given how close the airport is, and how well they handle their private clients, you should be good on timing."

"Will you and your men be here the whole week?" Dausi asked Charlie.

"Not me. I'm leaving once you get started. Gotta get back to my day job." He'd never told anyone in this life what he did in his real life. Or vice versa. "But Quinn and Sanam will stick around all week, providing security. I don't think anything will happen, but keep your bag packed just in case. They'll have a car ready to take you to the airport at a moment's notice in case Uncle Sam decides to poke his nose in."

Dausi rose and gave Charlie a surprisingly solid hug for such a small woman, and kissed him on each cheek.

"Thank you."

"You are very welcome. This country needs your wisdom and leadership, even if it is too stupid to realize it."

Charlie excused himself to confirm that everything was ready with the video link. He was out the door, heading back to Opa-Locka for his late-night flight back to the Bay Area, before Roshin Dausi began her first video conference.

All week, leaders in America from various social justice organizations focused on empowering women and girls had video conferences with Dausi. A few federal and state legislators were also on her schedule. To a person, they were impressed and stirred by this passionate, powerful young woman. To a person, they thanked her for "staying up late" or "getting up early" and for "arranging the calls for their convenience." And to a person, they were impressed with the speed and quality of the video conference to what they thought was Malawi.

Chapter Eighteen

Senator Royce Carrington liked ceremony as much as he liked order. He started the meeting, as he always did, at exactly 8:00 p.m. and by following the rituals set forth almost two hundred years earlier. After leading the gathering in the opening prayer and burning the old card, he wrote 2149 on a new one and saved it in his desk drawer.

Reverend Porter Brooks was standing near the bar, pouring himself a brandy and Julian Kingsley was sitting and reading the front page of the Wall Street Journal. He'd already polished off three beers and had another resting on the side table near his chair.

"All right gentlemen, let's get to work. We have a great deal to do. After eight long years, we finally have control over the White House. Even better, we have firm control over the Senate and are still up a few seats in the House. In short, after an eternity in the wilderness, we are once again in a position to affect the kinds of changes we want in this world."

Carrington spoke directly to Kingsley. "Julian, you haven't been with us for very long, and most of the time you've been a part of our endeavor it's been quiet given our lackluster performance the last two election cycles. Porter can tell you, things heat up considerably when we're in power."

Reverend Brooks, who had been working with Senator Carrington for over thirty years, added, "Royce is telling it like it is, Julian. It's showtime."

Kingsley asked, "So what happens now?"

Carrington got up and walked over to the bar to pour himself a glass of delectable CHASE Vineyards Cabernet. He swirled it around in his glass to let it breathe, took a sip, and let out an audible moan. The Senator loved the company's bounding rabbit logo, the perfect representation of youthful exuberance. He knew that the delectable Zin grapes, grown at the Hayne Vineyard in Saint Helena, grew on vines over a century old and were hand-tended with no chemical intervention. He loved their mouthwatering acidity and complex flavors. He took another sip as he sat on the edge of his desk.

"It is tradition that we spend this meeting deciding on our short-term legislative, judicial, and cultural priorities. We will discuss our options and I'll decide our gameplan."

Kingsley said, "You mean, 'we,' right?" He was used to being in charge, taking the lead, being the voice in the room to which people listened.

Carrington said, simply, "I don't misspeak, Judge."

Kingsley, by this time, had once again had too much to drink. He rubbed his nose vigorously and said, "Wait just a second. I've been carrying your water for the past eight years. While Democrats have held the Presidency and both houses of Congress, I've been leading the charge in the Supreme Court. I was the swing vote that got *Roe* overturned. I did that, not you."

Carrington got up and walked to where Kingsley was sitting. He stood directly in front of the man, looking down on him. He spoke in an eerily calm voice.

"This is not a negotiation. You're a valuable member of our effort here, but, simply put, your membership is at my discretion. You understand, don't you?"

Even during his years as an assistant to the Solicitor General in the Justice Department, Kingsley had never experienced the kind of hardball Carrington appeared to play. He felt the chill of Carrington's words and demeanor. By "membership," Kingsley seriously wondered if Carrington meant "life." The man could be downright scary. He nodded weakly.

"Good. I'm happy we got that settled," Carrington said, his voice dripping with condescension. "As I was saying, let's talk about our priorities." He looked at Reverend Brooks. "Want to start us off, Porter?"

Porter Brooks spoke passionately for ten minutes on the evils of homosexuality. As a professional preacher, his presentation was more sermon than well-reasoned argument. It was also a screed he gave at every opportunity.

Brooks switched gears. "Or, what do you both think about going back to the issue of immigration? We were making great strides during the Spencer administration, nine or ten years ago. In the past eight years, the liberals have rolled back much of our progress. Immigration is back up. Illegal immigration is still low, but people are still fearful of these people invading our country. What is wrong with these Tacohead-loving liberals..."

Carrington, irritated, said, "Porter! Do you really have to use that kind of language? It's unbecoming for a man of God."

Kingsley, who was cracking open another beer, ignored Brooks' indelicacy and Carrington's rebuke and said, "I'd rather focus on birth control or something like that. My name was ruined by the accusations made against me years ago. 'Me Too' my ass. There are several cases that need to be overturned... There's—"

"Porter?" Carrington prompted, ignoring the legal weeds through which Kingsley was about to wade.

"I still want to tamp down on the queers or the hordes of immigrants attacking us."

Carrington bristled but ignored Brooks' rhetoric. "What about abortion?" he asked.

"What about abortion?" Kingsley said defensively.

Carrington shared what was on his mind. "Overturning *Roe* was a good first step, to be sure. But abortion is still legal in over twenty states. It's legal without significant limitations in eight." He sighed. "We can and should do more here."

Reverend Brooks said, "I think what Royce is suggesting is that we work to outlaw abortion everywhere."

"Yes, I understand, thank you," Kingsley said. "You're talking about a federal law that bans abortion."

"That's right," Carrington said. "A 'sanctity of life' bill. Yes, that's the ticket. That's what we need to push."

Kingsley asked, "What about doing something to prevent the use of birth control?"

Brooks asked, "What are we going to do about the damn wetbacks?"

"Enough," Carrington said. "I've decided. First order of business this year is to get a "Sanctity of Life" bill passed.

"But, but" Kingsley stammered, "our five-four majority was based on the argument that abortion should be a state-by-state policy decision. I was able to get the chief to sign onto my opinion only because we agreed that it's a states' rights issue."

"Well, lucky for us, you're a clever man. You'll find a way." Carrington was not asking or suggesting. Kingsley thought back to his years as a political operative in the Justice Department. *Once a partisan, always a partisan*, he supposed.

Carrington stood up and paced the room. "Let's spend the rest of the evening working through the kind of language we want in the legislation, and who we can work with in the Senate and House. Julian, you can spend some time thinking about how you can defend the law when we can get the right case in front of you. Figure a year or two at least."

The men strategized until midnight. When the meeting finally adjourned, Carrington pointed at the Reverend and said, "We'll make the rounds next Sunday morning. Get someone to cover your sermon. Now, if you'll excuse me, I've got to call the President."

Chapter Nineteen

The hair and makeup woman touched up Oscar Alvarez's makeup with a few minutes to spare before airtime. She'd already finished with Senator Carrington and Reverend Brooks. Damn, she thought, Carrington was still sexy despite being in his seventies.

"All set, boss," she said to Alvarez, who was checking his social media feeds on his cell phone.

Alvarez thanked the woman and walked out onto the set. The production crew had brought his two guests out a few minutes earlier in order to get them wired up and comfortably situated. They were sitting at the glass table that was at the center of his set, and he walked up to each man and shook hands.

Alvarez took his seat and allowed the tech to affix his microphone and battery pack. The man did the work quickly and wordlessly, and was off set as the director counted silently down from five.

As the clock showed 8:00:00, Alvarez stared into the camera and started his show.

"Good morning. I'm Oscar Alvarez. Welcome to 'Tough Talk.' I'm delighted to have two distinguished guests with me this morning, Senator Royce Carrington, the senior Senator from Mississippi, and Reverend Porter Brooks, pastor of megachurch Christ's Fellowship Church outside of Nashville, Tennessee. "Welcome gentlemen."

"Good morning," Carrington said in his rich baritone.

"Thanks for having us on," Brooks added.

"Let's get right to the tough talk, shall we?" This was Alvarez's trademark phrase. "I understand you have an announcement regarding important legislation you want to introduce. Is that right, Senator?"

"That's right, Oscar. President Owens and I have met several times to discuss this, and we agree that now is the time for Congress to pass a 'Sanctity of Life' bill for the President to sign."

He could guess from the name of the bill, but Oscar Alvarez, a seasoned pro, calmly asked, "What would the legislation provide for?"

"Our Sanctity of Life bill will defend the lives of unborn babies across the country. Right now, abortion is far too available in various states and is still far too common. We must protect these children." Carrington's passion infused intensity into his every word.

"Fetuses, you mean?" Alvarez asked.

"Children," Carrington said. "I mean children."

"You're talking about a national anti-abortion law?"

"That's correct," Reverend Brooks said. "It would outlaw abortion in all fifty states."

Carrington added, "It would make abortion a federal crime. Both for the mother and anyone providing medical treatment."

Oscar Alvarez listened to his producer's voice in his earpiece. "And you're saying that President Owens would be supportive of this legislation?"

"Yes. He's been involved since day one, and his people are helping us craft the bill."

Alvarez faced the camera and said, "Here's a clip of President Owens from the campaign trail, just a few months ago. I'll show it and then I'd like to get your comments on the other side."

The producer rolled footage of Brock Owens from four months earlier while Owens was a presidential candidate. He looked into the camera and said, "Our nation has had enough of the culture wars over the past twelve years. The time has come to focus on the issues upon which all Americans can agree: strengthening our economy, creating jobs, keeping the country safe, helping repair the environment. If elected President, I will steer clear from divisive issues that others use to drive a wedge between people."

Alvarez loved that he worked with outstanding professionals. He looked at Senator Carrington and asked, "That was the President just a few months ago while still a candidate. How is his support for—and, apparently, involvement in—bringing this kind of legislation forward consistent with his promise to steer clear of these kinds of cultural flashpoints?"

"The President fully supports our efforts to get this law passed," Carrington said, ignoring Alvarez's question.

"It is critically important that we pass this law as soon as possible," Reverend Brooks implored. "Every day, thousands of babies are slaughtered. We must act to protect them."

Alvarez was about to speak when Carrington added, "Our goal is to get the Sanctity of Life bill passed and on the President's desk by March 15th."

"That's just over five weeks away," Alvarez said, unable to keep the amazement from his voice.

"Thousands of unborn babies will be killed in that time," Reverend Brooks said in his best Pastor's Voice. "This is an emergency. A humanitarian crisis."

Alvarez heard his producer in his ear again and said, "Senator, when the Supreme Court overturned *Roe*, the decision was based on the principle that abortion was a state's rights issue. Do you really think your bill would be held as constitutional?"

Carrington was a man who prepared for everything. He had his aides lead mock interviews all week, and he knew this question would come. Damn Julian Kingsley, and the four Justices who joined his opinion, for relying on the principle of states' rights to overturn *Roe*. Carrington paused and considered his response. He turned to look Oscar Alvarez in the eye, sure he was facing away from the camera, and said, "We shall see." Only Oscar Alvarez saw the twinkle in the Senator's eye.

After another whisper in his ear, Oscar Alvarez looked into the camera and said, "Don't go anywhere. We'll be right back in just two minutes with more tough talk."

Chapter Twenty

29 days before vote on the Sanctity of Life bill

For the past ten days, since Hope heard about the so-called Sanctity of Life legislation about to be rushed through Congress, she had tried—and failed—to keep her emotions in check. For better or for worse, her schedule was too hectic to allow her to fully process the situation.

Since she'd fixed her citations and submitted her paper describing the results of the latest trial of her artificial womb, she'd been inundated with emails and calls from researchers around the world. Faye had told her early on in her tenure at the lab that responding quickly and encouragingly to every inquiry was critical. While the artificial womb was "her baby," pun not intended, Faye convinced her that at some point it would only be a success if others joined her efforts.

Finally, on Wednesday evening, Hope had time for herself, away from the hospital, away from the lab, and away from work at the Pancake Shack. She put on a pair of shorts, her faded LSU t-shirt, and her running shoes and "ran the Dish" as it was called, in the hills near Stanford. The Dish, a popular recreational area for hiking and jogging open to the public from sunrise to sunset throughout the year, got its name from a still-functioning radio telescope in the area. Stanford students and others in the Bay Area had been coming to the area for decades.

Finished with her run, she sat at the top of the hill, pondering her future.

She stared at the text message from the private detective for the hundredth time. He'd found Derek. In some shithole swamp in the Florida Keys. For now. Apparently, Derek was even more of a dirtbag as an adult than he was as a high school kid, surprise surprise. The detective said Derek had a habit of moving around, leaving town after one brush with the law or another. *Okay, great, so now what?* She was almost three thousand miles away, in her final year at Stanford Med School, and, if she was honest with herself, more than a little scared of the man. *What if he sends someone else, only this time it's someone competent? Or who has a knife or a gun? What if he's turned into a full-on psychopath and comes himself?* Besides, the Sanctity of Life Bill was the proverbial bigger fish to fry. That was the real priority, she knew.

As the sun went down over the hills, Billy walked up and sat next to her. He was breathing hard and his shirt was wet with perspiration.

"Hi there," Hope said. "Thanks for meeting me."

Billy sucked in a few deep breaths and said, "Sure, no problem." He smiled. He noticed that Hope didn't smile back. She normally liked to tease him gently about being out of shape. That's when he figured something was really awry.

"What's wrong?" he said, reaching out and placing a hand gently on Hope's shoulder.

Hope shrugged his hand off. She was stewing.

"You haven't called me back in, like, forever," Billy snapped. "I just figured you were crazy busy. Like always." He realized suddenly that it had been since election night that she'd gone dark. "Is this about the election? I know you must be unhappy..."

"Unhappy? Unhappy?!" Hope was shouting. "'Unhappy' doesn't begin to describe how I'm feeling."

Billy noticed a group of Stanford students nearby. They were staring. "Keep your voice down, Hope." He nodded his head toward the students.

Hope hissed the words "I will *not* keep my voice down" through clenched teeth. Her reaction surprised Billy; she was normally reluctant to draw attention to herself.

"Talk to me Hope. What. Is. Going. On?"

Hope held her knees close to her chest. She rocked forward and back.

"Hope? What's going on? Please talk to me."

"Did you know that today is the nine-year anniversary of Angel's death?"

Billy knew; he'd wanted to plan a romantic getaway for Valentine's Day and had asked one of the nurses about Hope's schedule a few weeks earlier. The nurse, after confirming Billy knew about Hope's sister, told him the exact date of her death and discouraged him from planning anything on a day of the year that, for Hope, brought back such a painful memory. He'd nodded solemnly and thanked her.

"Yeah, I know," Billy said softly.

"Have you heard about the bill Senator Carrington and the President are pushing?"

"The 'Sanctity of Life' bill?" Billy asked. "Who hasn't?"

"It's going to pass. Republicans regained control over the House and they still have control over the Senate. And Owens is going to sign it."

"Maybe," Billy said. "Maybe. But there's no way it'd stand up in court. The Supreme Court would strike it down."

Hope turned to face Billy. "You don't understand, do you? Kingsley is a partisan hack. So are the others, frankly. They'll find a way to declare the law constitutional."

"But the court's legal argument for overturning *Roe* was that abortion should be a state-by-state decision. The same nine people are still on the court. How could they possibly now say that it's not up to the states?"

"You are so naive," Hope said. She reached out and clutched one of his hands in hers. "They will do anything they have to. Anything." After a long pause she added, "I need to stop them."

A frisbee landed a few feet away and interrupted their conversation. A sweaty guy in a Stanford t-shirt ran toward them to retrieve it. He apologized, picked up the frisbee, and ran back toward his friends. He wanted no part of the black cloud that hung over the man and woman and the serious conversation in which they were engaged.

Billy started to ask Hope what she meant when she said, "I can't concentrate on my research. I can't concentrate with my patients. I keep dropping plates and glasses at work. I—"

"So? What? What, exactly, do you want to do? You're the one who always has a plan, always works her plan. What's your plan?"

"I don't know!" Hope shouted. "And I hate not knowing what I'm going to do. But I have to fight these people. I have to."

"Are you talking about... dropping out of school?" Billy asked, astonished. "That's insane. You're almost done with your last year of residency. You are, literally, just a few months away from being a doctor."

"I have to do something," Hope said, practically in a whisper.

"Please don't do anything rash. At least think about it for a while. Talk to as many people as you can. Your boss at the lab. Your boss at the diner. Me. Anyone. Everyone. Please."

Some part of Hope knew Billy was trying to help her and knew he was right. But a much bigger part of her wanted to strangle him. Couldn't he see the danger? What would happen to millions of women and young girls? If Carrington's bill was passed, signed into law, and upheld by the Supreme Court, millions of women would be at risk. While she resented her mother for leaving when she and Angel were so young, she saw now what a danger to the country President Spencer had been, and that her mother was unimaginably brave to fight against him despite the cost. Now, what was about to happen was far, far worse for the country. Certainly for women. She realized she truly understood what her mother had done and why, that her mother felt that she had no choice but to fight, no matter the cost. It was Hope's turn to do the same.

In a flash, an idea came to her: she needed to demonstrate to the politicians in Washington that her artificial womb worked.

"Listen, Billy. I'm going to need you to look after Xander for a while."

Chapter Twenty-One

28 days before vote on the Sanctity of Life bill

Charlie was scrubbing the grill while Hope wiped off the condiment holders and ketchup bottles. He had the stereo system tuned to his George Ezra playlist and was dancing in place as he worked. Despite the fact that he'd started his day at 5:30 a.m. and that it was almost midnight, Charlie was still going strong. The man was a force of nature, Hope mused.

When the work was done and Charlie was taking off his apron, he walked toward Hope, who was mindlessly wiping down the counter for a third time.

"What's bothering you, kiddo?"

Hope stopped wiping, looked up and smiled. Charlie was always looking out for her. She shrugged, not really knowing where to start.

"Look, you've dropped so many plates and glasses over the past week, I thought I was hosting Greek weddings every day. So either you've suddenly developed a palsy of some kind or something's on your mind. I'm guessing it isn't the palsy."

Hope's smile widened. This man, her adoptive father in a way, always had a way of wrapping her in a sense of warmth. She took a deep breath and talked about the bill Senator Carrington and Reverend Brooks announced a week and a half before, and about how the President apparently not only supported the legislation but actually had a hand in crafting it.

"I know all this," Charlie said gently. Many might mistake his good nature, the permanent twinkle in his eye, and his profession as indicators of an uneducated man. Well, he thought, he was uneducated in the traditional sense. But that didn't mean he wasn't smart or didn't read. Or didn't care about politics.

"I feel like I need to do something, Charlie. Ever since Angel died, it's been my mission to find a way to help girls and women who end up in a similar situation. Rape is bad enough. But worse, I think, is the law. Men should not be in a position to tell us what women can and cannot do with our bodies. Especially in the cases of rape and incest."

Charlie raised his hands in an "I'm on your side" motion.

"Do you know about my research at the lab?"

"Yes, kiddo. I listen to every word you say. I may not always understand everything, but I know that you're working on a way to remove fetuses from pregnant women as early in their pregnancies as possible so they don't have to carry unwanted pregnancies to term."

Hope was, once again, pleasantly surprised by this amazing man.

"Well, I have a crazy idea," Hope said. She described her plan, such as it was. As she did so, she realized it was really more of a fantasy. Still...

"How long have we known each other now, kiddo?" Charlie asked. "About ten years?"

"A little less, I guess, but yeah, that's about right."

"In all that time, I don't think I've ever told you about Charlie Jr."

"You have a son?" Hope exclaimed.

"C.J. was an amazing young man. Smart as a whip, kind-hearted. A lot like you. Had his whole life in front of him." Charlie's eyes watered as he remembered his boy. "He joined the military, said he wanted to help bring peace to the planet."

Hope was at a loss for words.

"C.J. died in a training exercise down in San Diego, about a year or so before you first came to work here. Remember when President Spencer decided to send troops to the southern border? C.J.'s squad was doing training exercises for that deployment when another marine's weapon accidentally discharged." Charlie was openly crying now.

Hope walked around the counter and gave Charlie her fiercest hug, something he normally did for her. He looked down at her and smiled gently.

"A fucking training exercise. For what? For a political stunt, that's what."

"Thank you for telling me about C.J.," Hope said. "But... why are you telling me that story now?"

Charlie wiped his tears and inhaled deeply. His barrel chest rose and fell. "Because," he said, "I'm in. Whatever you want to do, I'm in."

"Oh, no, Charlie. I can't ask you to do that."

"Did you ask? I'm offering," he said. He puffed his chest out and put his hands on his hips. "I'm in. Just try and stop me."

Hope hesitated. Charlie was a middle-aged man, a short-order cook, a small business owner. What she had in mind was crazy.

As if reading her mind, Charlie said, "Listen, there's something else you need to know about me." He motioned to one of the booths and he and Hope sat down. "Many years ago, I was a lieutenant in the Army. My men and I were deployed in Afghanistan. The executive summary is that Uncle Sam screwed us and almost all of my men died one horrible, fateful morning."

"Oh my God," Hope said. She didn't really know what to say. "But... why are you telling me this?"

"Ever since that day, I've secretly helped people wronged by the government. The guys who survived from my squad help me."

"But you work all the time. How—"

"We're closed two days a week, remember? That's not so I can rest or because I believe in observing the Sabbath."

A thought flashed through Hope's mind.

"That morning I came in for a job... you were injured. You blamed it on the meat slicer, if I remember."

"A rare Friday night adventure down in L.A. I'd just gotten back, not thirty minutes before you walked in the door. Barbed wire can do some serious damage, that's for sure. I knew you were a keeper when you helped me that day."

"I remember thinking how strange it was that the machine looked so clean."

After a beat, they both laughed.

"But you have the restaurant. And, let me remind you, the Capitol Building is not here in California."

"I am aware, Miss Sassypants."

Hope grinned. Through the years, this was Charlie's nickname for her whenever he thought she was being sassy, as he called it.

"You're serious?"

"As a heart attack."

Hope hated that he joked about that, still, even after he'd had a minor cardiac event several years earlier. She wanted to admonish him for his bad taste, but instead said, "Well, that's good. Because for the first time in my life, I have no real idea of what to do."

"Lucky for you, ol' Charlie is on your team. My guys and I can help. I'll call them tonight and ask them to be here tomorrow. Let's meet again tomorrow night, midnight."

"Sounds like a plan," Hope said. *Sorta.*

Charlie turned off the stereo system and grabbed his coat. The two friends walked out the front door, and Charlie locked it. He turned to Hope and took her hands in his.

"Love you kiddo," he said, gently squeezing her slender fingers in his arthritic paws.

"Love you, too, old man." She gave him another hug before walking to her car.

Chapter Twenty-Two

27 days before vote on the Sanctity of Life bill

At midnight the following night, Hope and Charlie were done cleaning up, and sat in a corner booth sipping decaffeinated coffee when the bells on the front door chimed. A man walked in and spotted Hope and Charlie in the corner.

Hope's first reaction was, "Hubba hubba." Her second reaction was, "He looks like a sea captain!" The man appeared to be in his mid-thirties, had short, coiffed brown hair, and a bushy brown and gray speckled beard.

"Hey Q," Charlie said, waving. He stood and gave the man a big bear hug. Turning to Hope, he said, "Quinn, meet Hope. Hope, Quinn."

Quinn reached his hand out and shook Hope's hand. She liked that it was a firm handshake, that he hadn't softened it because she was a woman.

"Quintavius Lancaster at your service, ma'am," Quinn said. "My friends call me Quinn, and any friend of Charlie's is a friend of mine, but you may call me anything you'd like. Anytime." He smiled, and Hope was further charmed.

"Nice to meet you, Boris," Hope said, and Quinn exploded in a full-throated laugh.

"Told you you'd like her," Charlie said to Quinn, reading his friend's expression. Then to Hope he said, "Quinn's the best explosives guy on the planet."

"Demolition. We say 'demolition' now Charlie." Quinn let out another chuckle. Hope realized she was going to have to watch herself around this man. He was sexy as hell.

While Charlie and Quinn told each other bawdy jokes, the front door opened again. This time, a slender Indian man walked in. Like Quinn had done, he walked toward the table where the group was sitting.

"Hi Charlie. Hey Quinn," the man said.

"Mister Patel!" Charlie boomed. "Please, come join us. Hope, I'd like you to meet Mister Patel. Mr. Patel, I'd like you to meet Hope Hunter."

"Hello Hope," the man said. "My name is Sanam, but Charlie says he can never remember it. I think he's pulling my leg, as you say, but what can I do?"

Hope sized the man up. He wore small plastic frame glasses that didn't hide his rich dark chocolate eyes, and he had a neatly trimmed goatee. She found herself liking him immediately. "It's nice to meet you, Sanam." She looked over at Charlie as if to shame him.

"There's always one in every class," Charlie joked.

"What's your area of expertise?" Hope asked Sanam.

"People say I'm a sensors and switches savant. Say that fast three times." He giggled. "Charlie said you might need something unique. I'm intrigued."

Hope started to explain, but Charlie cut her off.

"Let's hold off just a bit," Charlie said. "I've got one more guy joining us." Through the years, Charlie had brought in various mercenaries now and again depending on the particular needs of a mission. Quinn and Sanam wondered who he'd invited this time.

It was already 12:15. "Well, he's late," Quinn said. "I don't like working with people who aren't on time. It's not professional."

Charlie didn't want to tell Quinn that he'd actually told the last man to meet at 11:45 p.m. He wasn't just fifteen minutes late, he was thirty minutes late.

Finally, at 12:25, another man came into the restaurant. After he entered, he stood just inside the door and nervously looked around, almost like he was casing the joint like a burglar would. After thirty twitchy seconds, he finally made his way to the group assembled in the back.

If Hope found Quinn attractive and charming, and Sanam likeable, this man repulsed her immediately. He had thinning, oily hair; acne-scarred skin; a scraggly goatee; and an overall demeanor that screamed drug addict. Or axe murder. Or both.

"Glad you could join us, Eddie," Charlie said. Eddie had worked with Charlie on a few of Charlie's side jobs, but none with Quinn or Sanam to this point.

Eddie Townsend introduced himself to everyone, and explained his profession, such as it was, proudly stating that he could get guns of any kind for anyone that wanted them.

"You sell guns to gang members? Nutjobs? Angry ex-boyfriends?" Quinn asked Eddie, a hard edge to his voice.

"I provide a service," Eddie said. "That service happens to involve guns. And, yeah, that's right, I don't discriminate. Turns out the service I provide is highly valuable, too, if you know what I mean."

Quinn, already upset at the man's tardiness, said, "Charlie, I can't work with someone who sells guns to just anyone, and that are almost certainly used to hurt innocent people." Quinn felt strongly that some people deserved violence be committed upon them. Hell, he, Charlie, and Sanam had been doing it themselves for years against some very bad people, although never with guns." He looked at Eddie and added, "No offense."

"None taken," Eddie said. He was used to people's reaction to his profession and, if he was honest, to him personally.

"Why don't you listen to what Hope has in mind? I think you'll understand why I felt the need to include Eddie here," Charlie said to Quinn and Sanam. He hoped they would accept Eddie's involvement in their project once they knew what Hope was thinking.

"Please, proceed m'lady," Quinn said to Hope. "Tell us why we are all here."

Hope took a deep breath and closed her eyes. This was it: the first step down a road she never imagined she would walk. She briefly explained the circumstances of Angel's death and her stalwart opposition to the proposed Sanctity of Life bill, then moved on to describing her intentions. "In short, I want to attack the U.S. Senate, while they are in session, and impregnate Senator Royce Carrington. Yes, impregnate. With a fetus. And I want it to be covered live on C-SPAN."

She stopped and took a read of the men at the table. She waited for what felt like an eternity until Eddie, the gun guy, said, "Fuckin' A, lady! That's some seriously fucked up shit!" After a beat he added, "I love it!"

Hope, who desperately wanted the group to support her plan, suddenly worried what it meant that this lunatic supported it. She turned to face Quinn and Sanam. "Guys?"

Quinn asked, "You need me to help with a forced entry?"

Charlie interjected. "I'm hoping that we won't have to actually ignite any explosives. I want them as a deterrent. Assuming we can get in, we can place the explosives on the chamber door from the inside and inform the police or FBI that we've rigged the doors."

Hope added, "We need your talents in another way too, Quinn." She took a sip of coffee and said, "I don't want this man to have the option of removing the fetus I implant. I want you to help with a small explosive that I can somehow attach to the artificial womb I insert. No abortions for women? Well, no 'abortion'"—she made air quotes with her hands—

"for the douchebag from the great state of Mississippi, either."

Quinn couldn't help himself. He started calculating how much C-4 would be needed, how much wire, …

Hope continued, "I need the smaller explosive to be deadly to the host, but in no way dangerous to anyone around him. No innocent should be injured or put at risk. That's non-negotiable."

"Is that why I'm here?" Sanam asked. "You need some kind of sensor or switch that will set the internal explosive off should the man attempt to remove his fetus?"

"Exactly."

Sanam shook his head, "I don't know. I'm not sure how to make that work. A tilt switch? A change in pressure? Maybe a—"

"I still don't like that we have to involve a gun dealer," Quinn said, cutting off Sanam's musings. He didn't like the looks of this Eddie guy any more than Hope did.

The group discussed the situation for over an hour. When it was approaching two in the morning, Hope finally said, "Well? Are you guys in or are you out? There's less than a month before these Senators pass their precious 'Sanctity of Life' bill."

Sanam spoke in a quiet, serious voice. "This seems to be a plan borne of anger, not of clear thinking. This worries me."

"I can't disagree with that," Hope said. "But this is my mission. I'm doing this, somehow, some way. So I'll ask again: are you in or are you out?"

Quinn banged a hand on the table and declared, "I'm in." Hope actually blushed. She—and Charlie— would never know that Quinn's niece had gone for an off-the-books abortion a few years earlier and would never be able to have children because of the botched procedure.

Eddie twitched and said, "Fuck yeah! Let's stick it to the man!" Charlie had promised him ten grand for his help.

"Sanam?"

"Count me in," Sanam said with as much enthusiasm as he could muster.

"Thank you guys," Charlie said.

Hope told the men that the group would meet again in the Spirit of Justice park in Washington D.C. in three days, on the following Monday.

"At noon, Eddie," she said, looking directly at the man. It was all she could do not to look away, he repulsed her so much.

"Yeah, yeah, whatever," Eddie said.

"Be there. On time," Quinn said to Eddie. How he hated unprofessional people.

"Make reservations at separate hotels in the greater D.C. area. Not in D.C. proper. Understand? Eddie?"

"Yeah, yeah, got it," Eddie said. He hated how people talked to him.

Charlie gave each man and Hope an envelope of spending money, and the meeting was adjourned.

Chapter Twenty-Three

Senator Royce Carrington sat in the back of the school's crowded "multi-use room" and tried to stay invisible. He wore jeans, a plaid wool shirt, and paint-splattered work boots, and had a Shreveport Swamp Dragons baseball cap pulled tightly on his head. The boots were from the back of his closet, from back when he was still willing and able to do some of the renovations around his house, and the hat was from a garage sale he'd visited on the way to the emergency School Board meeting. He hadn't worn the jeans in years.

Carrington looked around the room, which seating for about a hundred people but currently held about twice that. Clusters of people—mostly parents of students at the school as best he could tell—stood and spoke in hushed tones. Dozens had pink public comment cards, which they intended to submit so they could speak for two minutes in front of the School Board. Most fanned themselves with their cards in a failed attempt to stay cool in the hot, stuffy room.

Eventually, the members of the Board returned and took their seats on the room's raised stage, which served as their dais. After a few minutes, all were settled and the Board President banged his gavel and officially announced that the meeting was now back in open session.

A parent volunteer weaved through the crowd and picked up all of the comment cards, then made her way to where the Board Secretary sat and handed over the stack of cards. Every member of the Board knew from the size of the crowd and the height of the stack of comment cards that it was going to be a long night. The Board President made introductory remarks, pleading with anyone intending to speak to do so civilly and for audience members to refrain from any kind of outburst. He called the first speaker, Sam Doernbecher.

A fortyish-looking man with thinning brown hair and wire-frame glasses walked nervously to the microphone in the center of the room, about ten feet from the Board Members on stage.

"Good evening ladies and gentlemen of the Board, and members of the audience. My name is Sam Doernbecher. My daughter, Elizabeth, is a freshman here. We are practicing Christians in my household, but I do not believe that Mrs. Hyatt, or any other teacher here, has the right to share her faith with students at school. I support whatever punishment you feel appropriate, up to and including termination. Thank you."

Despite the Board President's opening comments, the room erupted in chatter. Most of the people in the room either booed or yelled at the man, who quickly took his seat and tried to ignore the vitriol being spewed his way.

The next eight speakers took the opposite view. One, an algebra teacher at the school and a good friend of Mrs. Hyatt, the woman at the center of the storm, said, "We should not be asked to compartmentalize our faith. If we truly believe in Christ and desire to follow Him, then our faith should impact every aspect of our lives, including what we do here leading our students." This caused most of the crowd to erupt in applause.

After another man had the audacity to state his opinion that Mrs. Hyatt should be fired immediately, the crowd became so unruly that the Board President had to bang on his gavel repeatedly in his attempt to bring order to the chaos. He eventually quieted the crowd before calling another teacher.

"My name is Brenda Barnes, and I teach American History. Mrs. Hyatt is my department chair and she is an amazing teacher who is being treated horribly."

The crowd applauded and Brenda Barnes waited for quiet before continuing.

"Every teacher at North Fairfields and at every other school in the country has preconceived ideas they bring with them into the classroom. But there's a big difference. Ours are the Truth. Why should other teachers be able to spread their false ideas and their false philosophies while we're being told to muzzle our True ones?"

After another burst of applause and delay, Barnes delivered what she thought was her coup de grâce. "God's truths are not just for Sunday mornings," she said before taking her seat, a proud and defiant look on her face.

Carrington sat, rapt by the spectacle of local democracy in action. Passions ran high on both sides of the issue, but at least in this room on this night, there were far more people supporting the teacher, Mrs. Hyatt, than not. He'd read in the local paper that, during a lesson on ancient Egypt, she'd shared her view that the teachings of Jesus were clearly the Truth compared to the polytheism of the Egyptians, and that a student told her parents and the parents complained to someone at the School District. The primary agenda item in tonight's emergency session was whether the School Board would reprimand, suspend, or terminate the teacher.

Eventually, everyone who wanted to speak had his or her opportunity to do so. Carrington found it interesting that, in his mind at least, most of the poor, uneducated parents used their two minutes to far greater effect than most of the teachers. After some back and forth about the need for a clear motion with a yes or no vote, one of the parent representatives on the Board made a motion.

"I make a motion that we terminate Mrs. Hyatt's contract with the school," Mrs. Potter, a parent representative on the Board, said.

"Second," said the Vice President, a heavyset woman wearing huge hoop earrings and garish pink lipstick.

"All right," the Board President said, "I'll go down the line, starting with Mrs. Potter. I'll go last. The motion on the table is whether to terminate Mrs. Hyatt's contract. An 'aye' vote is a vote to fire her. A 'no' vote is a vote not to fire her. Depending on the outcome of the vote, we may entertain other motions. Everyone clear on the motion?"

The seven members of the Board nodded their heads.

Six votes later, the vote was three to three and the teaching career of Mrs. Hyatt was in the hands of the Board President.

"I vote 'aye,'" he said somberly.

And with that, Mrs. Hyatt's fate was sealed. The crowd became so hostile that the security guards the Board President hired felt the need to step forward from the corners of the room to position themselves in front of the stage. Several members of the audience threw wadded up papers, empty bottles and cans, and other items at the guards and the members of the Board.

Despite his preparation in hiring the guards, the Board President was afraid for his safety and that of his fellow Board members. He quickly called the meeting to a close. Within a minute, all four members who voted to fire the teacher were out the door, rushing for their cars. The other three stepped down into the crowd to commiserate with a cluster of parents in the audience.

Amidst the chaos, Royce Carrington walked quietly out the back door with his cell phone on his ear. His call was to the head of a political action committee committed to promoting "Judeo-Christian heritage" in public schools.

"Hello, Markus. It's me, Royce. I'm in. Twenty-five million. I'll get a check to you tomorrow."

Chapter Twenty-Four

Monday, February 19 (three days later)
The Spirit of Justice Park near the Capitol Building
Washington, D.C.

24 days before vote on the Sanctity of Life bill

Hope asked Charlie to meet her at the Spirit of Justice park fifteen minutes before their meeting with the others. He was waiting for her at the western fountain when she arrived.

"Hiya kiddo," he said, waving to her as she walked up.

"Hey Charlie."

Charlie noticed that Hope was shivering. He reached out and wrapped her scarf tighter around her neck and fully zipped her jacket.

"Thanks. I swear I don't know how people here do it. I took the metro to the Capitol South Station and only had to walk a block or two. What do the people who have to walk farther do? I mean, holy moly it's cold."

Charlie rubbed his hands up and down Hope's arms and enveloped her in his coat in an attempt to warm her up.

"We'll get a hot bowl of soup after we meet with the guys," Charlie said. "I know a place nearby." He reached into his pocket and pulled out a thermos of coffee. "In the meantime, drink this."

Hope took the thermos appreciatively. "Thanks. I don't know what I would do without you." She took a sip and savored it. "Listen... are you sure about Eddie Townsend? The guy gives me the creeps. And he can't even show up on time."

Charlie knew people's reaction to Eddie. Hell, he felt repulsed by the guy too. But the man could get his hands on pretty much any kind of weapon Charlie had needed through the years.

"He's not the most punctual guy, I'll grant you that," Charlie said, "but he's connected and can get us what we need. Like you said, we don't really have a lot of time. Which means we don't really have much choice."

"If you say so." She took another sip of the piping hot coffee and thanked Charlie again.

At noon, Sanam Patel and Quinn Lancaster walked up from different directions, Sanam from C Street and Quinn from D street.

After everyone greeted each other, Quinn made a point of looking at his watch. It was 12:01 and Eddie Townsend was nowhere to be seen.

"Charlie, I do not like working with people who don't have their shit together enough to be on time."

"I know, I know. Hope and I were just talking about it. But we need the firepower he can provide. We're talking about the U.S. Capitol for Christ's sake. We're going to need more than a couple of pea shooters."

The group stood and people watched for a few minutes until, finally, Eddie Townsend strolled up like he didn't have a care—or an appointment—in the world.

"Greetings and salutations, gentlemen. And m'lady," Eddie said with as much suaveness as he could muster.

Quinn stared at Eddie until Eddie dropped his gaze.

Charlie started their conversation. "Okay, listen up. The vote on the 'Sanctity of Life' bill is supposed to happen in less than a month, on the 15th. That doesn't give us much time. We need to rush but at the same time go slow, if you know what I mean.

"We need to make sure we give ourselves enough time to scope out the area, the Capitol building, and the Senate floor itself, if we can. I propose we give ourselves a week to do some recon; we need intel on the building's layout, the Capitol Police, surveillance cameras, and exit routes. We'll meet here one week from tomorrow at a coffee shop somewhere nearby. I'll text a time and an address, but figure a coffee shop somewhere near here and probably in the morning." He looked directly at Eddie and added, "Be on time, Eddie, or I'll find someone else."

Hope looked at Eddie, who was half listening and half ogling a young mother walking with a baby stroller.

"Eddie!" she shouted.

"Yeah, yeah, I got it," he said. He hadn't heard a word, but Charlie would have his back.

The group disbanded and the other men went their separate ways. Charlie wrapped his arm around Hope's shoulder and pulled her close. He kissed the top of her head.

"Let's get some soup," he said. "I'm freezing."

Chapter Twenty-Five

Tuesday, February 20 (the next day)
U.S. Capitol Building and surrounding area
Washington, D.C.

23 days before vote on the Sanctity of Life bill

On Tuesday morning, Hope took the Metro into D.C., bought several maps from the Capitol visitor center, and walked around. She held one of the maps open as she walked, something she would not normally do, hoping it would give her a measure of "cover" for surveilling the Capitol area: just another stupid tourist trying not to get lost. She turned on the voice recorder app on her phone, put her bluetooth earbud in her ear, and dictated important observations so she could listen to them later.

Quinn woke up and made an online reservation to take a standard visitor tour of the Capitol and another of the halls of the Senate, but learned that neither tour would include entry into the Senate chamber. The automated chat bot providing support told him that, for that, he needed a pass, which he could get from a Senator. He called his junior Senator, a young woman, put his magnetism on level eleven, and charmed himself a pass for the following day. He needed to see the doors of the Senate from the inside.

Charlie spent Tuesday shopping. He found a local Goodwill, which had most of what he wanted: an old overcoat, a wool cap, and some old leather boots. He bought a few more items at other second-hand stores. A quick trip to a pharmacy netted him baby wipes. He completed his shopping spree with a final stop at a hardware store where he bought a box of firewood, some lighter fluid, a box of matches, and a small box of extra strength garbage bags.

Sanam spent the day in his hotel room, thinking. From the very first moment Hope explained what she needed from him, he was worried he wouldn't be able to come through for her. He had no qualms about helping her; as a dark-skinned man, he was constantly harassed by people thinking he was a Muslim terrorist from the Middle East, and he was convinced that these people's spite and ignorance was fueled by conservative politicians. Throughout the day, he drew diagrams, then crumpled and burned them each time he realized his ideas were unworkable.

Eddie had a few old contacts in D.C. He called them when he woke up at noon, made arrangements to meet on Friday, then watched porn on the hotel pay-per-view system the rest of the evening.

Wednesday, February 21 (the next day)
U.S. Capitol Building and surrounding area
Washington, D.C.

22 days before vote on the Sanctity of Life bill

Hope spent Wednesday listening to the audio notes she'd recorded for herself and poring over the map of the U.S. Capitol area and a second map of the floorplan of the Capitol building itself. How could they get in? How could they do so without having to kill anyone? God, she really, really didn't want to hurt anyone but the Senator. How could they get away? After hours of spinning, she realized she was way out of her depth. She needed to call Charlie and get his help. Around 4:00 p.m., she received a short text message from Billy that read "xander's ok. r u?" She did not reply; she didn't really know the answer to his question.

Quinn arrived on time for his tour of the Capitol. As the group walked and the guide gave her spiel, Quinn memorized as many layout and security details as possible. After a quick lunch, he took his second tour, this time of the halls of the Senate. Although he was distracted by the exquisitely decorated corridors and stunning works by Italian-born artist Constantino, his professionalism was strong enough for him to memorize how many guards appeared to be on duty and where they were stationed.

Charlie woke up at 4:00 a.m., collected everything he needed for the day into a garbage bag, hoisted the bag over his shoulder, and headed out of his motel. He walked east for an hour and just before sunrise arrived at an abandoned strip mall under a highway overpass, where he unloaded a piece of firewood, the lighter fluid, and the matches. He tossed the piece of wood on the crumbling concrete loading dock behind the mall, doused it in lighter fluid, and lit it. While the wood burned, he changed out of his regular clothes into the clothes he'd bought around town the previous day. The pants were paint-stained and the three garish shirts he'd purchased clashed awfully; he ripped holes in everything. Charlie stuffed his street clothes into a garbage bag and waited a few more minutes for the wood to char. After stamping out a few remaining flames, he broke off chunks of charred ash and rubbed them all over his pants, shirt, and overcoat, and his hands, face and beard. Seeing his reflection in a broken window, Charlie was convinced he looked the part he was trying to play. He found a tree just inside the tree line nearby and stashed the trash bag that held his normal clothes and the box of baby wipes. He took out a protein bar, scarfed it down, and made his way toward the Capitol, where the city would host one more loitering apparently-homeless man for the day.

Wednesday was a repeat of Tuesday for Sanam, and he worried that his pacing was wearing a path in the threadbare carpeting of his hotel room. Near the end of the day, he arranged a tour of D.C., figuring he should probably do some first-hand recon.

Eddie slept late again, took a train into the city, and wandered. At five in the evening, he found a strip club that served dinner. After a lousy twenty-dollar steak, a bottle of Stoli, and six hours of watching naked ladies, Eddie made his way back to his hotel and passed out.

Thursday, February 22 (the next day)
U.S. Capitol Building and surrounding area
Washington, D.C.

21 days before vote on the Sanctity of Life bill

At Hope's request, Charlie came over to her hotel. Charlie had picked a low-class joint, but Hope had thoroughly outdone him. "Holy Christ this place is a dump," he said once she'd let him in. "Decorated it myself," she replied. She smiled and hugged him firmly for several seconds. Letting go, she added, "God, it's good to see you." Hope nodded toward the maps on the small desk in the corner, and the two friends sat down to review the maps and forge some kind of plan. Later that evening, Charlie did some more shopping on the way back to his motel.

Quinn spent Thursday planning out the details of what he needed as far as explosives for the doors. This was "the big boom" matériel, as he thought of it, compared to the "small boom" explosive for use within the body cavity of Hope's intended victim, which he still needed to think through. He was finishing up his calculations when Charlie came by and dropped off a bag of supplies and told him to meet Hope the following morning.

Sanam took his tour, but was so distracted by his sensor problem, he didn't notice much of anything that would be of value to the team.

Eddie went back to the same strip club, had another steak, drank another bottle, dropped another five hundred dollars for lap dances, and passed out again.

Friday, February 23 (the next day)
U.S. Capitol Building and surrounding area
Washington, D.C.

20 days before vote on the Sanctity of Life bill

Friday morning, Sanam was in a near panic. He'd never failed in his entire life. A star student, he'd been accepted into and received his degree from the esteemed India Institute of Technology, and had never let a client down in his years of private consulting or in his work with Charlie and Quinn. He feared that he was not going to be able to figure out how to solve the puzzle before him, and the thought of failure shook him to the core. He called Hope.

"Good morning. I hope I didn't wake you."

"No, no. Been up for a while," Hope said. "What's up?"

Sanam explained his concerns.

Hope thought back to her first year in college when she was certain she didn't know a single answer to any of the questions on a calculus exam. But she'd closed her eyes, taken several deep breaths, and then tackled them one at a time.

In an attempt to calm Sanam, Hope said, "I know you'll figure it out," despite knowing no such thing.

Eddie, pissed that he had to set his alarm, met his contact at a nearby convenience store a few minutes after nine. The man told Eddie he could pick up his weapons and ammunition the following Tuesday, and they agreed on a time and place. Later that night, he was back at the club. He decided he really had the hots for the chick who called herself "Lexus." He spent a fortune to keep her with him most of the night, and the two talked while she moved her hips.

When Quinn arrived at ten, Hope had already had breakfast and three cups of coffee. She was eager to get going, curious what Charlie had up his sleeve. He'd texted her to expect Quinn and to spend the day with him. Her mind raced when Quinn walked in with a large garbage bag over his shoulder. He plopped the bag on the bed.

"Get undressed, lassie," Quinn said. When he saw Hope's face flash from heat to fear to anger, he quickly added, "Calm yourself, child. Bad joke." Dumping out the contents of the bag, he motioned at the items Charlie had purchased.

"Funny. Real funny."

"Seemed to me you were interested there for a second," Quinn said. He smirked.

Hope blushed. "Just tell me what Charlie has cooked up."

Quinn explained.

Forty-five minutes later, an elderly couple, one nobody at the front desk had ever seen check in or visit, left the hotel. The woman had grey hair, wore a matronly dress and sensible shoes. She had what looked to be bad varicose veins under her panty hose, an effect that took Hope twenty painstaking minutes with a ballpoint pen. The stooped man had white hair and a white beard, wore an oxygen mask, and walked with a pair of oxygen tanks trailing behind him.

It was time to see if they could get the oxygen tanks past the security check and into the Senate chamber.

Saturday, February 24 (the next day)
U.S. Capitol Building and surrounding area
Washington, D.C.

19 days before vote on the Sanctity of Life bill

In a rare stretch of sobriety and professionalism, Eddie decided he should probably help scout the Capitol building. He woke early, took the train to the Capitol, and walked toward the loading dock of the Senate Office Buildings located on D Street. After scouting the area for a while, he spotted his mark: a Hispanic janitor about his size leaving the building, his overnight shift apparently over. Ten minutes later, the man lay in a hedge unconscious and with a growing welt on the back of his head, and Eddie, donning the man's overalls and wearing his employee badge, made his way into the building. He pushed an empty trash can around for several hours—he refused to pick up trash, especially in this place of all places—until he worried someone might find the rightful owner of his uniform.

Hope spent the morning sitting at a small coffee shop across from a local Planned Parenthood, watching the women going into and coming out of the facility. After her third cup of coffee, she was almost about to go to the restroom when she spotted a young teen, probably only sixteen or seventeen, come out of the building. The girl was bundled up in a pink coat and was wearing pink earmuffs but seemed to be losing her battle against the arctic winds that were whipping across the entire East Coast. The girl walked over to a nearby bench, sat, and immediately began sobbing, clearly beaten down by more than just the wind. Hope rushed out of the coffee shop, walked over to where the teen was sitting, said hello, and asked the girl why she was so forlorn. The young lady let her grief flow. She explained that she'd been molested and made pregnant by her drunken uncle, who was also her legal guardian, yet had to carry the baby to term because Virginia's state abortion law did not have an exception for incest. Hope quietly explained that she had an alternative, that she could remove the fetus from the girl's uterus so she wouldn't have to continue carrying the pregnancy to term. The girl immediately stopped crying and barraged Hope with questions. Hope explained that the medical procedure would remove the fetus, but that it would not be abortion. She said nothing about her intentions or Senator Royce Carrington. Hope told the girl to think things over, wrote down her phone number, and told the girl to call by the end of the day if she wanted help. This was a part of the plan that Hope hadn't told anyone else on the team.

Quinn spent the day working through the "small boom" explosive device. Hope had been very clear: the device must be potentially deadly to the man in whom it was to be inserted but could pose no harm to anyone else. After some research online and some time doing the calculations, he felt confident he could deliver. He spent the rest of the afternoon fantasizing about Hope. The woman was crazy sexy and didn't even know it.

Eddie returned to his hotel, took a nap, and showered when he woke up mid-afternoon. After an early dinner, he headed back to his new favorite strip joint. He waited a few hours and watched the stage show until Lexus started her shift. Man, she was hot. Maybe he could convince her to give him a little something extra in the back room. The rules were bound to be more lax back there.

He didn't see Charlie follow him throughout the day and into the men's club.

Lexus was grinding on Eddie, facing away from him, trying hard not to think about the man's greasy hair and scarred face. It was a skill you picked up pretty quickly if you wanted to last in the business. She was just about to turn and straddle him face-forward, when a handsome older man sat down close to Eddie.

"Hello, Eddie," Charlie said.

Eddie jumped, causing Lexus to lose her rhythm. "Well hello there, good looking," she said to Charlie. "Want a dance?" She winked at him and Eddie flashed to anger.

Charlie took out a hundred dollar bill and waved it at the woman on top of his weapons man. "No, thank you, dear. In fact, here's a hundred if you give my friend and me a song or two to talk in private."

Lexus didn't hesitate. She snatched the Benjamin from Charlie's hand and rose up off of Eddie's lap. "Catch ya later, Eddie."

"Hey! I paid for this song. The song's not over yet."

Lexus looked at Charlie and gave him a "you're really a friend of this guy?" look. Charlie shrugged, tilted his head, and raised his eyebrows.

Lexus flicked a twenty at Eddie and sashayed away.

"How ya doin', Eddie?"

Although he was someone who scared most people, and who didn't scare easily himself, Eddie found himself very much afraid of Charlie, despite the man's cheery demeanor and the handful of jobs they'd worked together. "All good, Charlie. We're all set."

"Yeah? You've got everything?"

"Well, not exactly."

"What do you mean, 'not exactly?'"

Eddie explained that he was going to pick up the merchandise on Tuesday.

After a few more questions, Charlie got up to leave. "Keep in touch." Eddie nodded vigorously.

On his way out, Charlie passed the girl who'd been dancing for Eddie. "He's all yours again," he said. "But, before that, I've got another hundred if you'll answer a few questions about our friend." After a few minutes that netted him no useful information, he gave the girl his phone number and asked her to call him if Eddie told her anything interesting.

Sunday, February 25 (the next day)
Lincoln Memorial
Washington, D.C.

18 days before vote on the Sanctity of Life bill

The girl with whom Hope had spoken outside the Planned Parenthood office called Saturday night and asked if they could meet. Now, the following morning, at the bottom of the stairs that led up to the Lincoln Memorial, Hope sat with the young girl again. The girl had visited the website of Hope's research lab and had few remaining questions. She was eager to be spared the horror of her pregnancy. When Hope asked the girl if her uncle knew she was pregnant, the girl laughed derisively, saying her uncle was blackout drunk half the time when he was at home between his trucking jobs. When Hope asked the girl if she would promise to keep the pregnancy and procedure secret, she nodded her head resolutely and agreed without hesitation.

Chapter Twenty-Six

17 days before vote on the Sanctity of Life bill

At his direction, Hope met Charlie at a firearms training place east of the Potomac river, four or five miles from the Capitol building. She'd never been to a gun range before, and the place made her uneasy. She'd never even held a gun, let alone fired one. As she opened the front door to the place, the likely violence of her plan suddenly hit her. It scared her, and she hated how unsure she was of everything now.

Charlie, who was already in the store, greeted her and, as always, his presence helped calm her. They walked up to the counter.

"Hi. My daughter and I would like to shoot," Charlie said. Hope shot a look at Charlie but said nothing.

"Sure. Welcome. What'd you have in mind?"

"The Glock with a nine milimeter Luger cartridge," Charlie said. "She's still learning."

The man turned and grabbed two Glock pistols and two boxes of cartridges. He set them on the counter. He reached under the counter and pulled out two forms and slid them toward Charlie.

"Pens are in the holster there."

Charlie slipped something into Hope's hand under the counter. She glanced down and realized it was a fake ID, complete with her picture but someone else's name and personal details. The man never ceased to surprise her. She filled out her paperwork using her new ID. Charlie used his. Ten minutes later, they were at a shooting bay.

Charlie slowly and methodically gave Hope a lesson in how to hold, load, aim, and shoot the pistol. He was a patient teacher and she was a good student. Several hours later, they took their IDs back from the shop owner and walked out into bright sunshine.

Charlie fielded a few more detailed questions from Hope as they walked to a burger joint nearby. Over lunch, she was quiet and pensive until she finally whispered, "I don't know if I can do this."

"I don't know what you mean," Charlie said. He knew exactly what she meant.

"I don't think I can... kill someone." She barely spoke the final two words aloud.

"I'm going to do everything I can to make sure you don't have to. You should not have to live with that feeling, kiddo."

Hope could tell from how Charlie said it that he lived with that feeling himself. Another onion layer about the man she'd have to peel. Assuming she lived through the next few weeks.

Charlie paid the check and said, "Come on, one more stop."

He led her south to Cedar Hill Cemetery. As they walked, he explained the importance of being flexible and adaptive, that things rarely went as planned in a battle.

Hope didn't hide her discomfort. "I get it, Charlie, I do. That's what scares me the most about this whole crazy idea. I have no idea what I'm doing. That's not me. I'm a planner. I plan, plan, plan, then I work my plan. I get it from my mother. She drilled it into me every day until she left, and even now she's a distant reminder of what it means to make a plan and commit to that plan."

"Well, it's time you learn a bit about the power of being adaptive," Charlie teased. It was a trait that had kept him alive more than once.

Charlie gave Hope a primer on relevant military strategies, including the concepts of Blitzkrieg, shock and awe, decapitation, encirclement, and flanking, and stressed the importance of distraction, feinting, and other indirect approaches. For this last lesson, he told Hope they would play an unusual variant of hide and seek: he would hide and Hope would seek, but after a short delay, he would seek her, too. To win, she had to get within five feet of him before he spotted her. Each round, he gave himself a thirty second head start and then made noises to let her know approximately where he was. Each time, she listened carefully, triangulated, and made her way in a straight path, but he circled around and surprised her from behind. Each time, he gently suggested alternatives to the path she'd taken and to her overly-linear thinking.

All her years of studying science and math and all her years of med school worked against her, but Charlie was a patient coach. Finally by sundown, Hope was able to adapt mid-search, and was actually able to spot Charlie and win a time or two. She was dead tired, too.

As they walked back to the closest Metro station, they picked a coffee shop and a time for the team to meet the next day. Hope sent a text message to everyone with the details.

Chapter Twenty-Seven

16 days before vote on the Sanctity of Life bill

They all—except Eddie—sat at a large wooden table in the back of the coffee shop. Each had their custom-made coffee or tea drink in their hands, and they all waited impatiently for Mr. On-Time.

Nervous about their planned attack the next day, they made idle chatter for ten minutes. After finishing his latte with one final sip, Quinn tossed his empty cup into a nearby trash bin and said what was on everyone's mind. "Can we really trust him? I mean, *Christ*, this is three times already."

Before Charlie could answer, Eddie walked into the coffee shop and sauntered over to the table. He looked like he thought he was ten minutes early. He sat down and tipped his chair back to the point that Hope thought he would fall backward at any moment. "Howdy pardners," he said in a Southern accent by way of a greeting.

"Are you sure it's a good idea to have this conversation here, in public?" Sanam asked after Eddie sat down, ignoring the man.

"Spoken like someone who's often confused for a Muslim terrorist," Quinn said in a joking tone. He laughed and quickly added, "No, I think we're fine." To Charlie, he said, "It's actually a smart idea, Charlie. People planning dastardly deeds don't do it out in the light of day."

"Except for us," Charlie said with a devious twinkle in his eye. After a chug of his coffee, he added, "Okay, we have a lot to cover. I'll go first and talk about the entry plan and Eddie can talk about our hardware. Then Q can talk about the boom boom. After that, Hope, you can talk about the actual procedure you plan to perform. Finally, Sanam, you can update everyone on your progress with the sensor."

The team nodded their approval and Charlie began. "First, thanks to each of you—well, except for you, Sanam—for your intel. Your observations and comments have been very helpful. Especially yours, Eddie. Care to share how you were able to get such good info?"

After his shift as the world's worst janitor, Eddie had returned to the hedge and tossed back the man's badge. When the man finally came to, he was so worried about being fired that he simply made his way home and had his wife tend to his wound. The janitor would never, ever tell anyone that his ID was out of his possession, even for an hour or two. Eddie figured nobody here had to know about what happened either. "Nope," he said simply.

"Moving on," Charlie said, not liking the implications of Eddie's unwillingness to share the details. He pulled out a blueprint of the Capitol building and surrounding area.

"Whoa? Did you download that off the Internet?" Eddie said. "They can trace that, you know." His paranoia ran deep.

"No," Charlie said. "I have an old friend who works at the Capitol as a janitor. I asked him for a favor."

Charlie didn't see the little color there was drain from Eddie's face as he worried whether Charlie's friend was the man he'd attacked. Charlie continued, "Our best bet is a small entrance on the northwest corner, off Constitution, on the Third Street side of the building. That'll keep us well clear of the visitor center. I think all of us spotted the dozens of cameras in that area, inside and out. I spotted just one camera over the door I'm recommending we use.

"We should be able to make our way along the north side of the building until we get to the cloak room. From there, we can enter the Senate chamber. But I don't know for sure because none of us were able to get to that part of the building."

"This is nuts," Sanam said, voicing what everyone was thinking.

Quinn ignored Sanam's quip and said, "Assuming we can somehow disable any guards inside of that door and make our way to the Senate floor, another problem I can see is that this approach puts us about as far from the entrance doors as possible. We'd have to somehow make our way all the way across the room so I can arm the doors."

"I don't see another way," Charlie said.

"Then that's our plan," Hope said, hoping her feigned confidence would sell the plan to the others. She'd never been a "fake it till you make it" kind of person and hated that she'd become one.

Charlie provided more details about how they would approach, the tactics they would try to use to disable but not kill the guards, and how they would communicate once inside.

"For our exit, we'll cross Emancipation Hall and make our way past the north gift shop, the Senate Appointment Desk and the north coat check, and then out the north entrance."

When he was done, he turned to Eddie and said, "Okay, you're up."

Eddie looked at the eager faces of the others. This was the best part of his work. They might treat him with disdain and distrust, but they needed him and the service he provided. He was THE MAN and they needed him, just like all his other clients.

"I'll pick up our merchandise today after lunch," Eddie said. "We'll have something small for each of us and something larger for me and Charlie." Eddie didn't like the idea of meeting in such a public place, no matter what Charlie and Quinn thought. 'Small' meant Glock pistols and 'larger' meant DPMS AP4s, a semi-automatic civilian version of the U.S. Military's M4 Carbine, a weapon used by members of the U.S. military in Iraq and Afghanistan.

Quinn waited until two young K Street types walked by and were out of earshot. "I'm all set. I've procured what we need for the doors. Based on the plan to use it to deter entry by others, it's a modest amount of playdough. That said, take my advice: don't stand near the doors if you don't have to."

Eddie squirmed. Despite his involvement with all manner of firearms, explosives gave him the willies.

"And, Hope, I have two small devices for you. One for redundancy. You know what they say: two is one and one is none. I'll give them to you when we leave here." Quinn was referring to the charge that would go inside the Senator's body. "I'll keep the big stuff and bring it with me when the time comes."

"Hope?" Charlie prompted.

Suddenly it was her turn. She fought down the bile that formed in her throat. "How about a quick bio break?" she asked. "Five minutes?"

Charlie sensed that Hope wanted to use the toilet for a reason unrelated to urination or defecation. He worried about her; she was, for all purposes, the daughter he never had. He told himself to be sure to check in with her after the meeting.

While the others went to the bathroom or got a second cup of coffee, Eddie stayed put at the table. He'd seen two D.C. police enter the shop and was doing his best to remain invisible until they left.

When everyone was back at the table, Hope popped a handful of breath mints, took a deep breath and began.

"As I told you back in California, my research has been about creating an artificial womb in which a fetus can develop normally until birth. We've had tremendous success so far, and the lambs develop—"

"Lambs?" Sanam exclaimed. "What do you mean 'lambs'? Are you saying you've never used this on human fetuses?" He fiddled with his watch, this one a cheap Timex Ironman Classic he'd picked up in the airport.

Hope wanted to blame Faye, who always insisted she follow the long, tortuous research, publication, and review process, but she knew in her heart that what she wanted to do was way out of line.

"That's correct. But lambs and humans develop similarly," she said as earnestly as she could. "It will work." *It has to.*

"Well," Quinn said, "let's assume for our discussion that your device works. What's the plan?"

Hope wanted to kiss Quinn, this time in gratitude, not due to hormones.

"Once we have the room secured, I'll bring the donor and the Senator to the lower tier of the dais, so I can use the desk there. Where the Sergeant at Arms and the others sit."

It took Charlie a moment to process what Hope had said. "Wait a second? *Donor?* You mean a pregnant woman?"

Hope summarized her successful efforts to recruit the young woman from whom she would transfer an embryo into the Senator.

"You didn't say anything about an innocent girl being part of this," Sanam said. "We're talking about a possible combat zone. Likely, in fact."

"I have to agree with Sanam," Charlie said. "Hope, I love you, but I won't do this. Isn't there some way you can extract the fetus ahead of time?"

Hope was hurt by Charlie's comments. It was the first time she could remember that he did not support her unconditionally. Yet she had to admit he was right. Once again, she hadn't carefully thought things through. She hated how sloppy and reckless her thinking had been since she started down her new path.

After a long pause, she said, "Okay. Okay. I can perform the extraction surgery tonight. I told the girl to be ready at any moment. I can keep the womb viable overnight, but we should go first thing tomorrow morning."

A full minute went by as tempers cooled. Charlie stepped in and said, "Sanam, why don't you give us an update on the sensor?"

Sanam looked down, revealing his sense of shame. "I'm sorry. I still don't really know what will work. I have a few prototypes of various approaches, but I just don't know."

"Why can't you just wire them up to go off by cell phone," Eddie asked. "Like in the movies." He pointed at Sanam and added, "Like your fellow terrorists do all the time."

Sanam, normally mild-mannered, snapped. "I'm Indian, you idiot! And I'm Hindu, not Muslim!"

Charlie reached his hand out and rested it on Sanam's arm in an attempt to calm him.

Hope tried to smooth over Eddie's baiting. She looked directly at Sanam and said, "Just bring what you have tonight, all right?"

Charlie, sensing the wheels were coming off the meeting, asked the group, "Anyone have anything the want to tell the group, or ask?"

When nobody had anything else to say, Hope said to the table, "Okay. We'll meet one last time tonight at five at the western fountain in the park so we can walk through the routes Charlie described. Same place we first met here in town." To Eddie she added, "And, Eddie, don't be late." He sneered at her in response.

As everyone rose to leave, Quinn quietly handed a small grocery bag to Hope. It contained the two small explosive devices. "If you want, you can use one for practice," he said before breaking out into his deep, resonant laugh.

Chapter Twenty-Eight

Early in his career, Senator Carrington realized that being successful as a United States Senator involved more than "thinking big thoughts" and crafting effective public policy; he needed to be plugged into the zeitgeist and daily happenings around the country so that he could pepper his legal arguments and public speeches with the kind of color commentary that won over hearts and minds far better than raw data ever could. Decades earlier, as a first-term Senator, he committed to nurturing a network of friendly scouts around the country who brought him newsworthy tidbits and local stories of interest.

He'd flown on a pre-dawn flight from New York to Seattle and then down to the Del Norte County Regional Airport. After a fifteen-minute drive past Lake Earl, Carrington arrived at his destination:

Pelican Bay State Prison. Situated at the far northwest corner of California, along the Pacific Ocean and adjacent to the Oregon border, Pelican State is one of the supermax prisons in the country, home to over three thousand of the most violent male criminals known to mankind.

Carrington sat in his rental car in the prison's parking lot with one of his scouts, a young man named Charlie Wilson, who he'd met at a law enforcement conference two years earlier.

"I only have a few minutes," Wilson said, nervously looking at the prison entrance. He didn't like meeting here, but Carrington's travel logistics—the Senator was returning to the airport immediately after their conversation—made it necessary. He hoped he could grab lunch before he went back on duty.

"Thanks for taking the time to meet," Carrington said. Tell me what's going on."

Charlie Wilson, a twenty-eight-year-old former wide receiver at Florida State, hit the gym daily to keep his body fit and trim. He'd also finished in the top five percent in his class at the police academy. Yet the man somehow looked frail and scared to Carrington.

Wilson hesitated, unsure how to begin. Finally, he said, "There's been a lot of weird shit goin' down here the past few months."

"What do you mean?"

"I mean, we get our fair share of depression and anxiety, uncontrollable anger, that kind of thing. The occasional suicide, too. Hell, most of the inmates claim to have hallucinations half the time." Carrington knew that inmates in cell blocks C and D at the prison were kept in solitary confinement over twenty-two hours a day, seven days a week, and that inmates, their lawyers, and prisoner advocacy groups had argued over the years that this treatment constitutes cruel and unusual punishment. "But we're talking all kinds of crazy shit. Next level crazy shit."

"Why don't you start at the beginning?" Carrington suggested gently.

"Okay, sure. Well... We have a new prisoner, Crow Jeffries, who's been stirring up trouble ever since he got here a few months ago. Dude's a psycho. Killed two dozen kids and carved 'em up something bad."

Carrington winced, but Wilson didn't notice.

"Guy says he's a wiccan."

"A witch?"

"I guess. I don't know. Don't really want to know. What I do know is that the dude says he casts spells against the other inmates. It wouldn't be a big deal except... Well, except that they seem to be working."

"What do you mean, 'working?'" Carrington asked, incredulous.

"I mean, three different guys have died from heart attacks. We're talking guys in their thirties or forties. In decent shape."

"Couldn't their deaths just be from natural causes? I mean, I'm sure being caged up all the time causes serious health issues."

Wilson, trained well by the prison, said, "Mental health issues like I mentioned, sure. But nothing that should cause heart attacks. In all the years Pelican Bay has been operating, we've only had one other heart attack until this guy showed up."

"I don't mean to make light of the situation, but is that all?"

Wilson shook his head. He was seriously spooked. "Guys are mutilating themselves with their plastic forks. Banging their heads against their cell walls until they crack open their skulls. One guy went blind in one eye. Another lost his ability to speak for a month."

Carrington sat quietly and pondered the bigger meaning of what was happening. It was one of his gifts, the ability to search for and find the larger implications of seemingly small, insignificant events.

"The other prisoners are becoming violent, aren't they?"

"You have no idea," Wilson said. He turned and looked out the passenger side window of Carrington's rental car. "It's not just that they're threatening Jeffries. Hell, most of us might look the other way if that kind of thing happened. Dude's an animal." Wilson took a deep breath and continued. "It's that they're so agitated that they're getting into fights all the time now. It's crazy how much shit they can get into in just thirty minutes together."

Wilson turned back to Carrington and said, "The place is a powder keg."

For a flash, Carrington worried for Wilson's safety and that of the other guards at the prison, but his mind quickly moved to a much bigger concern. Carrington remembered a case decades earlier about a federal prisoner named Kerry O'Bryan who was also a wiccan. The man had been prevented from practicing witchcraft by prison authorities, who argued that allowing prisoners to cast spells might result in fights, something they needed to prevent. O'Bryan sued under the Religious Freedom Restoration Act of 1993, and eventually won his case when the Seventh Circuit overruled a district court's ruling.

Reading Carrington's mind, Wilson said, "He's suing under RFRA." Wilson was referring to the religious freedom act from 1993.

"I figured that's why you called," Carrington said. In the *O'Byran v. Bureau of Prisons* case, the lower court refused to accept the assertion that banning spells was necessary to realize a compelling government interest. Maybe this time, where actual violence and deaths were possibly directly attributable to Crow Jeffries's witchcraft, the Supreme Court might overturn *O'Bryan*. Carrington knew that federal agencies are only able to burden religious practices to the least extent necessary to realize a compelling government interest. Stopping Crow Jeffries from casting hexes might very well now be seen as satisfying the legal standard.

"Listen," Wilson said. "I gotta get back. We good?"

Carrington thanked the guard and gave him his leave. Wilson walked briskly back into the prison, his intense hunger overriding his skittishness about the voodoo going down in the place.

Senator Royce Carrington punched a speed dial button on his phone. When the voice on the other end of the phone greeted him, Carrington said, simply, "Pelican Bay State Prison in northern California. Prisoner by the name of Crow Jeffries. The man's apparently an animal, but you need to see to it that he wins his RFRA case." He hung up. It wasn't Crow Jeffries' religious freedom he cared about; RFRA was still one of the primary legal tools that could be used to further the religious freedom of Christians around the country.

Carrington dialed a second number, this time for his money manager.

"Find a handful of charities doing the best work defending religious freedom. Groups with the strongest track records of success on the issue and overhead rates under, say, ten percent. Distribute twenty-five million between them as you see fit."

"You want me to clear the details with you before cutting checks?"

Carrington didn't hesitate. He had no doubts about the man's trustworthiness or competence; if he had, he would have fired the man long ago.

"No. Just send me the details once it's done."

After hanging up, Carrington punched the start button in his rental car and pulled out of the prison's parking lot. As he drove to the airport, Carrington soaked in the physical beauty of the giant Redwoods, the unusual plants and flowers dotting the area, and the myriad strange birds circling the bright sky.

Chapter Twenty-Nine

Tuesday, February 27 (later the same day)
The Spirit of Justice Park near the Capitol Building
Washington, D.C. area

16 days before vote on the Sanctity of Life bill

The sun was low in a dim blue sky when they met at the fountain in the Spirit of Justice park. It was 5:00 p.m. and, once again, Eddie was late.

Before Quinn could complain, Charlie asked the group if there were any last-second questions, comments, or concerns. There were none. The group briefly discussed their return travel plans, assuming they all got out alive and weren't caught by the Capitol Police or the FBI. Hope found it surreal that she was having a conversation that included the phrase "if we get out alive."

In the low light, a man staggered toward the group. Suddenly, everyone realized that it was Eddie.

"Whassup bitches?!" Eddie bellowed.

"Oh Christ. Not only is he late, he's drunk," Quinn said.

Hope looked closely at Eddie. In the darkness, she could just make out that his pupils were dilated, and she could see from his chest rising and falling that his breathing rate was increased. As he approached, she also noticed small burns on his fingers and cracking and blistering on his lips.

"Not drunk. High," Hope said. "You high on crack, Eddie?"

"God, you are such a bitch," Eddie snapped.

Charlie stepped toward Eddie, poked him in the chest, and said "watch yourself."

"Jeez, can't you take a joke?" Eddie tried to back peddle. "I partied a little bit. So what? It's kinda my ritual when I take delivery. I got our stuff, man."

Sanam pointed at Eddie and said "Charlie, I am not putting my life on the line with a drug addict. It's too risky."

"I agree," Quinn concurred.

Charlie said to the group, "Listen, I get it. I do. But he'll be fine in the morning." He looked at Eddie and said, "Right?" Then to the group he also added, "Look, I need a second person who can handle an AR. Hope just learned how to use a pistol. Like literally yesterday. Q could fill in, but he's going to be busy with the doors. And, no offense Mister Patel, but you can't shoot for shit."

"No offense taken," Sanam said. Truth be told, he hated guns.

Charlie's phone buzzed. He took his phone out of his pocket and saw that he had a new text message. He didn't receive many. "Excuse me a second," he said to the group before stepping a few feet away. The argument continued.

Charlie saw that the text was from a number he didn't recognize. Still, he opened his texting app and tapped on the message. It read:

```
Hi Charlie. Eddie bragged that he's
into something big. He wouldn't say
what it was but I hope you're not
involved, whatever it is. You seem
sweet, not like Eddie. Call me if you
want, any time. Love, Lexus
```

Charlie jammed his phone into his pocket and rejoined the group. He cut in, raising his voice over the heated discussion in progress.

"Listen up," he said. "We have a problem. Mr. Townsend here has been a naughty, naughty boy."

"Yeah, we know," Quinn said. "Just look at him. He can't even stand up straight."

"I'm not talking about that," Charlie said. "Eddie, care to share anything with the group?"

Eddie looked at Charlie with a confused look on his face. He had no idea what Charlie was talking about.

After a few painful seconds of silence, Charlie looked directly at Hope and said, "Eddie made friends with a stripper at a local strip joint. Seems like he was a bit chatty with his new lady friend."

"Are you saying what I think you're saying?" Sanam asked.

Hope rushed at Eddie and palm struck him in the solar plexus. "You son of a bitch!" She started swinging wildly at the man. Quinn wrapped his arms around her waist and pulled her away.

"I'm out," Sanam said. "Charlie, I think the world of you, you know that. But I am not doing this." He reached into his pocket and handed a small pouch to Hope. "Here. Take this. I don't really know if it will work or not. It might. It might not. For what it's worth, I think it's more likely that it'll go off when it shouldn't than not go off when it should."

Hope started to try to convince him to stay when Sanam reached out and held Hope's hands. "I wish you luck. I really do. I hope you're able to achieve some level of revenge. Better still, I hope you're able to achieve some level of peace." He turned and walked into the night.

Quinn, too, calculated the risks were too high. He'd been uncomfortable with Eddie Townsend from the first moment he met the man. Eddie had been consistently late, was a druggie, and, now, it was clear he was loose-lipped to boot. In short, he was unreliable in a business where reliability was paramount. "I'm out too. Charlie, I'll call you in a week or two. I'm tellin' you now, though, under no circumstances will I *ever* work with that asshat." He motioned with a thumb toward Townsend.

Quinn turned to Hope. "You are one fierce warrior, young lady. And I mean that as one of the highest compliments I can give. You also have a good heart, and *that* is the *highest* compliment I can give. I'm sorry about your sister. Truly. Like Sanam said, I hope you get your revenge, and even if you don't, I hope you can somehow figure out a way to go back and live a normal, happy life." He kissed Hope on her forehead and smiled.

As he walked away, he raised a hand and flicked his forefinger as if to say, "later."

Charlie grabbed Eddie firmly by his biceps and shook him. "Listen to me carefully. I don't care what you do with the weapons you acquired for this job. Sell 'em. Dump 'em. I don't care. But we're done, you and I. We are aborting this mission because of you, and I don't think you'll ever fully appreciate the harm you've done. Do not ever contact me again. Understand?"

Eddie shrugged. He reached into his pocket and pulled out his crack pipe and lighter. He was lighting up before he disappeared into the darkness.

Hope stood, her shoulders slumped, her spirit drained. Her plan, however crazy and ill-planned it may have been, was dead.

Chapter Thirty

15 days before vote on the Sanctity of Life bill

Hope barely slept. Whatever sleep she did get came fitfully. She finally dragged herself out of bed at nine and took a long, hot shower, something she never did in California due to the nearly permanent state of drought there. She glanced at her phone and saw that Charlie had left her several voicemail messages. She ignored them. Billy had also texted several times, each message exhibiting more worry than the ones before. She ignored these too.

Hope went downstairs to the hotel's breakfast buffet and put a few items on a flimsy orange plastic tray, but she didn't touch her food. Instead, she sat and stared into space, her mind numb. At some point, she tossed her uneaten food into a garbage bin and bundled herself up in her coat, scarf, and gloves and took the Metro to the Mall. She hadn't meant to; she was operating in a haze.

Surrounded by thousands of tourists—school tours, mothers with their children in strollers, and senior citizens—Hope wandered. She walked past the National World War II Memorial, the Vietnam Veterans and Korean War Veterans Memorials, the Lincoln Memorial, and the Martin Luther King, Jr. Memorial. She sat for a while at the Tidal Basin, a two-mile-long pond that was once attached to the Potomac River, then continued past the U.S. Holocaust Memorial Museum, the Washington Monument, and the White House. When she passed the White House, she cursed former president Fred Spencer and the current President, Brock Owens, both of whom paled in comparison to the honor and courage of George Washington, former Presidents Barack Obama and Gabriella Davenport, and the handful of Presidents who, in her mind, had lived up to the role. When she passed the Capitol Building, it somehow seemed so far away, surrounded by a fog. When she passed the Museum of the Bible, she wanted to scream.

Hope found herself thinking she should go visit Bei Bei, the panda at the Smithsonian National Zoo, but didn't have the energy to brave DuPont Circle or walk that far north.

Several times, Hope almost bumped into tourists or professionals who worked in the area and sometimes had to make their way between government buildings. All she could do was apologize before moving on. She had to move on, she thought. But how? She was utterly lost.

Hope bought a hot dog from a street vendor and practically inhaled it. She hadn't eaten in almost twenty-four hours. Still hungry, she found another stand and bought an enormous pretzel. After scraping off most of the salt crystals, she devoured that too.

She found herself circling back to the Lincoln Memorial, which had always been her favorite of the many historical sights in town. Why? How did that come to be? Hope felt the flicker of recognition but couldn't bring the memory into focus. She hated that her once-sharp mind had turned to mush; it had been years since she was unable to remember something she knew was in her brain.

Hope sat at the base of the stairs that led up to the larger-than-life statue of Abe Lincoln. She knew that the words of his two most famous speeches—his second Inaugural Address and the Gettysburg address—were etched into opposing walls of the memorial. She'd memorized them for social studies class in middle school, to the amazement of her teacher. She also learned that the building's design by Henry Bacon included thirty-eight Doric columns, thirty-six of which signify the states in the Union when Lincoln died. She never did figure out the significance or symbolism of the other two. She people watched for an hour until the sun started to set.

Just as she was getting up to walk back to her hotel, utterly defeated, she saw a man selling large transparent balloons with smaller red Lincoln-shaped balloons inside. A mother with her two children walked by the balloon vendor, and the two children pleaded with their mom to buy them each a balloon. Suddenly, Hope remembered why she loved this memorial so much, beyond its historical significance and its sheer beauty: her mother.

She flashed back to a memory: She and Angel were pestering their mother for cotton candy during her eighth grade field trip. Her mother was a chaperone, and had brought Angel along. The trip was one of the last things they did as a family, before her mom left for Washington to fight against then-President Spencer.

For years, Hope had honored the distance her mother had put between them, and only contacted her twice, once when Angel was raped and again the day Angel died. Now, given the stakes and her commitment to do whatever it took, she didn't hesitate for a second. She was desperate.

After a few minutes rehearsing what she wanted to say, she called the number for Senator Mary Roberts. She knew the number by heart, and was momentarily thrilled that her brain wasn't completely gone. At this time of night, the call went to voicemail, as she hoped it would. She put on her thickest Louisiana accent, hoping she still remembered how it sounded after so many years in California.

"Hi there. My name is Regina Staubach. I'm one of your constituents from the great state of Louisiana. My brother and I are usually too busy with our real estate business to travel out of state, but I happen to be in Washington D.C. for a conference. I'm a big fan of the work you do, Senator, especially your work on immigration reform, and I'd like to come by your office to make a donation to your re-election campaign. I can meet tomorrow morning. I'm afraid that's the only time I'll be in town and available, as I fly back to Baton Rouge at noon. Please call me back." Hope gave the number of the prepaid phone she'd purchased for the trip, thankful Charlie had recommended it. She feared that despite the years her mother might remember her real cell number.

Hope quickly dialed Charlie and asked him to be ready to meet her downtown at some point in the morning and to bring his new ID. She told him she'd text him a time and place as soon as she could, and hung up before he could ask any questions.

Finally, she recorded a voicemail greeting on the prepaid phone. She used the same Louisiana twang and the same name she'd used when calling the Senator's office: the name on the fake ID Charlie had made for her, Regina Staubach.

Chapter Thirty-One

Thursday, March 1 (the next day)
Senator Mary Roberts' Office, U.S. Capitol
Washington, D.C.

14 days before vote on the Sanctity of Life bill

Hope was counting on the fact that politicians do not risk losing possible donations from prospective donors. Sure enough, she received a call on her prepaid phone at two minutes after nine the following morning.

It took all of Hope's patience to let the call go to voicemail and wait until her phone indicated that she had a message. She listened to it, deleted the message, and immediately texted Charlie.

> 11:45 a.m., Senator Mary Roberts'
> office. Dress nice.

Hope quickly showered and put on a navy blue pair of pants, a white blouse, and a red jacket. It was the one nice outfit she'd brought with her. She took the Metro to the Capitol South Metro Station and walked to the Capitol building. It was the first time on the trip that she would enter the building without a disguise. As she approached, she saw Charlie, wearing a coat and tie, standing just outside the entrance. She ran the last few feet between them and gave him a tight squeeze. She tugged on his tie and said, "Never thought I'd see the day." She had never seen him in anything other than jeans and a t-shirt under his greasy apron. He gave her a "what the hell are we doing here?" look, but she grabbed his hand and led him into the building.

Hope and Charlie went through security screening just inside the north entrance. Hope gave her assumed name to the guard at the Senate Appointment Desk while Charlie stood quietly, wondering what was going on.

"Driver's license, please," the guard requested like an automaton. Hope handed her doctored license to the guard. She tried to trust that Charlie had chosen someone reliable to make the fake ID—someone considerably more reliable than Eddie Townsend—but she found herself struggling to breathe normally. Charlie noticed and made a "breath" motion with his hands and inhaled and exhaled through pursed lips.

"Are you together?" the guard asked Hope, lifting his head in a slight nod in Charlie's direction.

Charlie turned and faced the guard. "Yes." He handed over his own falsified identification.

The guard returned their driver's licenses and said, "Please wait here. Someone will be out to get you." He turned to the man standing behind Charlie and said, "Next." Hope and Charlie pocketed their IDs and stepped aside.

A few minutes later, a pimple-faced intern in a poorly fitting blue polyester suit came out to fetch them. "Regina Staubach?" he said as he approached Hope, surprised at how young the woman was. She introduced Charlie, remembering to use the name on the fake ID he'd just given to the guard.

"Please follow me. The Senator is quite busy today but is very much looking forward to meeting with important constituents such as yourselves."

Charlie shot Hope another look that said, "What the hell?" Hope could only squeeze his hand and silently urge him to go with the flow. *Wow, I never imagined I'd embrace a phrase like that in my entire life.* She was winging it now, and it simultaneously scared and thrilled her.

The intern led Hope and Charlie through a wandering path until they finally made their way to the office of Senator Mary Roberts, the junior Senator from Louisiana. The young man stopped just before the entrance to the office and said, "Here you go. The Senator's staff will assist you until she returns from the floor vote that's going on right now. It was nice to meet you." He shook their hands and scurried down the hallway.

Hope took a deep breath and steadied herself against the door jamb. She looked at Charlie, the only real source of comfort she'd known for nearly a decade. His kind eyes and warm spirit gave her the strength to enter through the door.

"Hope?" the woman at the small, messy desk in the antechamber exclaimed. "What are you doing here?"

Charlie looked at the woman. She had a narrow face, straight shoulder-length brown hair, and thin lips. Her lipstick was too pink for her age, he thought. Charlie looked at the woman's name plate, which read Tanya McAvoy. He'd never heard of anyone named Tanya or McAvoy in Hope's life. Still, the woman somehow seemed familiar.

"Hello, Mom," Hope said. It was only the second time she'd seen her mother since Tanya left for Washington the day after Fred Spencer was elected President, over twelve years earlier, and the first since Angel died.

Tanya looked around to see if anyone else in the office was around. Especially the Senator.

"What are you doing here?" Tanya repeated.

"It's nice to see you, too."

Charlie stood quietly, not wanting to interrupt this family reunion, such as it was. So this was Hope's mother. Charlie knew that Hope had practically raised herself and, while she was alive, her younger sister. Why on earth did this woman leave Hope alone? He found himself disliking Tanya McAvoy immediately.

Tanya McAvoy was never really cut out to be a mother. When the girls were toddlers, she found herself perturbed by having to worry about and care for them every second of the day. Now, years later, she had stopped thinking of herself as one altogether. "I thought you were a donor." She checked her notepad. "Someone named Regina Staubach."

"Surprise," Hope said sarcastically.

"Hope," Tanya said in a quiet, menacing voice, "We agreed that you would not interfere with my important work here."

Hope looked around at the cramped room, which wasn't much more than a closet. The room held two other small desks besides her mother's, both of which were currently unoccupied. Hope glanced at the heavy wooden door to the Senator's office. She wanted to say, "What important work? The important work happens behind that door," but she held her tongue. Instead, she replied, "No. *You* decided. I was *thirteen*. Angel was only *eleven*. And you just picked up and disappeared."

Tanya noticed Hope's glance at the door to the Senator's office and read her daughter's mind. Despite the fact that Hope hadn't said anything out loud, she stung from Hope's unspoken judgement about her standing in the office. "You were almost fourteen and Angel was almost twelve," she said, as if rounding up their ages justified her decision. She smoothed her shoulder-length mousy brown hair and added, "And look, you've turned out to be a strong, confident young woman."

Charlie found himself simultaneously mortified by this woman and begrudgingly willing to grant that Hope had, indeed, grown up to be independent, competent, and a natural leader. He reached out and touched Hope's shoulder. She jumped at his touch.

"Maybe you should explain why we're here, kiddo," he said gently.

"Tanya," Hope said, her disdain dripping as she purposely used her mother's first name, "I need your help."

"Go on."

"I am trying to stop the 'Sanctity of Life' bill. Surely you must know about it."

"Yes, of course. Senator Roberts and I are working hard to defeat it."

Hope stared angrily at her mother and said the thing she knew would hurt her the most: "You don't have the votes. Surely you must know this. The bill is going to pass unless something is done. Something big."

Tanya's shoulders sagged. She knew Hope was right.

Hope thought she heard a rustling sound come from behind Senator Roberts' door, but wasn't certain. She hoped her mother hadn't heard it; if she had, she almost certainly would have immediately thrown her and Charlie out.

"I have a plan," Hope said, knowing as she said it that this was far from the truth. She briefly explained her research and her idea of showing Senator Royce Carrington first-hand what it meant to be made pregnant against one's will. "I need your help getting into the Senate chamber. That's all. After that, you don't have to be a party to anything." While Hope spoke, Charlie slowly moved to stand closer to Hope, who stood at the edge of Tanya's desk.

After a few minutes, Hope's impassioned plea ended and the room was silent for several moments. Her mother finally spoke.

"You are nuts. Nuts! I cannot support what you're doing. I cannot help you. I *won't* help you. Don't ruin this for me, Hope. I'm trying to make a difference, from the inside." *Legally.*

It was Hope's shoulders that sagged this time. What was she thinking? Her mother had been focused on her own life plan since that fateful day when that douchebag Fed Spencer, with his absurd handlebar moustache, got elected. Hope, Angel, and a traditional family structure be damned. A small voice in her head asked, *How is that description of your mother different from the way people would describe you, Hope?* She shook the thought away.

"Dad would be ashamed," Hope blurted out.

"Don't bring your father into things. He left the day after your sister was born, leaving me alone to raise you both. My plan to run for office died that day." She nodded toward the door to the Senator's office and added, "I saw your eyes before and you're right. That's where the real work happens. That was my goal, but your father saw to it that that was not in the cards for me."

"Are you blaming Dad—or me and Angel—for you not being a member of Congress? For the fact that you're on this side of that door?"

"That's not what I'm saying. Your father and I had a plan. Or so I thought. When we first got married, he was totally on board. But then your dad just wouldn't join the military—he was a spineless pussy. All he cared about was his stupid music. He set my plan back by years." It took her two full seconds to stretch out the last word. "Then, when he left, he killed it for good."

Hope turned to Charlie. "Mom always told us, 'Always have a Plan.' The way she said it, you could tell the 'P' was capitalized. Angel and I were obstacles to her plan. So was our dad, apparently."

She glanced at her mother. The woman didn't try to argue, and Hope's heart sunk. She continued speaking with Charlie. "Then when Doucheface was elected, she left for Washington the next day. The very next day. She said that since we lived in such a rural area and that I was already in high school, nobody'd know she was gone. She sent five hundred dollars every month to help with expenses. Christ, what a joke! I've been working since I was twelve to help pay for things, things like clothes and food."

Hope turned to her mother and sealed her emotions away. "Goodbye, Tanya," she said, again purposely using her mother's first name. "Thank you for your time this morning. Tell Senator Roberts that Regina Staubach couldn't make it to her appointment. Or that she decided not to donate. Or whatever, I don't really care."

Hope motioned to Charlie, signaling him that it was time to go. Charlie put his hands into his pockets and followed Hope out. He was deeply saddened by Hope's icy relationship with her mother.

As Hope and Charlie walked out of the office, neither noticed Senator Mary Roberts as she listened through a crack in the door to her office. Tanya, who sat with her head in her hands, didn't notice either, and her boss carefully, silently closed her door.

When Hope and Charlie exited the building, Hope made it about ten steps before she bent over and put her hands on her knees. She had failed. Again. She was suddenly so tired she could hardly stand.

Charlie wrapped his arm around Hope's waist and steered her toward a nearby bench. "Come, sit," he pleaded.

When they were seated on the bench, Hope began to cry. "It's over, Charlie. It's over," she said through tears and snot. A breeze whipped her hair around, and a light drizzle began to fall.

Charlie lifted her chin with one hand and reached into his pocket with the other. He palmed his large hands around the object he withdrew from his pocket and flashed it in front of Hope's face.

"Nope." He grinned and his eyes danced.

He had swiped Tanya McAvoy's badge.

Hope's face brightened immediately. She wiped the snot from her nose with a crumpled tissue from her pocket, then jumped forward and crushed Charlie, who fell backward from the impact.

Hope snapped into overdrive. "Tomorrow. 10 a.m. Go buy a suit. A nice suit." She got up with renewed energy, already thinking through all that she had to accomplish in—she checked her phone for the time— less than twenty-one hours. She started to walk away, got a few steps away, then turned and walked back to where Charlie was sitting.

"Love you, crazy old man."

"Love you too, kiddo."

Chapter Thirty-Two

14 days before vote on the Sanctity of Life bill

Hope pushed thoughts of Tanya McAvoy out of her head. God, it was hard to believe the woman was her mother. She'd had years of training partitioning her mind, of putting her emotions into boxes and time-shifting when she opened them. She called on that training now. Strangely, the one emotion that she couldn't fully curtail was anger that her mother was using her maiden name, not her father's last name. *A shrink would have a field day with me,* she thought. *The man left when I was two years old and this is what I'm most upset about?*

As soon as she left Charlie outside of the Capitol, Hope called the young girl who wanted to shorten her pregnancy. She asked the girl to come to her hotel at 9:00 p.m. Hope wasn't truly comfortable with the idea that she had to perform surgery in her hotel room and so late in the evening, but she had no choice. She knew that her mother had almost certainly realized her badge was missing. The only question was what Tanya would do about it. Would she inform security? If so, would they disable the badge? Would she figure out that it was Charlie who'd stolen it and call the police? The only thing Hope could do was hurry and hope that things would work out. She recalled all the times her mother had said "Hope is not a strategy" to her when she was growing up, and tried to shake the thought away.

Her surgical appointment made, she spent the rest of the day shopping. First, she purchased a navy blue pant suit, choosing the color so she could wear the pair of shoes she already had. She slipped the tailor five twenties to get the pants tailored while she waited. She also purchased a powder blue blouse, the color as close to the Democratic party's blue as she could find. She was going be making a statement, and she did not want to be wearing Republican red when she did. Second, she purchased a small watermelon from a neighborhood fruit stand. She brought her haul back to her hotel room, then headed back out.

Hope walked to a medical supply company and purchased a new oxygen tank and a small two-wheel oxygen tank carrier. As soon as she walked into her hotel room, she emptied the tank completely. An hour later, she was wearing her old lady disguise, with the added detail that she now wore the oxygen tubes and pulled the now-empty oxygen tank. She walked slowly to a nearby hospital, excruciatingly aware of each minute that passed. Finally, she made her way into the hospital and to its OB-GYN pod. Undetected, she walked out fifteen minutes later with her tank filled with sevoflurane, an anesthetic she'd used many times during her residency. The extent to which people trusted the elderly never ceased to amaze her.

It was eight by the time Hope was back in her hotel room. She had an hour before her young patient arrived.

Hope removed the small bag containing the two explosive devices Quinn had given her from the small safe in the closet of her room. She took one out and put the other one back in the safe, which clacked securely after she closed its door. With a knife she'd swiped from the breakfast buffet, she dug a small tunnel into the center of the watermelon and carefully inserted the explosive device into the hole, ensuring that the fuse trailed out. She walked into the bathroom and gently set the watermelon, hole down, in the center of the bathtub.

Hope suddenly pictured Quinn's magnetic grin, his crazy beard, his larger-than-life personality. She focused on his quiet competence, or at least what she thought was his competence. But how did she know he was, in fact, an expert? She didn't, really.

She stripped the sheets from her bed and carried the mattress toward the bathroom, propping it up next to the door. Hope pictured the maneuver she intended. It was something she was always good at: forming a detailed mental model of human anatomy and of medical procedures in time and space. Convinced she was ready, she lit a match, leaned into the tub, and lit the fuse. She flicked her wrist to put out the match and quickly retreated out of the bathroom. Three seconds later, the mattress was in position blocking the door and she was across the room, squatting behind the dresser.

A few seconds later, Hope could barely make out a muffled *pfft* sound from the bathroom.

Slightly embarrassed by the precautions she'd taken, Hope moved the mattress away and entered the bathroom. The watermelon was still sitting in the center of the tub, but was bulging outward, like it had expanded by a half an inch or so. She reached into the tub to lift the watermelon but when she went to pick it up, it disintegrated into thousands of small pieces. Juices and seeds slipped through her fingers. Hope's last thought before cleaning up the mess in the bathtub and re-making her bed was to silently offer an apology to Quinn for having doubted him.

Chapter Thirty-Three

Thursday, March 1 (the same evening)
Delivery University
Murdock, Virginia

While Hope Hunter was blowing up a watermelon in her bathtub, Senator Royce Carrington was on stage at Delivery University in Murdock, Virginia, participating in a debate on abstinence-based sex education. Leroy "Roy" Wainwright, the school's fifth president, was moderating. The Slather Convention Center was packed with students, faculty, and members of the press, and they were being treated to a lively, heated debate.

Dr. Marcia Huang, a tiny woman with long, shiny black hair that fell to the middle of her back and an MD–PhD from the Yale School of Medicine, said, "Federally funded abstinence-only programs continue to rely on curricula that, quote, contain false, misleading or distorted information about reproductive health, unquote. That quote is from a 2004 congressional study. Similar studies since then have, sadly, confirmed that the misinformation and distortions have gotten worse."

Peter Norquist, a public policy analyst at the Kaelin Institute, a conservative think tank, once again interrupted Huang. "Democrats continually deny these programs the critical funding they need. With more funding—"

Huang returned fire. "Federal funding for these programs increased to record levels under President Spencer. In his time in office, funding was over five hundred million dollars annually. During that time, teen pregnancies and incidents of sexually transmitted diseases were at an all-time high. During the eight years of President Davenport's presidency, these programs were re-tooled to include information about contraceptives and—guess what?—the rates of teen pregnancy and STDs dropped sharply. These programs didn't lack funding, they lacked academic integrity. They lacked efficacy."

Roy Wainwright interjected. "Now, now, Miss Huang, there's no need for attacks on people's integrity."

"That's 'Doctor Huang'," Huang admonished Wainwright.

Wainwright blushed but said nothing.

Senator Carrington said, "Let's not lose track of the fact that sex education began in public schools in the 1960s, promoted by the sex education arm of Planned Parenthood."

Huang knew that Carrington saw his statement as a dig against Planned Parenthood. She saw it differently, believing that every individual, regardless of age or marital status, should choose for themselves when he or she becomes sexually active. Sex education—real sex education—unequivocally helped them make these choices.

Huang faced the audience, knowing she was likely speaking to an auditorium full of deaf ears. "That's a good thing, right? Did you know that research shows that so-called 'virginity pledgers' who pledge to remain a virgin until marriage are just as likely to engage in premarital sex as their peers, have STD rates similar to other teens and, worse, are less likely to use contraception if they do engage in sexual intercourse? How is this the public health outcome we want?"

"Condoms are untrustworthy, both against pregnancy and STDs," Norquist said.

"That is false. The U. S. Center for Disease Control has found that, quote, latex condoms provide an essentially impermeable barrier to particles the size of STD pathogens, unquote. Yet you continue to push your false narrative. So does at least one of the curricula you favor."

Carrington jumped in and said, "All of you here should visit the website 'number of abortions dot com'. You can watch, in real time, the count of babies killed every second of every day. Dr. Huang calls it choice. I call it what it is: genocide."

Huang quietly asked Carrington, "Why does that site contain a statistic for 'black babies since '73 in the U.S.'?" The racial bias was uncalled for and unforgivable in her mind.

Carrington deftly declined to answer Huang's question. Frankly, he didn't agree with the decision to add that statistic to the site; the data was powerful enough without bringing bigotry into the picture. He changed the subject, and said,

"Sincerely held religious beliefs and heritage surrounding sexuality should be honored."

Huang countered, "Are you suggesting that the religious beliefs and heritage of, say, Muslims should be honored, too?" Before Carrington could answer, she added, "And what about those who believe in a great and powerful flying toaster that tells them to have sex all the time? That marriage is a sin?" Gasps came from the crowd at this.

Peter Norquist tried another attack. "Parents should be the primary sex educators of their children."

"I agree," said Huang. "We're here discussing whether there's a valid public interest in also having sex education taught in schools and, if so, what that sex education should cover. My argument isn't that parents shouldn't take the lead. They should. My argument is that abstinence-only sex ed leads to far worse public health outcomes."

Norquist said, "School-age children should refrain from sexual activity until they are married."

"Why? If your argument is that that's what your holy book says, then what if my holy book says we should fuck like rabbits? Pardon my French." More gasps from the audience.

"Miss—Dr. Huang!" Wainwright said, objecting to Huang's profanity.

"But," Huang continued, "if your argument is aimed to inform public policy, I ask, simply, 'why'? The data clearly shows that this is not good for children or society."

Norquist huffed and squirmed in his chair. "Abstinence until marriage eliminates health risks," he said definitively.

"In theory, sure," Huang said. "I choose to live in reality. I think you owe it to society, and teens in particular, to join me there."

Carrington could tell that Dr. Huang was a far better debater than Peter Norquist would ever be. He said, "Delayed gratification is essential to maturity."

Huang surprised Carrington and the others by saying, simply, "I agree."

"Learning to develop friendships without physical intimacy is a critical skill that leads to healthier marriages," Carrington said.

"I agree," Huang repeated. "But," she added, "I repeat my plea: join me in the land of reality. You're making theoretical arguments that don't hold up in the real world."

Norquist said, "Children should be able to pursue their dreams without the distraction of the consequences of sexual activity."

"I agree," Huang said for a third time. "One of the best ways for them to avoid those distractions is to use contraception to minimize the risk of pregnancy and disease."

Roy Wainwright surreptitiously checked his watch. It was time to wind down the event.

"Well, on that note, I think we need to bring things to a close. I want to thank my guests, Senator Royce Carrington, Mr. Norquist, and Miss Huang, for being here and joining us for this spirited conversation. Students, as you leave here and go back to your dorms and apartments, I want you to realize that having multiple sexual partners can be dangerous to your physical and emotional health. Abstinence is the only sure way to avoid these dangers. And, remember, pornography is a clear and present danger to you and to society." After a pause and a request for a round of applause for the evening's guests, he finished with, "Thank you, good night, and God bless you."

Huang, fuming from Wainwright's almost certain purposeful use of 'Miss' instead of 'Doctor,' sat and wondered how the hell Wainwright made the leap to pornography.

Norquist rose and shook Carrington's hand and then Wainwright's. He walked to the side of the stage and began packing up his personal effects in preparation for his late flight home.

Carrington waited for Norquist to exit the stage before approaching Wainwright. After shaking hands with the University president, he said, "Thanks for hosting."

"My pleasure, Senator."

"Two things," Carrington said. "First, find someone other than Norquist the next time you put one of these on. And for that matter, invite someone other than Dr. Huang. The sad fact is that she wiped the floor with him." *And me*, he admitted to himself.

Wainwright nodded his assent.

Secondly, "Here's a thirty million dollar check to Delivery University to further the cause of abstinence-only education. For me, the bottom line is this: we need to do everything we can to prevent abortions in this country, and despite all of Dr. Huang's so-called facts and studies, I believe the best way to do this is to keep teens from having sex before marriage." He handed Wainwright the check.

As Roy Wainwright shook Carrington's hand and thanked him for the donation, Dr. Marcia Huang, who watched the exchange and guessed correctly what had just transpired, shook her head in disgust before walking out to her rental car.

Chapter Thirty-Four

13 days before vote on the Sanctity of Life bill

The events of Friday morning would forever remain a blur to Hope.

When Hope came to Charlie's hotel room at 8:00 in the morning, she wheeled her suitcase in behind her, and as soon as Charlie closed the door, she carefully lifted it onto the bed and unzipped it.

"Tank all set?" she asked.

The previous evening, Charlie had bought a propane tank and an acetylene torch and sliced off the very bottom of the oxygen tank he'd purchased earlier. With the rubber heel attached, the tank looked normal, but was, in effect, a steel hiding place.

"All set," Charlie said. He removed the rubber heel from the tank.

Carefully, Hope inserted an artificial womb containing the transplanted fetus from the young woman from whom she'd extracted it the night before.

"Is that the baby?" Charlie asked.

"The fetus, yes. eighteen weeks."

Charlie said a silent prayer for its safety.

Next, Hope inserted her scalpel and other medical instruments as well as various medicines she would need for the surgeries.

"That's it," she said. "Close 'er up."

Charlie had watched Hope carefully. "No sensor or explosive?"

Hope thought back to what Sanam had said, that it was more likely that the switch would go off when it shouldn't than the other way around. Despite the nature of what she was doing, she had, after all, agreed to uphold the Hippocratic Oath to "do no harm." She did not want innocent people to die, or even to be at risk.

"Given the risk that Sanam's switch might go off by accident, I can't risk using it. And if I can't use the switch, I can't use Quinn's explosive device." The disappointment in her voice was obvious.

Charlie attached the rubber heel to the tank.

Hope's emotions were all over the place. Her initial plan, which called for an assault on the Senate floor, was a failure. Yet she felt relieved that at least she wouldn't have to shoot anyone. Her visit with her mom had been heartbreaking; the distance between them was simply too far to bridge. Yet Charlie had saved the day by swiping her mother's badge. Now, here she was, standing with Charlie just outside the Capitol building, about to go through with her latest, risky, ill-conceived plan.

"Ready?" she asked.

"Born ready," Charlie said. It was his standard answer to that question since she'd met him so many years earlier.

"Think it'll work?" she asked, hopeful.

"Not really, no," Charlie responded. He'd faced death before, and he would either live or he would die. Hope's cause was worth dying for. Hope was worth dying for. And if he died, he'd see his son again. After a beat, he added, "Love you, kiddo."

"Love you, Charlie," Hope said. She took a deep breath to steel her nerves and added, "Here we go."

Hope wore her new business suit, and Charlie was wearing the old man disguise that Quinn had used back when Hope and Quinn had done their reconnaissance run. While Hope thought the whole get-up made Quinn look eccentric, she had a pang of sadness when she realized she was seeing a version of Charlie not too many years into the future. The man was already in his mid-fifties, she had to constantly remind herself.

Hope and Charlie made their way toward the security screening checkpoint. This was a crucial moment. One of Charlie's tanks held the sevoflurane. The other, which Charlie had connected through tubing to his nose, was the empty tank that contained the artificial womb containing the embryo, and all of Hope's surgical gear.

Hope went through security without a hitch, despite several dozen of Charlie's nylon, 250-pound tensile strength cable ties in her purse. Then it was Charlie's turn.

He really hammed it up, Hope thought, putting on a show as the crotchety old man who didn't like the hassle of the security guards touching and prodding him and his oxygen tanks.

"Careful with those, sonny. That's my life in there. No ox-y, no breathe-y. No breathe-y, no life-y. You understand that, sonny?"

Whether it was due to lax security or because the guard was sick and tired of Charlie's incessant complaints, Charlie made it through security without incident. He caught up to Hope, who stood quietly off to the side. As he walked up to where Hope was standing, Charlie raised his eyebrows and opened his eyes wide as if to say, "Whew." She gave him a tight-lipped smile.

Their tour started a few minutes later. As the group passed the north gift shop and the entrance to the Senate, Hope and Charlie made eye contact. At just the right moment, they hopped onto the escalator going down to the lower level of the Capitol building.

They quickly made their way across the Hall and between the two orientation theaters. Soon they were in the Exhibition Hall. Led by instinct and Charlie's finely tuned sense of direction honed by years in the Army, they finally found a stairwell and went up a flight of stairs. If Charlie was right, they were just outside the Senate chamber, on the side of the chamber where the Democrats sat. Hope thought of this as "stage right."

"Hand me the cable ties," Charlie said to Hope. She handed the heavy-duty fasteners to him, and he pocketed them. He carefully removed the plastic tubing from his nose, but left it connected to the tank. He handed the oxygen tank carrier to Hope and said, "Just rip off the black heel from this one," he said, pointing to one of the tanks. "Pull hard."

Hope took the carrier by its handle. "Good luck," she said, touching her fingertips to his cheek.

"Give me five minutes to get the main entrance doors secured," Charlie said. "Stay invisible until then." Before she could respond, he walked through the side entrance and into the Senate chamber, and toward the main doors. Because the Senate was in session, the doors were all closed. Good, he thought. That will save me some time.

Hope crossed through the side door just behind Charlie and tried to blend in. Her suit helped, which was her goal. A great many of the seats were empty, as was often the case, and so Hope quietly sat along the side of the chamber and waited for Charlie. From her seat, she could see her target, Senator Royce Carrington, and several of his cronies. Closer, on her side of the aisle she could see Senator Mary Roberts, her mother's boss. The woman was gorgeous, with shocking platinum blonde hair, piercing blue eyes, perfect skin, and just a touch of expertly applied makeup. She was speaking quietly to several other Democratic Senators and Hope couldn't help but sense how confident and composed the woman was.

If it weren't for a bored high school student in the visitor gallery, Charlie might have been able to finish securing all of the doors. As it was, the young girl's cell phone battery had died just moments earlier and she was no longer able to amuse herself with her social media feeds. She looked up and saw Charlie moving from door to door, doing something that somehow seemed strange. She wasn't sure what the man was up to, but it didn't seem right. "If you see something, say something," her parents and teachers always said.

"Hey!" she screamed. "There's a suspicious man in the back, near the doors!"

Hope's heart sank immediately. She knew that once again, she had failed. Worse, she and Charlie were likely going to go to jail.

The Capitol Police were on their game, and were able to enter the Senate chamber through one of the few doors that Charlie hadn't yet secured. He knew he was doomed, but Charlie did his best to fortify as many doors as possible, hoping he could somehow protect Hope.

A split second after the police entered the chamber and tackled Charlie, Hope sensed someone beside her. She spun, thinking that she would not go down without a fight. She balled up her fists and was prepared to punch whomever it was when she realized it was Senator Mary Roberts. The Senator whispered, "Follow me. Quickly." The room was in chaos. Police rushed in and Senators and aides ran in panic or crouched in the aisles.

Before Hope could respond, Senator Roberts was already walking toward a side exit, nearer the dais than the one through which she and Charlie had entered. Hope stood and rushed to keep up with the Senator. As she walked, she reached down and gave two full twists to the tank that contained the anesthesia. By the time Senator Roberts led her to the exit of the building, the tank was empty.

When the women were at the exit door, Senator Roberts motioned to the exit and simply said, "Go. Now." Hope didn't get to ask Senator Roberts why she was helping her escape, and didn't notice Senator Roberts unclip Tanya's badge from her suit jacket before she rushed out of the building and into the harsh sunlight and crisp air of another beautiful fall day in the nation's capital.

Chapter Thirty-Five

13 days before vote on the Sanctity of Life bill

Too scared that she would be caught, Hope didn't dare just crumple into a ball somewhere and cry, didn't dare run to the train and then from the train to her hotel. She stumbled in a kind of trance, and bumped into more people than she could count. Somehow, though, she made it back to her room.

As soon as she closed and deadbolted her door, she turned on the TV, tuned to CNN, and stood watching. News reports of some kind of unusual event at the U.S. Senate were already out. The Capitol building was on lockdown, and Hope gave another silent thanks to Senator Roberts. Practically hyperventilating, the anchorman announced that an unnamed man had been arrested. It had to be Charlie. Hope's legs gave out.

She fell to the ground and cracked the back of her head against the frame of the bed. She let out a yelp.

Hope reached behind her head and her hand came back bloody. She crawled into the bathroom and snatched a washcloth from the vanity and pressed it against her injury. She yelped again.

Curling up on the bath mat outside of the shower, which was still damp from her morning shower, Hope broke down and wept while keeping pressure on her wound.

Some time later, Hope regained some measure of composure and managed to walk down the hall, fill up her ice bucket, and bring it back to her room. Along the way, she swiped a handful of fresh washcloths and put the Do Not Disturb sign on her door. She wrapped some ice in one of the washcloths and held it to the back of her head. After a few minutes, she checked her wound by taking a picture of it with her phone. It was just a small cut, thankfully. She popped two Tylenol and curled up again, this time on the bed.

Her mind raced, spinning and spiraling. Within just over two weeks—sixteen days, she realized, doing the math in her head—she'd gone off the rails. She had been just a few months away from finishing her residency, from graduating Medical School! She'd almost certainly alienated Faye at the lab; she'd simply left her boss and friend a note that said she would be away for two weeks to a month, with no explanation. And despite her uncertainty about Billy, the man *was* sweet and patient, and did look a bit like Prince William. She hadn't answered any of his texts since she'd been gone. What could she say? "Oh, don't worry, I'm off doing something idiotic and will likely be in prison soon, but have a great day."

She had failed so spectacularly it left her unable to process her situation. For her entire academic career—from elementary school to med school—she was always able to get straight As. She'd been trained by her mother and by "the system" to make sure she made very, very few errors. And none of those mistakes could be significant; there is no room for making a big, hairy, audacious mistake in the U.S. school system. Yet, when she took stock of the past two weeks, she felt like she should congratulate herself for just how spectacularly she had failed. Space Shuttle Challenger ball of fire failed.

Not that her efforts really ever had a chance. She flashed on that thought clearly now. What was she thinking? That a ragtag team of five people stood a chance to pull of her hair-brained scheme? It didn't help that Eddie Townsend turned out to be a crackhead, of course, but her plan was doomed before she even started. How did she not see that? At least Quinn and Sanam got away, she thought, assuming Eddie didn't blab his mouth off at some point. But Charlie. Poor Charlie. He was her only true friend in the world, agreeing to go through with her plans as she made them up by the seat of her pants, knowing the likely outcome yet staying by her side through everything. Poor Charlie.

She realized she must have dozed because the next thing she knew, the sky had grown dim. She shot upright and checked her phone to see what time it was. She quickly crammed her belongings into her suitcase, carefully placed the artificial womb in her carry-on bag, washed her face and brushed her teeth, and went downstairs to check out. Charlie had instructed everyone to make their hotel reservations through the end of the weekend so they could lay low if needed and Hope had done as he recommended. Now it looked like she would not need the full reservation. Standing in line at the shoddy front desk in the rundown lobby, she teared up again, realizing that Charlie was likely in a cage while she was about to fly back to California. Still, she knew what she needed to do, and her first stop was back home. She dumped a garbage bag full of her surgical equipment in the dumpster behind the hotel before she got into her rental car and headed for the airport.

Chapter Thirty-Six

12 days before vote on the Sanctity of Life bill

Except for waking once at some point and eating half of a tuna fish sandwich, leaving the rest uneaten on her kitchen table, Hope slept most of Saturday. It was almost dark out when she finally woke and took a shower. She was unpacking when she heard a knock at her apartment door. She figured the only two people it could possibly be were Charlie and Billy, but Charlie was most likely in a jail cell, and Billy probably wouldn't talk to her ever again, given how badly she'd ignored him for the past two weeks. Could it be the police or FBI? Would Charlie have told them about her? No. Could they have identified her from video surveillance, despite her fake ID? Possible.

"Who is it?" she asked through the locked and chained door, trying to keep her voice from cracking.

"Hi, Hope. It's me, Billy. Can I come in?"

Hope, realizing she'd been holding her breath, took a few breaths to regulate her breathing, then unchained the door, turned the deadbolt, and opened the door.

"Come in." She closed the door behind Billy after he crossed into her apartment. What kind of glutton for punishment was this sad sack?

"Before you yell at me," Billy said as soon as Hope turned from the door, "I know you don't like it when people come over unannounced." He glanced at her apartment, which he had never seen in any condition other than spotless, and saw the half-eaten sandwich and an empty glass on the table. He also saw the unpacking in progress in her bedroom.

"Just get back?"

"No. Late last night."

"Jesus. Are you alright?" Billy knew that if Hope had been home for a day and hadn't already unpacked and had left dirty dishes out, something was likely very wrong. And given what she'd confided in him, he feared that things could be very, very bad indeed.

"I'm fine. Really," Hope lied. She was just so tired, and didn't want to deal with... with whatever this was with Billy. Even on her best day, Hope knew she was damaged goods.

"Christ, Hope!" Billy said, his voice raised for the first time Hope could remember. "You summon me to talk with you two or three weeks ago up on that infernal mountain," he said, referring to the hill atop which the 150-foot-diameter dish sits. "You tell me you're going to drop out of med school just a few months from the end of your residency. I mean, who does that? Then you suddenly ask me to watch your cat. Then... nothing. You go dark. You don't even have the decency to return a single fucking text message." He was angry and, for the first time, showing it.

"I don't know what to say," Hope said, lamely.

"First, how about 'sorry.' Sorry for worrying you. Sorry for being so selfish and focused on your capital 'P' Plan for not letting me know you were still alive."

Hope dropped her head and wrapped her arms around her shoulders. She knew Billy was right. Well, except for assuming she'd had anything resembling a plan in Washington, or had one now.

Before Hope could say anything, Billy continued. "Second, how about telling me how you are? How you really are." Billy's voice was still raised, and tears welled up in his eyes. "I've been working crazy hours at the hospital—the new network backbone goes live on Monday, not that you care—and I had to spend yesterday and today helping my mom, who has to go through another round of chemo, not that you care. So I have no idea what's happening with you, with your 'extracurricular activities.' I stopped by, like I've been doing every day for the past three weeks to feed Xander and clean his shit box. So, great, you're back. Glad to see you're alive."

"Billy—"

"Save it. I gotta go. Have a nice life, Hope." He dropped the key she'd loaned him on the small table near the front door.

And with that, Billy left, gently closing the door behind him.

Hope sat at her kitchen table for what felt like an eternity. Several times, she picked up the remaining half of her sandwich, only to let it drop to the plate untouched. Billy was right about everything, she realized. She had not been fair to him, no matter what her excuses or reasons.

"I've really cocked things up, haven't I?" Hope said to Angel's urn. "I blew it in Washington and I blew it with Billy, too, didn't I?" Angel didn't answer.

Finally, around 11:00 p.m., she finished unpacking. Most of her clothes went into her laundry bin. She hung her new blue suit in her closet, thinking of the money she would save from not having to dry clean it, despite its wrinkles, while wondering whether she would ever get another chance to wear it.

Suddenly, she realized she hadn't heard Xander the entire time she'd been home. She looked at the bowls of food and water that sat just inside the kitchen. Both were full. She'd asked Billy to feed Xander up until the fifteenth, the date of the planned vote on the 'Sanctity of Life' bill, figuring that one way or the other, things would be over by then, and she was confident Billy had come reliably. A thought popped into her head: What would happen to Xander when she went away to prison?

She looked around the kitchen and living room, calling out Xander's name. She did not see him, and got no response. She checked in her bedroom, including under the bed. Again, nothing. Finally, she went into her tiny bathroom. God, she hated how cramped the tiny room was. When she walked past the counter and shower, to where the toilet was, she saw Xander, laying curled around the back of the toilet. He did not respond when she called out his name.

Hope carefully reached around the toilet and pulled Xander into her lap. Angel's kitty, purchased that fateful day at the fair, was gone, and so too was her last remaining living connection to her baby sister. For what felt like the umpteenth time in the past few days, Hope curled up in the fetal position and sobbed.

Chapter Thirty-Seven

11 days before vote on the Sanctity of Life bill

Hope spent Sunday morning making calls to all of the waitresses and cooks who worked at the Pancake Shack. Without telling them the details, she told them that Charlie was likely going to be away for quite some time, but that she wanted them to re-open the restaurant and keep it running for him. She instructed everyone to meet her at the restaurant the following morning at nine. She could only imagine the legal bills Charlie was going to face, and figured that he'd be happy to have the extra money. Plus, it felt like it would be a symbolic victory of a sort.

During the day, Hope scrubbed her apartment. A layer of dust had settled after more than two weeks away, plus she was embarrassed that Billy had noticed what a sty her place was. Really, though, Hope admitted to herself the truth: her cleansing rituals, both at home and in the operating room, were therapeutic. Cleaning now, given everything that had happened and was going to happen, gave her a sense of control and order despite her life having spun out of control.

Her knees sore and her hands raw from too much Pine Sol, Hope showered and put on her jogging gear. She drove to the Dish area, parked, and stretched. She ran up the hill, walked back down, and ran up again. Exhausted, she sat on a flat patch near the top and watched as the sun set in the distance. She willed herself not to cry.

"Excuse me, is this seat taken?" asked a voice from behind her. She turned and saw that it was Billy.

"What are you doing here?" she asked. Quickly realizing he might think she didn't want him there, she added, "I mean, hi. It's nice to see you." After a beat she added, "I honestly didn't think I'd ever see you again... I thought you didn't want anything to do with me."

Billy sat down a few feet away from Hope. "I finally watched the news for the first time in days. I heard the news from Washington, and figured it had something to do with you. You know the man they took into custody, don't you?"

Hope nodded. "Charlie." Billy and Hope had eaten together at the restaurant several times, and she'd introduced Billy to Charlie, who'd ribbed her about Billy's boyish good looks for months.

"How are you here? I mean..."

"It's a long story. I'll tell you someday. But it's only temporary. I've got one thing to do tomorrow and then I'm going to the FBI. I need to get Charlie out of jail, or at least explain that he wasn't the mastermind." She laughed at herself for using that word. As if anyone, especially her, qualified as a mastermind for such a series of unfortunate events.

"Did you accomplish what you set out to do?"

"Ha!" Her derisive laugh escaped.

"It's not like you to leave something undone, a goal unachieved." Billy plucked a handful of burrs from his khakis.

"Thank you, I think," Hope said. "No, I'm done. I have to turn myself in. If I can get Charlie out, I'm willing to pay the price for my idiocy."

"You can't. You just can't," Billy implored. He wiped his hands against his pant legs. "God, I hate it up here. All this long grass and dirt. And bugs. Yuck. Give me an ice cold, sterile data center any day over this."

It occurred to Hope that this was not the first time Billy had met her up here.

"Thank you. For everything."

"There's nothing to thank me for. In case you hadn't noticed, I'm crazy about you. Have been since I first saw you. Likely always will be."

Hope blushed.

"But that's not why I'm here. We can talk about us—whatever that means—later. Right now, we need to talk about how you can still win."

"I can't win. It's over," Hope said, resigned to her fate.

"It's not over until the bill is signed into law. You owe it to yourself to fight until then. If you don't, you'll never forgive yourself."

Hope wanted to argue, but she knew he was right. "How'd you get so smart?"

"Always been, always will be. You just never noticed, smartypants."

"What should I do? Tell me what to do." She hated herself for how weak she sounded, but she needed whatever help she could get.

"Can't you find this bastard and implant a fetus privately, not on camera in front of the world? That part of your original plan was nuts, by the way."

Hope ignored the well-deserved criticism and replied, "We never got the switch to work. And without the switch, the explosive device is pretty much worthless. It's not like I can follow him around and light his fuse if he tries to enter a hospital. I threw everything away."

"Did you—"

"Yes, I disarmed the device before I tossed it into the river. I'm not a monster, you know."

"This I know," Billy said, smiling. God, he had a really cute smile, Hope thought. After a beat, Billy said, "Go back to first principles. Why all that tech in the first place?"

"What do you mean?"

"I mean, why did you want to arm the womb with the sensor and the explosive?" Before saying the last word, he looked around to make sure nobody was near, and even then he practically whispered the word.

"Without some kind of safeguard, he could have simply gone in and had my womb removed. He would have been able to undo everything with a simple surgical procedure. I wanted him to have to go through 'pregnancy'"—she made air quotes with her fingers—"for the full nine months and then have to watch as the unwanted baby came out of his body. I wanted him to have to *feel* that repulsive feeling, have that memory seared into his brain."

"Tell me how you really feel," Billy said.

Hope smiled. God, she was beautiful, Billy thought.

"There's just one thing you're forgetting," Billy said, unable to keep the excitement from his voice.

"What's that?"

"Assuming the 'Sanctity of Life' bill passes, it will be the law of the land. Federal law. Abortion will be illegal across the entire country."

"Including for him!" Hope exclaimed. The idea that the "Sanctity of Life" law, if passed, would also apply to her victim just hadn't occurred to her.

"Yep. I think a pretty good case could be made that that's what he would be doing: aborting a fetus."

"Oh, Billy! I could kiss you!"

"I think it's about time," Billy said, smirking.

"When this is all over, I'll do more than that. And that's a promise," Hope said, for the first time as excited by the thought as she was terrified. She stood and smacked off the long grass and dirt from her shorts and legs. "Of course, I might not see you for twenty years to life." She tried to laugh but couldn't. "Listen, I've gotta go," she said. "I only have a little over a week to somehow pull off a miracle."

"Call me," Billy said. It wasn't a question.

"I will," Hope said. It was a promise.

Chapter Thirty-Eight

Saturday, March 10 (six days later)
Senator Royce Carrington's Home
Village of Oyster Bay Cove, Nassau County, New York

5 days before vote on the Sanctity of Life bill

Senator Carrington once again began the monthly meeting at exactly 8:00 p.m.

"Almighty God, we bow before you, and recognize you as our great Savior. We lift our hearts in praise to you, and as your beloved children and your redeemed servants, we lay our lives before you in worship. We ask for your strength that we may be bold proclaimers of your Word. Amen."

Reverend Porter Brooks prayed "amen."

After ceremoniously burning the old card from the previous month's meeting, Carrington wrote the number 2151 in his usual elegant style on a fresh card and saved it in his desk drawer. One more monthly meeting of the Benevolent Overlords Society.

"Want anything?" Carrington asked the Reverend. He poured himself a brandy at the bar.

"No, I'm good, thanks," Brooks said, lifting his tumbler of scotch. Carrington always stocked a Laphroaig Islay Single Malt Scotch Whisky that Brooks liked to say was as close to God as anything on earth. He loved its rich floral notes, and its smoke and licorice flavors.

"Well, with Julian absent, if you want a beer, you'll be able to have one without having your hand bitten off. That guy is like a frat boy at a kegger half the time."

"Can't say I'm a fan of the man's drinking, either," Brooks said.

"Asking him to join our group may have been a mistake," Carrington said. His tone was ominous. He sat in the Dragon Chair and caressed its intertwined serpentine dragons.

"He did deliver on the *Roe* overturn, something we thought might never happen."

"Good riddance to that abomination. More than fifty years," Carrington said. He shook his head and said a silent prayer for the millions of babies killed since that ruling came down in 1973.

"And we'll likely need him to uphold the 'Sanctity' bill," Brooks said.

"He is useful," Carrington said, as much to remind himself as to reply to Brooks.

Brooks lifted his glass in a mock toast and took a sip. *Why didn't Jesus turn water into 20-year-old scotch?*

"I'm still furious the majority decision he wrote was based on a states' rights argument. That's going to make getting the Court to uphold our bill as constitutional that much harder. Maybe even impossible."

"Maybe that was the only way he could get the others to join his decision. In any event, he seems to be willing to do whatever it takes when the time comes, and he can be very persuasive," Brooks said, optimistically.

"Well, we'll cross that bridge when we come to it." Carrington said. "In the meantime, I need you to make a few calls. We need to twist a few more arms in order to get this baby—no pun intended—over the finish line."

"Who?"

"Pennebaker, Smith, Graham. Probably Abbott and Reynolds in the House too."

"Tell me what you need me to do..."

When Hope returned to her apartment after seeing Billy at the Dish on Sunday, she was flooded with optimism and adrenaline. Vim and vinegar, her mom would have said back when she was around. But truth be told she hadn't really known what to do, how to take action. Still, one thing was clear, she had to do something.

Start with the things you can do, even if they are little things, she told herself.

She texted everyone at the Pancake Shack and told them to hold off, that she would contact them again when it was time to open the restaurant. She took a shower and packed a bag with a few days' worth of clothes, assuming that she'd be getting on a plane soon. She just didn't know her destination.

Hope fired up her web browser and searched for whatever personal information she could find on

Senator Royce Carrington, Reverend Porter Brooks, and Julian Kingsley. At this point, she was willing to impregnate any one of them. She was wading through the millions of pages of search results when her phone chimed. She got up and grabbed it from her bedside table. One text message. From Sanam.

```
RC and PB mtg at RC's home. 3/10 eve.
Oyster Bay Cove, NY. Study NE corner.
Professional courtesy given my epic
fail. Sorry to have let you down.
```

Hope shrieked with joy. She immediately closed all of her search tabs and visited her favorite travel reservation site. Five minutes later, she was booked on an early morning flight to LaGuardia. Waiting until midnight, she made an unannounced visit to her research lab and, within two minutes, raced out with exactly what she needed for her trip.

In the morning, after a few hours of fitful sleep, she showered, changed, grabbed her suitcase, kissed Angel's urn, locked her apartment, and ran down the stairs to her car. She broke a large number of traffic laws on her way to San Francisco International Airport. Six and three-quarters hours later, she touched down in New York.

Now, she was crouched in the woods just to the east of Senator Royce Carrington's house. The place was enormous. She wished she could dismiss the place as gaudy, but she had to admit, the home was gorgeous and, somehow, understated despite being larger than her entire apartment building. For the past few days, she'd scoped out the neighborhood, found Carrington's house, and figured out the best route to carry in and cache her equipment in the woods nearby. Despite the unusually mild spring weather, Hope was chilly; she'd been hiding in the woods for over three hours.

At ten minutes before eight, she heard a car approach, a door open and close, and crunching gravel. Thirty seconds later, she heard a rapid series of beeps and one longer, higher pitched tone. A few minutes later, she heard a second car and more crunching gravel. She waited silently to see if anyone else would arrive. No one did. At 8:10, it was go time.

Slowly, she carried her equipment toward the house. Even if Sanam hadn't told her that Carrington's study was in the northeast corner of the house, she probably could have guessed it. She'd immediately noticed the complete lack of windows on most of the north and east sides of the home. The walls were made from beautiful stone slabs, cool to her touch.

After ten minutes, she had her gear piled a few steps east of the kitchen doorwall on the north side of the house. She figured that would be her entry point. From there, she could simply follow the interior wall to Carrington's study. It made sense that's where the man would conduct business or social events—men love their caves, even when those caves are well-appointed wood-panelled rooms within stone mansions.

The wind picked up and Hope shivered. She could barely feel her fingers and she realized, now, too late, that she should have worn her wool gloves. She would have to leave enough time for her fingers to thaw before conducting her surgeries, assuming she got that far. She was fully prepared for failure and somehow, for the first time in her life, was at peace with that possibility. She wished she'd brought one more tank of anesthesia.

Hope carried the two oversized tanks of sevoflurane she did bring in her arms to the southeast corner of the house. She'd seen earlier that this is where the air conditioning units sat. As she walked along the eastern side of the house, she paused briefly and stared at the stone wall, as if trying to see her enemies with x-ray eyes. She squeezed the tanks tightly against her chest, not wanting to drop one or clang them together and risk being heard.

This was the tricky bit. Too little anesthesia and the men would not go under. Too much and they could die. She couldn't risk using too little; she needed the men incapacitated. Despite being confident about her self-defense skills and being in excellent shape, Hope figured that she was no match for two adult men. Especially Royce Carrington who, despite his age, still seemed vigorous. Plus, Carrington might have a weapon. On the other hand, she didn't want to kill them. She wanted them to suffer.

She connected her tubing to the smaller air conditioner, helpfully marked "Study" with a black Sharpie by Carrington himself years earlier, and turned the knobs on the tanks.

Ten minutes later, the tanks were nearly empty. It was now or never. Hope disconnected the tubing and carried the tanks, much lighter now, over to where the rest of her equipment was collected. She grabbed her medical bag and made her way to the door wall. She was prepared to break in, but the glass slid open without resistance. Thankful that Senator Carrington was apparently more concerned with privacy than with security, she paused once she was fully inside and listened as carefully as she could. She stood perfectly still, silent, until she was convinced there was no one else in the house and that the men weren't moving about. She didn't know that Carrington's study was soundproof, even from within the house.

In the dining room, Hope noticed the enormous circular black marble table surrounded by high-back muted vermillion leather chairs, and fresh tulips on the table. Carrington had good taste, the asshole.

Hope tiptoed her way to where she figured the study was. She stopped momentarily just outside the door. If she had been religious, she would have said a prayer. She was not, so she inhaled deeply, turned the handle, and opened the door, ready to face her nemeses, asleep or awake.

The two men were out cold. She quickly walked over to where they were sitting and checked their pulses. Alive, although the Reverend's breathing was shallow. Hope quickly went back out and closed the door behind her in order to trap as much of the sleeping gas as possible in the study. Breathing again, she lugged her equipment into Carrington's house and staged everything right outside the study door. She donned the gas mask she'd purchased at a local sporting goods store that sold survival gear, and entered, again closing the door.

Hope worked quickly and efficiently, hoping all of her preparation would warm her hands so she wouldn't have to waste any time waiting for the feeling in her fingers to return. She ran her arm over Carrington's desk, spraying its contents onto the floor. She didn't care that she'd broken over $100,000 worth of the Senator's fancy tchotchkes. She noticed a framed picture of Senator Carrington with former President Fred Spencer, taken at what looked like a hunting lodge. She stomped on the frame, grinding the broken glass into the study's plush oatmeal-colored carpet.

She set up her drip bags and laid out her medical instruments and the artificial wombs on a chair next to the desk. That's when she first realized how ostentatious the chair in which Carrington was seated was. God, it was horrible, in stark contrast to the overall good taste used to decorate the rest of the house. It was the kind of trophy a rich person acquires so he can have a trophy and show his trophy and brag to others about his trophy.

She dragged the two men onto the desk. She had little trouble with Carrington, who was still trim. The portly Reverend was a different story. She'd planned for this eventuality, though, and took out a large transfer belt with handles and put it around Brooks' waist. It provided just enough leverage for her to hoist the man up on the table, although she did crack his head into one of the desk's legs. She laid the men side by side.

Her fingers were close to being ready for surgery, but not quite. She flicked her hands as fast as she could, trying to get more blood to flow to her most precious body parts. It wasn't that she cared about accidentally nicking the patients, other than that she didn't want to cause a severe internal injury; it was that she didn't want to risk the embryos inside the wombs.

Just as she thought she was ready to begin, Carrington stirred.

Chapter Thirty-Nine

Improvise. Improvise. Improvise. That was her new mantra. For her entire life until about a month ago, it was Plan, Plan, Plan. Now, she seemed to be doing her best to string together a series of partially cobbled-together plans as best she could in the face of enormous uncertainty and then, when those plans went haywire, fly by the seat of her pants. Again, she had the thought that her new modus operandi was both scary and thrilling.

Hope quickly rushed out into the hall and carried the two tanks into the study. Was there enough sevoflurane left in them? Only one way to find out.

Hope took out a handful of cable ties left over from their aborted attack on the Senate. It made her think of Charlie. Poor Charlie. *I'm coming, soon, and hopefully they'll let you go.* She looped ties together into long chains, flashing back to the green and red Christmas construction paper chains she made in the second grade, and tied Carrington spread eagle on the desk. She secured each limb to a corner of the desk and, for safety, took out another large handful of ties, made two more chains, and tightened them across the man's thighs and neck and under the table. She repeated these steps on Reverend Brooks. Finally, just as Norman Underhill had done when he attacked her in the hospital parking garage, she put a bandana over her face and donned a red RESISTANCE baseball cap, being sure to tuck all of her hair into the cap.

She gagged the two men with rolls of gauze and waited out of sight. She saw the well-stocked bar and was tempted to toss back a whiskey. No, she needed to be at her best.

Carrington came to first. Over the course of a few minutes, he slowly realized his situation and struggled hopelessly against the half-inch wide, extra-strength cable ties. His eyes widened in fear. He had no idea who had knocked him out and incapacitated him. Hopefully it was just a burglar; material things could always be replaced. *But why would a burglar tie me down on my desk?* The thought unnerved him.

A few minutes later, Reverend Brooks stirred and went through a similar process of recognition and fear. His screams were muffled by the gauze roll Hope had crammed into his mouth.

Finally, once both men were fully aware of how at risk they were, Hope moved forward until Carrington and Brooks could see her.

"Good evening, gentlemen," Hope said, eerily calm.

Carrington struggled to free himself from his bindings, but eventually gave up. Brooks actually wet himself.

"Please listen carefully. I was going to leave a key decision I have to make tonight to chance, but I've decided to let your answers to some important questions decide for me. One of you is going to be unhappy with what happens this evening. The other, more so."

Hope pulled out a vial of clear liquid and two syringes. "To encourage your honesty, I've brought this. It's sodium thiopental, commonly known as Sodium Pentothal. It's the closest thing to a 'truth serum' we have. Thank you, Abbott Laboratories."

Confusion was obvious on the men's faces. Hope injected the men and waited ten minutes for the drug to make its way through the men's bloodstreams and for them to regain consciousness. She removed the gauze rolls from the men's mouths.

Hope began, "There's a Jataka story of the Buddha, in one of his previous incarnations as the sage Mahosadha, who must arbitrate between a mother and a mythical being in the shape of a woman who has kidnapped the mother's baby and claimed it as her own. To resolve the dispute, the Buddha drew a line on the ground and asked the two women to stand on opposite sides of the line, each holding one of the infant's feet and one of its hands. The one who won the tug of war, pulling the baby's whole body beyond the line, would get to keep the baby."

"That's barbaric," Senator Carrington exclaimed. The sodium thiopental was suppressing his higher cortical functions and he could sense that he lacked his normal iron control.

"Horrible," agreed Reverend Brooks.

"Really? Not seeing it, huh? Okay, let's try the Chinese story of the the Chalk Circle. A beautiful sixteen-year-old girl is sold into a house of prostitution by her destitute family after her father's death. A wealthy and childless man takes her into his house as a second wife. The girl bears him a son, but this makes the man's first wife jealous. So the first wife poisons her husband and blames the young girl for the murder. The girl is arrested and beaten until she confesses, despite being innocent. Just before she is about to be hanged, Bao Zheng, known for his moral fortitude, intervenes and places the baby in a circle of chalk between the man's wife and the young girl. Each is ordered to pull the child toward her.

"Why are you telling us these terrible stories?" Brooks asked.

"Wow. All right. Let's choose a story you know, from Sunday School. King Solomon—you've heard of him, I'm sure—has to rule between two women claiming to be the mother of a child. He tells the women that his 'solution' is to cut the baby in two, so that each woman can receive half. One woman doesn't contest the ruling, but the baby's actual mother begs King Solomon to sheathe his sword and give the baby to the other woman, which is how he comes to know she is the true mother of the infant."

"Such wisdom," Reverend Brooks said, his voice thick with reverence.

"Finally we're getting somewhere," Hope mumbled, exasperated. "So, to confirm, Reverend, you think this story shows that King Solomon had great wisdom, is that correct?"

"Yes, of course."

"And if you were in his position, would you have done the same thing?"

"I would hope to be that wise."

"And had the woman not begged the King, what should he have done? What would you have done?"

"A king must be a man of his word," Reverend Brooks said without hesitation.

Hope turned to Carrington, who had turned his head and was looking, aghast, at his friend.

"And what about you, Senator? Would you have cut the baby in half if neither woman objected? To be a man of your word?"

Carrington's reaction surprised her: He turned his head away from Brooks and began to cry. She discreetly wiped his tears and gave him a few moments to gain his composure.

"Never. I could never..." Carrington's voice trailed off into a whisper.

"Look at Mr. Tough Guy now," Brooks mocked, noticing Carrington's emotion. Disdain dripped from his voice.

"Thank you both. I appreciate the candid conversation." Hope said. "For the record, I have to say that I am appalled that neither of you recognized the parallels between the Jataka and Chinese tales and the more popular story of King Solomon." She knew that biblical scholars see the King Solomon story as a re-telling of this standard folktale, which had been documented almost two dozen times by the time of the bible. "You may want to invest a bit more in some history lessons and a little less in your bible studies."

Her rebuke over, Hope crammed the rolls of gauze back in the men's mouths and walked over to the two tanks and set them near the desk, then reassembled the tubing. She attached the tubing to both men's nostrils.

"Next comes the part you won't like."

Carrington struggled, again to no avail. Brooks trembled, certain he was going to die. Hope's next comments made him realize it would be far, far worse.

"I am going to impregnate you both. That's right... impregnate. As in 'make pregnant.' I am going to insert an artificial womb into each of your abdomens, each containing a fetus."

Reverend Porter Brooks started to moan through his gag. Senator Carrington glared at Hope, the hatred beaming from his eyes.

Hope pulled her phone from her pocket, tapped and swiped a few times, and turned the phone so that first Carrington and then Brooks could see it.

"This is a small explosive device I am going to attach to each of the wombs I insert. Connected to each is a sensor that will detonate the explosive should you attempt to remove the womb before thirty-five weeks pass." Adrenaline was coursing through Hope's veins now. "That's right. No abortions for women? Then no abortions for you either." She hoped her bluff was convincing. She only needed to fool the men for five days, which was when the vote on their bill was scheduled. To increase her odds, she'd shielded her artificial wombs in a stainless steel and titanium mesh, hopefully making them radiopaque, or opaque to X-rays or similar radiation.

"Ready?" Hope paused as if to wait for their responses. Their gags muffled their pleas. "Great. Good to hear. Here we go."

She turned the handles on the tanks of anesthesia.

Chapter Forty

It was well past midnight by the time Hope completed her surgeries. It took another hour for her to haul all of her equipment back to her rental car and another to dispose of it. Along the way, she called the Nassau County police from a prepaid phone and told them that Senator Royce Carrington and Reverend Porter Brooks were in need of medical attention at Senator Carrington's home.

By 4:00 a.m., she was back in her motel room and slept like the dead until her alarm woke her four hours later. She packed and drove to the airport.

At the airport, Hope nervously waited to go through security. She didn't think it was likely, but it was possible they would whisk her out of line and into some detention cell somewhere. The TSA agent spent considerably more time with her than normal, but perhaps it was because she couldn't stop fidgeting. Once through security, she headed straight to a bank of television sets in one of the gate areas. None of the major news networks were reporting anything about an attack on Senator Carrington's home. She found a bookstore-newsstand place and checked the papers, but then sheepishly realized that these would have been printed the previous day. She did her best to control her hyperventilation. She had a cup of coffee and a muffin for breakfast and immediately afterward rushed into a women's bathroom and vomited.

Hope boarded the plane without incident and took her cross-country flight back to California. She was too keyed up to sleep on the flight, and by the time she arrived back at her apartment in Redwood City by mid-evening, she was exhausted. She slept soundly through the night.

When Hope woke the next morning, she felt a strange calm. She'd done what she'd done. It was time for what came next and she was willing to pay the price. She only hoped her actions weren't in vain. She'd find out sometime in the next four days.

Hope had done something illegal. Something wrong. Something monstrous. Yet she felt like her actions were justified, and that feeling scared her.

Hope walked to the kitchen, drank a glass of water, and sat at her table. She thought about the detailed instructions she'd left behind for Carrington and Brooks.

She hadn't had time to figure out how to make a self-sustaining womb, with enough nutrients for the fetuses throughout their maturation. In any event, she figured it would require too many calories, which would take too much space within the men's bodies. Instead, she'd rigged up a feeding tube to each artificial womb, letting them protrude slightly from the men's bodies. The Senator and Reverend could "feed" their babies through the tubes. She left clear directions on how to use the tubes and keep them clean, and provided information about the types of nutrients to provide, and on what schedule. She was confident that if the men followed her instructions, the fetuses would remain healthy and grow normally.

Hope was worried about the men's bodies rejecting the artificial wombs. Rejection was a fact of life in these kinds of surgeries, but while in school she'd learned about some cutting-edge work being done on anti-inflammatory polymers. It was now possible to coat medical devices with a biomaterial made from a family of polymers found to reduce inflammation, specifically when it interacts with white blood cells. The coating calms the body's immune response, reducing or eliminating the risk of implant failure. She'd coated the artificial wombs she implanted in the men with one of these polymers. Hopefully, that would keep rejection at bay. Of course, unlike, say, a heart transplant recipient, these men would only have her devices inside of their bodies for a limited time, by design. No more than nine months. The two rich and powerful men should be able to receive adequate medical care during that time. As well, in her instructions, she spelled out a specific regimen of anti-rejection medication.

Hope was careful not to include anything in her letters about the explosives and sensors. No need for there to be any physical evidence of her bluff.

Hope made herself a sandwich with the last can of tuna in her cupboard and mixed herself a cup of peach iced tea from her favorite powdered mix. She sat at her table and picked at her food until she finally decided to give up. She tossed the uneaten half of her sandwich down the garbage disposal, gulped down her tea, rinsed her glass, and put it into her dishwasher.

Hope brushed her teeth and brushed her hair, and laughed at her vanity. Well, if they play the video on the nightly news, I might as well look presentable, she thought. She got her small tripod from her drawer of electronics, mounted her cell phone on it, and set it across from her on her kitchen table. She set her prepared remarks in front of her and pressed the RECORD button on her phone's camera application. She took a deep breath and began.

"Hello. My name is Hope Hunter. Yesterday, I impregnated Senator Royce Carrington and Reverend Porter Brooks. That's right; the two men are now pregnant—'with child' as they say. Let me try to explain why I took the extraordinary steps I've taken.

"Almost ten years ago, my sister, Angel Hunter, was raped. She was only fourteen years old. As fate would have it, she was raped on the very day that *Roe v. Wade* was overturned. Because of Louisiana's trigger law, all abortion became illegal in the state that day. Angel was forced to carry the baby and give birth, against her will. A little less than eight months later, my sister died from complications during childbirth. This was a travesty of monumental proportions.

"But overturning *Roe* was apparently not enough for these right-wing extremists. Both Senator Carrington and Reverend Brooks are personally responsible for the so-called 'Sanctity of Life' bill that is coming up for a vote at the end of the week. This law, if passed, will outlaw all abortion in the United States. All abortion, period. Even in the case of rape or incest. That outrages me. It should outrage every single person in this country.

"My only regret is that Julian Kingsley, Associate Justice of the Supreme Court, was not present at the time, as I believe his ruling to overturn *Roe* was done for personal and political reasons. And, of course, I wish that I could have somehow held President Brock Owens, who admits to having a hand in crafting this terrible legislation, to account as well.

"Behind my actions is one simple belief: If men had to deal with the possibility of being pregnant and of being forced to carry unwanted pregnancies to term, the laws of this country would be radically different. Misogyny is real. It permeates our government at the highest levels. If our laws—written and passed almost exclusively by men—also applied to men, things would be different. I believe that with all my heart. And so I decided to test my faith, as it were.

"I am not asking for mercy. I am not bragging. I am explaining my actions, in the simplest terms I can think of. My hope is that they have the desired effect. And soon. Thanks for listening."

Hope got up and pressed the STOP button. Sadness permeated her recorded video, she knew, but that was an honest, raw emotion that now almost overwhelmed her.

Satisfied with her recording, she closed her camera app. She rubbed her eyes and tried to shake away her melancholy. After calming herself, she opened her texting app and quickly texted everyone on the staff at the Pancake Shack and asked them to meet her at the restaurant the following morning at ten. It was time to open the restaurant for Charlie, she told them. She didn't say that she would not be with them when they did.

Hope spent the remainder of the day curled up on her couch binge watching "The Handmaid's Tale," a TV series from years earlier that dramatized a society in which women are brutally subjugated, and by law are not allowed to work, own property, handle money, or read. She figured she might not have access to Netflix wherever she was going, and she'd always wanted to watch the award-winning series that sadly seemed less and less like fiction every year.

By midnight, Hope was sound asleep. She dreamed that after flying while being tied to an enormous bundle of helium balloons, she landed gently in a meadow filled with orange poppies and purple geraniums as the knots slowly, magically loosened. She lay perfectly still in the long, cool grass, and the balloons drifted away.

Chapter Forty-One

Monday, March 12 (the next day)
Hope's Apartment
Redwood City, California

3 days before vote on the Sanctity of Life bill

A hummingbird chirped in the large oak tree behind Hope's apartment. It sounded like an over-eager kid playing laser tag. God, how Hope normally hated that sound, despite how cute the tiny busybodies were. Yet this morning she somehow didn't mind.

Hope put on a pot of coffee, showered, and changed. She texted the waitstaff and cookstaff at the Pancake Shack to confirm they would meet her at the restaurant at ten. As she scoured the Internet for news of her activities at Senator Carrington's house, everyone responded that they would meet her as scheduled. She was not surprised; Charlie was the kind of man who hired high-character people and instilled loyalty. *Hang on, Charlie, I'm comin'.*

After an hour failing to find a single article about her activities two nights earlier, Hope closed her laptop, rinsed out the coffee pot and her mug, and grabbed her keys. She thought about taking Angel with her but settled for an awkward hug of the urn. It might be the last time she would be with her sister, she realized. Would they let her keep the urn with her in prison?

Ten minutes later, she opened the door to the restaurant for the first time in over three weeks. She left the "Sorry, We're Closed" sign on the door; they would open the restaurant tomorrow if all went well. She was sorry she wouldn't be there to see it.

Hope made her way into the kitchen. Except for a thin layer of dust, the place was spotless, just as Charlie always left it. His fastidiousness was one of the many things she liked and admired about him. That he was willing to die or go to jail for her was, of course, another. God, how she loved that crazy old man.

As Hope was scrubbing the grill and countertops in the prep area, she heard the bells on the door. It was only 9:30 and she wondered who had arrived early; perhaps it was a team member expecting her to be here and willing to help her get a head start.

She was about halfway through the opening that led from the kitchen to the public area of the restaurant when she saw who had arrived. It was that creep Norman Underhill, the guy hired by Derek, who had grabbed her ass here in the restaurant and then attacked her in the parking garage. She reached out with her left arm, which was still on the kitchen side of the opening and slowly explored the countertop with her left hand until she found what she was looking for: a cleaver.

She quickly moved it to her right hand and stepped fully out of the kitchen. She was behind the counter, about twenty feet from the man.

Norman Underhill saw the cleaver in Hope's hand and the look on her face. He quickly raised his arms in a "I'm putting up my hands officer, don't shoot" motion and said, "No, no, no. Wait. Wait. I came here to apologize."

Hope lowered the cleaver, but only a little. "Go on."

"I really, truly do apologize. For the garage, of course, but also for fondling you here at the restaurant. I should never have listened to Derek, that asshole."

Hope was shocked by Underhill's changed demeanor. She was happy to hear the apology of course, but found herself wondering.

"Why the sudden change of heart?"

"I realized I was wrong, that's all."

Hope decided to push. "I don't believe you, Norman. Come on, you can tell me. Why the change of heart?"

"Honestly?"

"No... lie to me," Hope said sarcastically. Softening, she said, "Yes, honestly. I think you owe me at least that much."

"Well, I, uh... there was, uh, this blog post I read about some men who were forced into being pregnant. It, uh, you know, made me rethink a lot of things, ya know?"

She'd searched for over an hour and hadn't found anything. But it appeared that the story was out, at least in some form. Maybe one of the EMTs talked to someone who talked to someone...

"I appreciate the apology, Norman. I really do. I wish you would have come to that conclusion on your own, but I guess I'll take what I can get," Hope said.

"Well, that's it. That's all I wanted to say. I won't bother you again." Underhill turned to leave.

"Hey, Norman. Where'd you find that article? What website?"

Norman spun around and answered her. He gave her the name of a right-wing conspiracy website she had never heard of.

After Underhill left, Hope returned to the kitchen and put the cleaver down. She noticed that her hand wasn't shaking at all. She wasn't sure she liked what that meant.

The crew arrived a few minutes after Underhill's visit, which Hope did not mention. There were hugs all around, as the crew was a family in many ways. Certainly Charlie always treated them that way. Hope assigned jobs to everyone, and they got to work.

José, one of the line cooks, made lunch for everyone, then wiped the griddle down again. The group sat and told stories about how they'd spent the few weeks since they'd last been at the restaurant. Hope lied and told everyone she was still busy at the hospital and at work. Nobody questioned her; it's what they expected of her.

By three, the restaurant was spic and span. Hope made a work schedule for the next two weeks, being sure not to schedule herself. When one of the other waitresses noticed and asked her about it, she demurred and said something about the fact that she might not be able to make any shifts for a while.

Hope locked up the restaurant. Standing just outside the door, she pressed her hand against the cool glass of the door. *I'm coming, Charlie. I just hope it helps.*

She swiped her phone and opened her email app. A few taps later, her confessional video was en route to CNN. She hopped on her bike and rode to the nearby Caltrain station and boarded a train to San Francisco. She'd thought about driving but couldn't contemplate the astronomical parking fee she would owe if she had to leave her car parked in some $20-a-minute lot in the City while she served twenty years in prison.

Chapter Forty-Two

3 days before vote on the Sanctity of Life bill

The FBI office in San Francisco was a modern, glass building a block and a half east of Van Ness Avenue and about four blocks north of Market Street. The office was just to the southwest of the Tenderloin area, a gritty place Hope tried hard to avoid whenever she visited the City. She had never before seen the building, let alone needed to visit it. Let alone turn herself in at it.

Hope left her bike in a bike rack off of Golden Gate Avenue, the street on which the office was located. She opened the door to the building and walked in.

The office was quiet. She noticed a few agents sitting at desks in a bullpen area on the other side of a high counter that ran the length of the main room. Most were heads-down at their computers, while a few stood talking quietly. A fluorescent light flickered in the far corner.

"May I help you," asked a woman at the front desk who seemed interested in anything but helping people.

"I'd like to talk to an FBI agent."

"What about?"

"I'd like to confess to a crime. Several, actually."

The woman, a twenty-year veteran of the FBI, had seen her share of cranks and crazy people. This woman didn't look crazy, but that didn't mean she wasn't.

"Oh really?"

"Yes. Really," Hope said, returning the woman's sarcasm. Given what was about to happen to her, what did she care if some woman with an attitude didn't like her?

"Take a seat over there," the woman said, motioning with her arm to a waiting area.

"Thanks so much for your help," Hope said, not meaning it, and not hiding the fact. The woman didn't even bother to look up; she simply went back to the stack of paperwork on the desk in front of her.

Hope walked over to the waiting area and sat in one of the bright orange molded plastic chairs which, while hideous, were actually pretty comfortable. She looked up at the bank of muted TVs on the wall.

The TV airing CNN showed a handsome news anchor talking in an overly animated way. The chyron on screen read "Is it possible for men to get pregnant?" So, her video had made it into the right hands and had been considered credible enough to report on, even if they did not include the names of Senator Carrington and Reverend Brooks, and weren't airing her confessional video yet. Hope wished she could hear what was being said.

The TV airing MSNBC also appeared to be showing coverage of the story, while Fox News was airing footage from the 2012 Benghazi attack and a chyron that stated, "New evidence Hillary Clinton prevented rescue." Hope moaned. The story was the gift that kept on giving for Fox, even after all these years.

Hope was looking up at the TVs when a lanky Hispanic man with a completely bald head approached.

"I'm told you would like to speak to an FBI agent? And that you'd like to confess to a crime?"

Hope stood and shook the man's hand. "Yes, that's right. My name is Hope Hunter and that"—she pointed to the TV set airing CNN—"is me. It's true. It's real," Hope said. "It happened. And I did it."

The agent had CNN on in his office at all times and had seen the breaking news.

"Tell me more."

"Until very recently, I was a resident in medical school. And a few days ago, I impregnated Senator Royce Carrington and Reverend Porter Brooks at Senator Carrington's home in New York."

The man couldn't believe what he was hearing.

Hope repeated her synopsis and added, "I'm here to turn myself in."

They left Hope sitting alone in the interrogation room for almost two hours. At least that's what it felt like. She couldn't tell for sure, since they took her cell phone from her and there was no clock in the room. The room was just like what she'd seen on TV dramas: empty save for a metal table in the center of the room with an uncomfortable metal chair on each side. A large mirror dominated one of the walls, which she assumed was of the two-way variety, allowing observers to watch and listen.

Finally, two agents walked into the room. One was the bald agent to whom she had spoken in the waiting room and who had taken her here. The other, probably in his mid-sixties, wearing a rumpled suit and a garish multi-colored tie, looked like he might be the first man's boss.

The older man began speaking while the bald man walked around behind her.

"I'm Special Agent-in-Charge Miller. You've already met Special Agent Alvarez."

"Hello."

"Special Agent Alvarez tells me you have quite a tale to tell."

"I'm here to admit to my crimes, if that's what you mean."

"Mind if I record our conversation while we talk?"

"No. Not at all."

"And you don't want an attorney present?"

"No, thank you."

Special Agent-in-Charge Miller didn't know what to make of this woman. In his forty years with the bureau, he could count on one hand when someone walked in to confess, and did so without a lawyer. And those were uneducated junkies who were, frankly, not fully aware of the significance of their actions. This woman looked like she was competent, not impaired by drugs or alcohol, and even claimed to be a recent medical school student.

Miller wasn't one to miss an opportunity. If what Alvarez told him this woman had admitted to was true, he would likely receive one last citation before his retirement in a few months. He pressed the RECORD button on the camera.

"Please state your name and address."

Hope did so. Then, for the next hour and a half, she told her story. She provided much more detail than she had in the tape she sent to CNN. She explained about the rape, unwanted pregnancy and death of her sister, Angel. She explained that when she heard about the possibility of a national anti-abortion law, she felt compelled to act. She provided a detailed explanation of her actions at the Senator's house, and of the medical procedures she performed. The only two details she omitted were that she'd threatened the men with explosives that would go off if they attempted to end their pregnancies and any details about the origins of the embryos she'd surgically implanted.

A few times, Special Agent-in-Charge Miller asked a clarifying question or two, but otherwise was happy to sit in silence and let Hope speak. Finally, she finished her confession and the room went silent.

Hope didn't know what to make of Miller. He sat like a sphinx, silent and still, through most of her confession and again now that it was over. She couldn't read him at all. She supposed this was a skill honed from his many years on the job.

Miller finally rose from his chair and ran his palms down his suit coat as if that would iron out its countless wrinkles. After a few moments, he realized his effort was fruitless and stopped.

"Take Miss Hunter into custody, Special Agent Alvarez," he said to his colleague. To Hope he said, "I'm going to do everything in my power to expedite your case and to make sure you get put away for life as soon as possible." A flash of anger had escaped, and Hope noticed it. Miller noticed Hope notice, and his anger only grew more intense.

Hope smiled at Miller. "Would it be possible for me to get a bite to eat first? I'm starving."

Miller punched the RECORD button to stop the recording and stormed out of the interrogation room. Special Agent Alvarez, still stunned by Hope's admission, his boss's rare display of emotion, and Hope's *cajones*, gently took Hope by the arm and helped her stand.

"Let's go," he said. Then, with his mouth just behind Hope's right ear, he added, "I'll get you a pack of peanuts or something on the way." His niece had recently had an abortion in the Central Valley, and he knew she was lucky to live in California, one of the few states where abortion was still legal. He tried not to think about what he would have done to help her had she lived elsewhere.

Chapter Forty-Three

2 days before vote on the Sanctity of Life bill

Senator Royce Carrington spent Sunday and Monday recovering from the surgery some mad woman had performed on him. His abdomen had fifteen stiches running across what his private physician said was a pfannenstiel-style horizontal incision, and he felt lethargic for the first time in his life. Assuming what the woman said was true, he had an artificial womb inside of his body. He was "pregnant." Unsure if what she'd said was true and given the delicate nature of his situation, Carrington did not want to tell anyone other than his doctor about what had happened, at least not yet. He convinced his doctor to allow him to spend a few hours at work on Tuesday morning, promising that he would immediately go back home and rest for a few more days.

The Majority Leader was dumbfounded when Carrington called him Monday night and told him what he wanted him to do: call an early vote on the "Sanctity of Life" bill. The man asked Carrington if he didn't just want to let the bill die rather than calling a vote, but Carrington was adamant and the man relented; he might be Majority Leader, but only because Carrington didn't want to be, and because Carrington had helped him get the job.

Now, at Carrington's request, the two men were on the Senate floor.

"Hi Royce," the Senator from Ohio said as he walked up to Carrington's desk, where Carrington was sitting. He'd spotted Carrington come on to the Senate floor and head straight to his seat, something that was unlike Carrington, who usually prowled around the room like a feral cat. "You all right?"

"Fine, fine," Carrington lied. "Just a little under the weather."

The Ohio Senator doubted Carrington's explanation, if he could call it that; Carrington was famous for having an iron constitution, for never being sick. But he let it slide and walked over to talk with a colleague from West Virginia. A few other Senators came to greet Carrington, each also curious as to why the man was seated. Carrington told the same lie to each of them.

The Leader shocked almost everyone in the Senate chamber when he declared that the Sanctity of Life bill would now come to a vote. They weren't expecting the vote until Thursday.

They certainly weren't expecting the result of the vote, either.

When the vote closed, the bill was defeated fifty-two to forty-one, with one abstention and six no-shows. Carrington had called Senators Pennebaker, Smith, and Graham and asked them, despite the urging they'd received by Reverend Brooks just days earlier—at Carrington's request no less—to vote no on the bill. Carrington promised he would explain at some point. More importantly, he'd indicated clearly that he would owe each of his colleagues, and this was worth more to them than the outcome of any particular vote. They joined all forty-nine Democrats in voting "nay" on the bill.

Senator Mary Roberts, one of the staunchest opponents of the bill, couldn't contain her joy when the final tally came in. She texted Tanya McAvoy, who she'd come to realize had a complicated past:

> Sanctity bill defeated! Carrington himself asked for an early vote and voted NAY. Strange world we live in. We'll celebrate later.

Roberts didn't reveal her belief that the woman pretending to be Regina Staubach likely had something to do with today's miracle, or that she suspected the woman was Tanya's daughter. Well, she figured, Tanya wasn't the only person in Washington with secrets.

A few minutes before noon, his hopes of a national anti-abortion law shattered by his own hand, Senator Royce Carrington made his way quietly off the Senate floor and to a waiting car. He needed to lie down. He had morning sickness.

Tuesday, March 13 (later the same day)
Correctional Treatment Facility
Washington, D.C.

Hope tried to be a model prisoner. She had no beef with the guards, the prison, or the legal system. She was, as far as she could tell, the only woman here that had admitted her crimes. Plus, she figured her life would be easier if she went along, and did so as obediently and as quietly as possible.

Lunch was some kind of stew. Again. She'd only been in prison for two days and already they were serving the same meal. She couldn't complain, though; it actually wasn't all that bad. Still, she expected she'd miss fresh fruits and vegetables, and soon.

On her way back to her cell, a guard approached her. It was one of the women who seemed to have responsibility for her wing of the prison. The woman snuck something into her hand.

"Here. This is for you."

Hope looked down and saw two chocolate chip cookies that appeared to be freshly baked. A look of confusion covered her face.

"I was watching CNN in the break room. The news just hit. The 'Sanctity of Life' bill went down! That dreamboat Senator Carrington apparently asked for an early vote and then voted against his own bill. It's all so confusing. But one thing I know: it's wonderful!"

Hope wasn't sure she heard right. "The bill, it's—"

"Dead. Dead dead dead," the guard whispered. "And word is that you're the reason why." She smiled, which made Hope realize that in just two days she'd already come to miss the simple act of someone smiling. "So, here. These are for you. But, shh. Don't tell anyone now, ya hear?"

Hope quickly reached out and gave the woman a hug, and immediately retreated.

"Go on. Get outta here," the guard said kindly. Then, more loudly, in case the walls had ears, she added, "Back to your cell, prisoner."

Chapter Forty-Four

Hope was lying on her cot reading a biography of Winston Churchill when a guard approached.
"Visitor for you, Hunter."

Hope was confused. The only person she thought might possibly visit her was Charlie, but he was in jail or maybe in some terrorist detention facility somewhere being waterboarded. Her mother had made it clear that she valued her position and purported power more than her relationship with Hope; There was no way Tanya would come. And while Quinn and Sanam had been willing to help her, she didn't expect them to raise their heads, either, especially here in the belly of the beast. Plus, it was almost 9:00 p.m., which she assumed was well past the end of visiting hours. She put a bookmark into her book, pivoted to a sitting position, then stood.

"Open 117," the guard shouted. The door to Hope's cell slid open.

"Let's go," the woman said to Hope. Hope let the guard guide her to the visiting area, which was dead quiet except for one guard standing at attention behind where the prisoners sat and one man sitting in one of the visitor's chairs: Charlie.

Hope hadn't had any visitors, so she looked around the room for the first time. She decided it looked exactly like she expected one should look based on movies and TV shows. Drab gray carpeting and walls in desperate need of a fresh coat of paint. Two long lines of chairs, separated by partitions, on either side of a long plexiglass wall. A few posters on the visitors' side indicated that firearms and explosives were not allowed. How ridiculous, Hope thought, since visitors presumably had to pass through security to get here. She felt the ghosts of broken dreams fill the room.

Hope sat across from Charlie and took stock of him. He looked nonplussed, as if nothing unusual or significant had happened recently. She picked up the phone handset, which she assumed would allow her to talk with Charlie. He picked up his as well.

"Hiya, kiddo," Charlie said. Hope could feel the warmth of his familiar greeting wrap around her and hug her, even if his arms could not.

"Oh Charlie! I'm so glad you're okay. I was so worried about you. Are you... are you out of jail? Are you free?"

"Free as a bird. Funny how things work out when they don't work out," Charlie said cryptically, fearing recording devices or eavesdroppers on the line. He hoped that Hope understood he was talking about the fact he didn't have a gun or the modified oxygen tank with the explosive device when he was arrested.

"But—"

"But nothing. I'm just an idiot who tried to put on an old man disguise and pull a stupid prank. They got me for trespassing on government property. And attempting to block a fire exit, or something stupid like that. Who cares?" Charlie laughed, as if being charged by a crime was no big deal. "And nobody ever complained about anything being missing," he added, hoping Hope would understand that he was referring to the fact that he had swiped her mom's identification badge but that Tanya hadn't reported it. Neither would ever know for certain why Senator Mary Roberts had snatched it off of Hope's suit when she helped Hope escape, or ever know she'd dropped it in one of Tanya's drawers and never said a word to anyone. Charlie had told the FBI that he simply walked in from the lobby, hoping not to have to mention Hope's mother's badge, despite the woman being a self-centered bitch as far as he was concerned. He was actually surprised and perplexed that they hadn't questioned him further about that part of his story.

"I was so worried about you," Hope said. She'd been trying to figure out how to tell the authorities that Charlie had nothing to do with things, that she'd made him come with her.

"Shh. I'm good, kiddo. I'm good," Charlie lied. In fact, he wasn't certain his legal risk was over, but he didn't want Hope to worry about him, especially given the legal difficulties she faced herself. "Listen, when is your initial appearance in court?"

"I have no idea. The FBI agent in charge, a guy named Miller, seemed to have a hard-on for me. I think he's threatened by strong women."

"I'll find out. In the meantime, how are you? I mean, really?"

"I'm okay. I mean, I'm already sick of the food, but it'll be fine. So far, the guards have treated me fairly, if not well."

Charlie put the palm of his hand on the glass and Hope reached up and placed hers as if to touch his.

"I'll be here every day to visit you."

"You don't have to do that. Besides, you have to be at the restaurant, which, if I recall, is in California."

"I wasn't asking," Charlie said. "And besides, it appears that some enterprising young lady who shall remain nameless has organized the team and re-opened the restaurant. I think they'll be fine without me for a while. I can sign checks from here."

Hope smiled, so gratified to have this incredible man as a friend.

Charlie stood and Hope followed suit. "Listen, I gotta go. I'll see you tomorrow during regular visiting hours. And, hey, kiddo..." After glancing at a security camera, Charlie turned to Hope, beamed his brightest smile, and fully raised his arms in an exaggerated "touchdown" motion. Hope knew he was congratulating her and telling her he was proud of her.

"Thanks, Charlie."

"Love you, kiddo."

"Love you too," Hope said. Just as Charlie was about to hang up and leave, she asked, "Hey... How did you arrange to meet me tonight?" She motioned around the empty room. "I mean, you a big shot around here?"

"Nope. After tonight, I'm like every other Joe Shmoe. But tonight they owed me a favor. You see, I gave 'em a lead on a certain gun dealer who works in the area." Charlie tilted his head and gave Hope a wry smile. "Mr. Eddie Townsend was recently picked up with possession of a small arsenal. The Feds don't like that sort of thing. Not one bit. He's down the street at the D.C. Central Detention Facility." Before Hope could say anything, Charlie said, "See you tomorrow, kiddo," hung up, and left. He didn't feel the need to tell Hope about the gruesome threat he'd had Quinn and Sanam deliver to Eddie to keep him from talking.

Chapter Forty-Five

Royce Carrington was not used to rest or relaxation. Yet, given his condition and his insistence on calling the vote the day before, he was bedridden. Not one for taking orders, even from doctors, Carrington finally agreed to take a few days off only after nearly collapsing while making himself coffee in his kitchen and pulling two stitches.

As the sun rose to its apex in the clear blue sky, he sat propped up in his bed, surrounded by the day's New York Times, Wall Street Journal, and Clarion-Ledger as well as dozens of magazines. His copy of the latest Jon Meacham biography on Gabriella Davenport sat unopened on his nightstand. He disagreed with the woman on pretty much every important policy issue, but he admired her. Her story was a compelling one: from poverty to Harvard to successful entrepreneurship to the

White House, with plenty of well-meaning—if misguided—liberal do-goodism along the way.

Saturday was a shock, and for the first time in his life, Carrington was having a hard time concentrating. As he read a headline about yet another conflict in Afghanistan, he flashed to waking up strapped to his desk and being confronted by that infernal woman. As he tried to read the article, which likened the U.S. policy to the children's game Whack-a-Mole, he flashed to waking up the second time, with fresh stitches running along his abdomen. He put the paper down and picked up the Davenport bio. At eight hundred pages, it was quite a tome, and within minutes he was too tired to hold it upright. He hated himself for being so weak.

Carrington got out of bed and stood at the French doors that led out from his master suite onto a second-floor balcony with a stunning view of the Long Island Sound. As he stared out of the windows, contemplating the natural beauty of the area and God's many creations—including, he supposed, the woman who'd attacked him—his mind calmed. God was always there for him, showing him the way forward. *The baby inside me is one of God's creations, too.*

He knew the baby growing inside of him could have become one of the nearly one hundred million victims of abortion in the United States had he not orchestrated the overturn of *Roe*. The fetus must have come from *somewhere*. From *someone*. For a brief moment, he feared it might be a crack baby, already unhealthy due to its mother's drug use.

Carrington stood soaking in the warmth of the sun and the beauty before him and took five deep, cleansing breaths. As he calmed himself, an idea began to form in his mind, but it was just out of reach, somehow unravelling each time it started to form. *Please, God, do not forsake me.*

The Senator got back into bed, as even standing for a few minutes was difficult. He picked up his phone and called his housekeeper, Rosa, who was downstairs cleaning the rest of the house. He asked that she bring him up some lunch.

A few minutes later, a bowl of homemade chicken noodle soup and fresh rolls were on a bed tray across his lap.

"Is there anything else I can get you sir?"

"No, thank you. This is perfect."

Rosa smiled and turned to leave. When she got to the door, she turned back and said, "Mr. Carrington, may I ask you a question?"

"Of course."

"What will you do with the baby?" Rosa asked. She was a devout Catholic.

Royce Carrington didn't hesitate. "My beliefs are sincere, if that's what you're asking."

"Good. Very good," she said. After a beat, she added, "You are lucky that woman saved your baby's life."

In his weakened state, it took Carrington a moment to understand what Rosa was saying. The blurry thought that was in his mind earlier snapped into focus.

"Yes, I am indeed. Thank you, Rosa. When you finish up downstairs, let yourself out. I have to make some phone calls and then I'm going to rest. I'll call you if I need anything."

Once Rosa had closed the door, Carrington dialed his money manager.

"How much do I have left in my foundation fund?"

"A little under ten million," the man said. He couldn't believe that Carrington had donated ninety million dollars in a little less than a year and a half.

"That's what I thought. I want to give another grant and that's not nearly enough. Can you pull together another hundred million from my personal accounts and move it to the foundation?"

Carrington's money manager wasn't sure he heard correctly.

"A hundred million?"

"That's right."

"That's almost half of what you have left in your personal accounts, after the hundred you've already put into the foundation. Are you sure?"

Carrington laughed. "Yes, I'm sure." *So I'll only have a hundred million left. Poor me. Whatever will I do?*

Calculating his reduced fees, which were based on the value of his client's investments, the man was not as sanguine. Still, he hadn't landed clients like Senator Carrington by questioning them.

"What's the charity? Who are the lucky S-O-B's who are going to get the big fat check?"

"Oh, it's not a charity."

Ten minutes later, Senator Carrington was on the phone with Dr. Faye Young.

"You want to do what?" Faye asked for the second time.

"I want to donate to your lab, Dr. Young," Carrington repeated.

"And you want to donate one hundred million dollars?"

"That's correct,"

"Is this some kind of a prank?"

"I can assure you it is not."

"What's the catch?"

"There's no 'catch' but I do insist that the funds be used on a specific research project."

"Which project?" Faye asked. She had a feeling she knew which one.

"Your work on an artificial womb," Carrington said as he ran his fingertips over his incision.

Of course, Faye thought. "You should know that my lead researcher on that project has temporarily stepped away from that work." She had no idea if Hope's absence was temporary or not. In fact, she hadn't heard from Hope in over a month, and she feared the worst: that her young protege was somehow involved in the events in New York a few days earlier.

Carrington quickly grabbed his laptop and reopened the browser tab opened to Dr. Young's research lab. He clicked on the "Staff" link and there she was: Hope Hunter, the woman who had attacked her.

"Are you there Senator?" Faye asked after several seconds of silence.

"Yes, yes, sorry," Carrington said, recovering from his shock. He made a quick calculation. The right course of action was clear. "That's fine. I would very much like to support and accelerate your research in this area. I think an artificial womb would provide an important alternative to abortion."

Dr. Faye Young, a graduate from ultra-liberal University of California, Berkeley, and daughter to two parents of the sixties, did not like Senator Carrington's politics one bit. The man—like too many powerful men in Washington in her mind—was far too eager, and sadly able, to impose his religious beliefs on women across the country. Yet, the man had a point. If Hope's research could be perfected to the point where it could be used with human embryos, it could perhaps be used as an alternative to abortion. And, perhaps more importantly, the man had one hundred million dollars he was willing to give to the lab. Faye took her fundraising responsibilities seriously.

"I'll have my secretary get back to you with the necessary paperwork," Faye said coolly.

"Thank you. That would be great," Carrington said. After a pause he added, "Oh, and there's one other condition. You must promise to keep my identity private. If I find out that anyone but you knows about my involvement, I will sue you personally for every penny you've got. And the hospital, too."

"As I said, I'll have my secretary get back to you with the necessary paperwork. Have a nice day," Faye said before saying something she would regret.

Chapter Forty-Six

Monday, June 25
U.S. District Court
Washington, D.C.

Three months after Hope's arrest

The last one hundred and five days had been simultaneously horrible and bearable, mundane and eventful, stressful and relaxing. Hope knew that it was a very bad idea for her to be counting her days in prison, but she couldn't help herself. While some prisoners used the paper and pencils provided to them to write letters to loved ones or to draw, Hope simply tallied the days she'd spent caged up since turning herself in. She spent almost all of her time reading books she was able to take out from the prison's surprisingly well stocked library. After finishing most of the biographies in the library, she moved to reading books from the much larger collection of self-help titles on meditation.

She hated being confined to a cage most of the day, but, thanks to a suggestion by a friendly guard, she read book after book on finding inner peace and tried to meditate her way to a place where she could tolerate her situation without going crazy. Most days seemed to drag on interminably, but the occasional fight or other bout of drama kept her on her toes. It was stressful to have to navigate the various cliques and gangs, but she'd found a way to carve out her own identity without offending anyone, at least so far. She mused, frequently, about how trivial her issues with the Pamela Pack had been back at Stanford. None of those girls had a shiv made MacGyver-style from a razor and a toothbrush.

She'd made her initial appearance in court the day after turning herself in, in the middle of March. For weeks after, she'd had nightmares about the hulking federal agents who brusquely brought her into a courtroom and shoved her into her chair, and, worse, the shiver of despair she felt when she first looked into the soulless black eyes of the federal magistrate judge. By comparison, the Assistant U.S. Attorney, who tried to act tough, wasn't nearly as intimidating. When the judge formally read the charges against her, he announced the statutory maximum sentence for her crimes: eighteen years in prison. She still had nightmares about that, despite her attempts at meditation.

When informed of her constitutional rights and asked if she could afford counsel, she requested a public defender, filled out some paperwork to prove she was poor enough to qualify, and was assigned a short, pudgy attorney with short blond hair and rosacea named Christian Nash. The young man looked to be a few years younger than she was, and he had a disconcerting habit of biting his nails all the time. Despite her lack of confidence in the man, she followed his advice and did not seek bail when the AUSA indicated he wanted Hope detained.

A week and a half later, she was back in court for her preliminary hearing, this time in a different courtroom, just a half a mile and a ten-minute walk from the U.S. Capitol. The district court judge for her case, Judge Lorraine Jackson, a tiny woman with cropped blonde hair and horn-rimmed glasses, reminded her of Faye at the lab: friendly but stern. She was informed that the grand jury signed off on her indictment, which meant they believed there was sufficient evidence to force Hope to face the charges against her.

Over the next five or six weeks, Hope found herself back in the courtroom once or twice a week as her lawyer made one pretrial motion after another. The little confidence she had in the man waned further after each of his motions was shot down, effortlessly, by the AUSA.

Nash's first motion was a motion to dismiss the case because Porter Brooks claimed that he was pregnant because of Hope's actions, yet, Nash argued, it was biologically impossible for a man to get pregnant and therefore the case had to be thrown out. Judge Jackson shot Nash a "really, counselor?" look when informing him that she would not interpret the charge quite so literally.

Nash tried to argue that Hope's confession should be excluded, despite the fact that she had given it freely and was not under duress or the influence of drugs or alcohol when she'd given her statement at the FBI office in San Francisco. After this motion was denied, Nash tried to get a change of venue, arguing that since the events in question happened in New York, Hope should be tried there, not in Washington D.C. The AUSA argued that under 18 U.S. Code § 2, Hope's crimes were an offense against the United States. Judge Jackson denied this motion, as well.

Unable to hide his desperation, Nash attempted an insanity defense under 18 U.S. Code § 17, but this went nowhere when Hope, asked if she was fully aware of the consequences of her actions, assented without hesitation. He moved to dismiss one final time after reading in the newspaper that Brooks wouldn't testify in open court. Judge Jackson swatted down this motion like all the others.

When Nash was out of motions, Jackson asked for Hope's plea. On her behalf, Nash stood and gravely said "not guilty." Hope didn't really understand how she could plead not guilty when she'd admitted to the crimes, but she was swayed by Nash's advice despite her concern about having her future in the hands of such an inexperienced lawyer. The judge consulted her calendar and announced that the trial would begin six weeks later. She was back in her cell a half an hour later.

In the third week in June, she was back in Judge Jackson's courtroom in U.S. District Court for her trial. After such a long wait, she was surprised at how quickly everything suddenly moved. Her trial lasted only four days, starting on a Wednesday and ending the following Monday.

Now, on the last day of the trial, Hope sat awaiting her verdict. It had been a little over six months since her foray in New York, since she had walked into the FBI field office in San Francisco and been taken into custody, and since Senator Royce Carrington had done a one hundred and eighty degree turn and voted down his own national anti-abortion bill. Her time in the Correctional Treatment Facility—prison—already seemed like a lifetime and she hadn't even been sentenced yet.

Hope sat at the defense table with her public defender in the same courtroom they'd been coming to for the past four days. The room could be summed up with one word: wood. Wood paneling on the walls, wooden tables for the plaintiff and defense, and wooden desks for the judge and court reporter. An American flag hung limply from a flagpole in the corner. Walking paths had been carved into the threadbare yellow carpeting.

Reverend Brooks, the complainant in her case, had not been coming into court, and was not present now. Hope guessed he must be too embarrassed to be seen in public while six months pregnant. Interestingly, Senator Carrington had not filed charges against Hope, and had been at work on the Senate floor, distended belly and all, for the past several months.

Based on her good behavior while in custody awaiting trial and her past as an outstanding student at Stanford University Medical School, they allowed Hope to appear in court wearing street clothes instead of her prison jumper. She was not in cuffs either. She wore black pants and a simple white blouse. She wore no makeup, and was still the most beautiful woman in the room to Billy, who waved to her from the front row of the public seating area. Hope waved back nervously to Billy, and to Charlie and Faye, who were also in the courtroom. Charlie and Billy had attended each day of the trial. Faye must have flown out over the weekend. She was the only woman in the packed courtroom not wearing a CHILDREN OF HOPE baseball cap.

As she sat and waited for the proceedings to begin, Hope found herself thinking once again that the courtroom was eerily similar to the one she'd been in when she was called for jury duty a few years earlier back in Redwood City, California. That case was about a robbery, and there was overwhelming evidence that the defendant was guilty. The case was settled just before Hope and the rest of the jury would have deliberated. She found the case boring and would have convicted the man after just the first hour of testimony. She couldn't help but think that the jurors in her trial had a far more interesting trial to adjudicate; they'd have a story to tell for the rest of their lives. She only hoped they would not jump to a conclusion about her as quickly as she had about the defendant in the case for which she was a juror. Her fate was in their hands.

The case had ended the previous Friday afternoon. The jury of five women and seven men, after spending just two hours together Monday morning, reached its verdict. Everyone had been called back into court after lunch. In prison, Hope was served stew yet again.

When the jury was brought in and seated, Hope tried to read their faces. Most of the women looked sympathetic, but she wasn't sure. Maybe they were just pitying her for the judgement that was about to come. The men, except for an older African

American man and a slight, professorial-looking man, seemed openly hostile to her. The heavyset guy wearing a flannel shirt and paint-stained khakis, as he had done each day of the trial, stared at her to the point that she was uncomfortable. Worryingly, he was the jury foreman.

When the judge entered from her chambers, the bailiff announced, "All rise. The U.S. District Court is now in session, the Honorable Judge Lorraine Jackson presiding."

Judge Jackson stepped up on the dais and sat down, and everyone in the courtroom took their seats. Jackson took a moment to organize the folders and papers in front of her; a decade of service in the Army implanted an insatiable need for right angles, crisp bed corners, and socks and belts rolled counterclockwise, never clockwise.

"Ladies and gentlemen of the jury, have you reached a verdict?"

"We have, your Honor." Hope didn't like how the man glared at her as he said this.

The bailiff walked over and took a small piece of paper from the jury foreman. He carried it to the judge and handed it to her. She peeked at the paper, then refolded it.

Charge by charge, the judge asked the jury their findings. Charge by charge, the jury found Hope Hunter guilty as charged.

Hope was numb. She was here to take responsibility for her actions, yet she had hoped beyond hope that somehow she wouldn't have to spend decades of her life behind bars. Her attorney, the pimple-faced public defender, seemed to need more consoling than Hope did, so she helped the poor young man regulate his breathing until she was taken from the courtroom.

Judge Lorraine Jackson thanked the jury for their service. After checking her oversized paper desk calendar and attempting to smooth one of the corners that was, annoyingly, curling up, she said, "Sentencing to be held Monday, September tenth." She banged her gavel and walked to her chambers. No one in the courtroom could see the heartbreak in her eyes.

Chapter Forty-Seven

Monday, September 10 (three months later)
U.S. District Court
Washington, D.C.

Three months later
Six months after Hope's arrest

Hope sat awaiting sentencing in the same courtroom in U.S. District Court where the jury had found her guilty eleven weeks earlier. While she'd established a rhythm of sorts in her time in prison, she was thankful for the change in scenery. She sat at the defense table with her public defender, who once again nervously bit his nails. The wood paneling and wooden furniture was the same, but the flagpole in the corner had been replaced by a newer, shinier model.

As for her trial, Hope was allowed to appear in court wearing street clothes instead of her prison jumper, and without cuffs. She wore the same black pants and white blouse she wore the last day of her trial. When she was led to her seat, she waved to Billy, Charlie, and Faye, who were once again in the courtroom. As was true during Hope's trial, Faye was the only woman in the packed courtroom not wearing a CHILDREN OF HOPE baseball cap.

Judge Jackson entered from her chambers, and the bailiff announced, "All rise. The U.S. District Court is now in session, the Honorable Judge Lorraine Jackson presiding." Judge Jackson stepped up on the dais and sat down, and everyone in the packed courtroom took their seats. Jackson organized her papers, as she always did, flicked an annoying speck of dust from her robe, and addressed Hope and the entire courtroom.

"As I'm sure everyone in the court can appreciate and, as was stated several times throughout the trial, this is a difficult case, and a difficult decision. Let me just say for the record that I have reviewed everything, including the sentencing memorandum submitted. And, before I forget, I would like to thank counsel for their professionalism throughout this trial." The two lawyers bowed their heads slightly, graciously accepting a rare compliment from Judge Jackson.

Judge Jackson took a sip of water, placed her glass precisely in the center of her Ruth Bader Ginsburg coaster, which she made sure was at right angles on her bench, and continued.

"The facts of this case appear to be incontrovertible. The defendant surrendered herself to the FBI and, on her own accord, admitted her actions. Yet I believe there are mitigating factors in this case. The defendant has no history of criminal conduct. In fact, she was, until very recently, a model student and citizen. She was also under great personal stress, given her family's tragic history."

The judge paused and added, "In effect, the defendant sexually assaulted her victims while they were unconscious. This case, in its essence, is not much different than traditional rape cases heard by courts around the country every day. Obviously the details are unique, but the essence remains the same." Jackson paused and steeled herself to say her next line exactly as she'd rehearsed, despite not believing a word of it. "As in all rape cases, the victims will be inconvenienced for just nine months or less."

Gasps, shouts, and cries came from the audience in the courtroom. Half were furious that it seemed the judge was saying that *permanent* injury was the standard for criminal sentences. Half loved the irony of the judge's comments, which echoed the arguments of pro-life activists through the years. Jackson let the hubbub die down.

Judge Jackson knew that Hope's convictions carried a potential sentence of eighteen years in prison. The AUSA in the case recommended eight years in prison, while probation officials recommended only a "moderate" county jail sentence.

Jackson, who had envisioned this moment in her mind every day since Hope's jury had found her guilty on all charges, said, "The role of the Court at sentencing is, essentially, to follow the roadmap that our system of criminal justice sets out for the Court in sentencing decisions, which I will do to the best of my ability." She took a deep breath and continued. "Based on these rules and associated constraints, my decision is to sentence the defendant to six months with time served."

Hope had been in prison awaiting sentencing for six months. Judge Jackson was, in effect, saying that Hope had served her prison time.

The courtroom erupted. Many immediately flashed back to the light sentence given to Brock Turner in the case *People v. Turner*, formally *People of the State of California v. Brock Allen Turner*, in 2015. Turner sexually assaulted an unconscious woman. His convictions carried a potential sentence of fourteen years in prison and prosecutors recommended he serve six years. Instead, on June 2, 2016, Santa Clara County Superior Court Judge Aaron Persky sentenced Turner to six months' confinement in the Santa Clara County jail. He had already served half of that time. People were outraged then, as it appeared they were now. Lorraine Jackson was prepared to take the backlash she would receive for her sentencing. And the praise.

Judge Jackson pounded her gavel. "Quiet. Quiet please." She waited for the courtroom to quiet down and proceeded.

"The question I have to ask myself, consistent with the Rules of Court, is: Is prison for this defendant an appropriate antidote to the poisoning of Reverend Porter Brooks' life? Is incarceration in federal prison the right answer? In trying to balance the factors in the Rules of Court, I conclude that it is not and that justice would best be served, ultimately, with my judgment here today.

"I will now go through some of the factors I have taken into account." The judge took another sip of water. "First, the Defendant was not armed and did not use a weapon. Second, the victim, while arguably vulnerable during the crime, is not, generally, a member of a traditionally vulnerable class. Third, while the Defendant inflicted physical and emotional injury, there was no real degree of monetary loss to the victim. Fourth, this crime was arguably committed because of unusual circumstances, which are not likely to reoccur. And fifth, the Defendant did not take advantage of a position of trust or confidence to commit the crime."

A middle-aged man in the audience stood and yelled, "This is an outrage!" A U.S. marshall quickly escorted the man from the courtroom. His red baseball cap was knocked off of his head as the marshall dragged the man from the room.

Lorraine Jackson waited for the bedlam to recede. Her demeanor shifted and she looked directly at Hope.

"All of that said, what you did was horrific, young lady. As a medical school student, you agreed to follow the Hippocratic Oath, to do no harm. There is no doubt that knocking two men unconscious and performing surgery on them without their consent constitutes 'harm.'" She sighed. "It gives me no pleasure to do this, but I must. I hereby place an injunction on your ability to practice medicine in the United States. You may not practice medicine ever again in this country."

Hope was not surprised by this part of the judge's ruling.

"My injunction is backed by the full coercive power of the Court. If it is found that you ever so much as prescribe an aspirin to anyone, I will personally find you in contempt of court and throw the book at you. Am I clear?"

"Yes, ma'am," Hope said.

"However, I will allow you to continue your research—assuming your boss will still employ you—on two conditions. One, that you agree to focus on helping women who can't carry their pregnancies to term, not on impregnating men. And, two, that you agree to follow every single best practice and norm for your research, and not get ahead of yourself ever again. Am I clear?"

"Yes, ma'am," Hope repeated.

Judge Lorraine Jackson liked when defendants showed her the respect she deserved.

"I am also sentencing you to three years of probation. I am not sentencing you to a lifelong obligation to be lawfully registered as a sex offender and, further, I am not ordering you to complete a state approved rehabilitation program for sex offenders. I do not believe your particular case warrants those penalties. Do you understand just how much harsher a penalty I could have sentenced you to?"

"Yes, ma'am, I do," Hope repeated yet again. "Thank you."

"Well, in that case, we are adjourned." She banged her gavel, closed her notebook, and walked off the dais and into her chambers, ignoring the chaos that once again filled the courtroom.

Hope turned to her lawyer and asked, "Does this mean what I think it means?"

The man-boy could once again hardly breathe, but managed to say, "You're... you're free to go." He put his head in his hands and sat that way for quite a while. It was his first win as a practicing attorney after ten consecutive losses.

Hope turned to the gallery and saw Charlie, Billy, and Faye. Charlie had a huge, crooked grin on his face. Billy looked like a weight had been lifted from his life, which, she supposed, it had. Faye, forever stern, was not smiling, but Hope noticed that her eyes were moist.

Hope ran to Charlie, who wrapped her in a powerful bear hug. She squeezed back with all her might.

Releasing herself, she kissed him on his cheek.

"Oh, Charlie!"

"I know, kiddo. I know," Charlie said. He subtly nodded his head in the direction of Billy Valentine, who had supported Hope just as much as he had, even if she didn't fully realize it yet.

Hope turned to Billy, reached up and held his head with both of her hands, and kissed him on his lips. It wasn't a full-on smooch, but it was the first time they'd kissed.

"Let's have a real date," she said. "This Friday. Pick me up at six?"

Billy smiled his Prince William smile and energetically bobbed his head.

Finally, Hope turned to Dr. Faye Young, her friend and mentor. And boss, still, maybe?

"I am appalled by what you've done. I hope you realize that," Faye said.

"I do."

"Are you going to apologize?"

Hope considered the question. "Honestly, I don't know."

Faye wasn't happy with Hope's answer, but let things go for the moment. She appreciated that at least Hope hadn't offered up an insincere apology. And, besides, there was the not-so-small matter of a hundred million dollar research grant that was directly attributable to Hope Hunter's high profile actions.

"Come by tomorrow at nine. We can talk about you coming back to work at the Research Lab. On a probationary status."

Hope, not reading all of the reasons behind the pained look on Faye's face, reached out and hugged her, catching her mentor by surprise.

"I'll be there."

Chapter Forty-Eight

That Friday, Billy made reservations for two at Trattoria Don Giovanni, a tiny Italian restaurant in downtown Palo Alto. The owner, a jovial man who wore long, colorful ties over his protruding belly, welcomed Billy and Hope with hugs when they arrived for their seven o'clock table. They'd come to the cozy hole in the wall with incredible pasta and rotisserie chicken several times before Hope had gone to Washington and then to prison.

"Bentornato! Bentornata!" Welcome back.

"Thank you, Giovanni. We're happy to be back." Billy and Hope looked at each other and their eyes agreed: happier than you'll ever know.

Giovanni sat the couple at a table for two near the window. A waiter soon approached with a basket of breadsticks and small containers of butter and olive oil and balsamic vinegar.

"Anything to drink tonight?"

Hope normally didn't drink when they went out, but of course that was because she usually had a shift at the hospital or work at the lab early the following morning. Billy glanced at her and then turned to the waiter. "A bottle of Chianti, please."

When the waiter left, Billy said, "I like your hair," taking Hope's hands in his own.

Hope had curled her hair for what felt like a special night, in a sort of salute to Angel. She was self-conscious about it and blushed at the compliment.

"Of course, I like it straight, too," Billy said, nervous his compliment would be weaponized against him. He squeezed her hands and Hope smiled.

When the waiter arrived to take their order, Hope ordered the rotisserie chicken, her usual and the house specialty, and Billy ordered linguini and clams, one of his favorites. They sipped their wine and talked while they waited for their food.

"Thank you again for coming to the courthouse every day," Hope said. "It really was unnecessary."

"You're welcome again," Billy replied. "And, yes, it was necessary. I get to decide that, not you." He smiled, grabbed a breadstick, dunked it in the oil and vinegar, and took a bite.

"How did you get so much time off from work?"

"I almost never take any vacation days. You were always busy with your residency and at the lab, so I knew you wouldn't be able to go anywhere with me. Plus, you know, it's not like we were at that point in our relationship." Billy sighed. "I really don't have any desire to go on vacation alone. Plus I like my work."

Hope reached out and pulled Billy's hands to the middle of the table, their fingers curled together. "Well, once you replenish your balance of vacation days, count me in. I'm going to have a great deal more free time now."

"That would be nice," Billy said. "I'd like that very much."

"Me too." Hope was surprised to realize that she meant it. Billy really had been one of the good guys through everything, especially considering the distance she'd put between them.

Dinner was delicious and slow-paced, as Billy hoped it would be. They finished off the bottle of Chianti and he ordered a second. He found himself wondering if alcohol consumption at restaurants went up with the recent adoption of fully automated cars, as they had when ride sharing services were introduced.

Billy and Hope shared a flourless chocolate cake for dessert, their spoons occasionally clacking as they went in for bites of the decadent treat.

As they finished the cake, Billy reached into his pocket and showed Hope a hotel key. Hope met his eyes, reached out for his hands again and squeezed them, and nodded her head.

"Are you sure?" Billy asked.

"Yes," Hope said. "I love you, Billy."

Billy's smile could have lit a small Italian village. "It's about damn time. Been way ahead of you on that front. Oh, and call me 'William' from now on. I reserve my full name only for a woman in love with me."

It was Hope's turn to beam her magnificent smile. So that's why he insisted I call him Billy before.

Four Seasons Hotel
East Palo Alto, California

Decades earlier, East Palo Alto had been the ugly little sister to the beauty that was her neighbor, Palo Alto. Then, slowly but surely, the city made strides to reduce crime and become more upscale, and the city took a major leap forward in 2006 when the Four Seasons Hotel opened along Highway 101.

After paying the bill and a quick five-minute ride, William led Hope to the suite he'd reserved at the luxurious hotel.

"Wow," Hope said, looking at the nicest hotel room she'd ever seen.

"Wow indeed," William said, looking at Hope.

Hope blushed at the compliment. "Listen, William, I, uh, haven't ever done this before."

"Shh. We'll go as slow as you want, and you'll tell me how you're feeling, what you need, and what you want."

Hope loved this man with all her heart. She turned to him and kissed him passionately. The kiss lasted several minutes, as they stood in the center of the suite. It was their first real kiss, and Hope's first real kiss since that day way back at the Louisiana State Fair over eleven years earlier. Todd had been cute, she remembered, but William was a man, and a man that loved her.

"Wow," Hope said again.

"Wow indeed." William said.

Billy wrapped his arms around Hope's waist and started to turn slowly. Hope realized what he was doing and stretched her arms around his neck. They slowly danced there, in the center of the room, with no music, and Hope thought it was the most romantic thing she could imagine. After several minutes, Billy stepped back and said, "God, I love your body."

Hope demurred, saying, "Really? I've always thought my breasts were too small."

Billy grinned. "Oh, believe me, I will definitely show them the appreciation they deserve." He looked toward the bedroom but didn't move.

Hope realized he was asking her to lead, if she was ready. She was. She slowly led William to the bedroom by her fingertips. She was clearly nervous, but she did not hesitate.

Later, when Hope screamed during their lovemaking, it wasn't in pain or fear; it was from release, and the first joy she'd felt in years.

Chapter Forty-Nine

Sunday, September 16 (two days later)
Zeline Yearwood's house
Perryton, Texas

Charlie, Quinn, and Sanam formed their opinion of Miss Zeline Yearwood's house as they approached: shithole. A half flight of bare concrete steps led up to the front door, which had a ripped screen door bouncing in the wind. The 1,100-square-foot house had moldy, peeling siding over a tan brick base. The yard was nothing but straw and dirt.

They entered the side door to the one-and-a-half car garage and began their search. Within a minute, Quinn had found what they were looking for: a loose piece of drywall that, when moved, revealed a cache of handguns, marijuana, condoms, and bundles of cash. Quinn pocketed the cash and put the drywall back in its place. "Okay, let's do this."

The men quietly closed the door to the garage and made their way to the front of the house. The street, which only had a few other homes scattered along its length, was deathly quiet. As they approached the front door, they could hear angry yelling inside the house. It was an hour after sundown and a chill was in the air.

From inside, they heard a man's voice say, "How many times do I have to tell you, you stupid bitch? Have my dinner ready when I come home from work. How hard is that?"

"That our man?" Quinn asked Charlie.

"Yep. Quite the charmer, huh?" It had taken him two years to track the son of a bitch down.

"Let's do this," Sanam urged. "It's freezing out here."

Charlie knocked on the door and stepped back. After a few moments he realized the couple was still arguing and not coming to the door. He knocked again. Just before the door opened, he could have sworn he heard a loud smacking sound.

The door swung open and a man wearing a wife beater t-shirt and patchy stubble on his face said, "Whadda *you* want?"

"You Derek Johnson, originally from Houston?" Charlie asked, already knowing the answer. The man, now twenty-eight, looked almost exactly like his high school yearbook picture and his old pictures on social media. Well, except for his forehead, which had already receded, and the beer belly, which had already formed.

"Yeah. I'll ask again: Whadda you want?"

"May we come in?"

"No, you may no—"

Before Derek could finish his objection, Charlie forced his way past him and into the house. Quinn and Sanam followed.

"Hi," Quinn said, a wide grin on his face, when Derek gave him a "who the fuck are you?" look.

A woman, presumably Zeline Yearwood, came out of the kitchen. She had a bag of frozen peas against her cheek. Charlie boiled inside, realizing he was right about the smacking sound he'd heard.

"Who... who... who are you?" Zeline asked.

"Zeline?" Charlie asked.

"Yes."

Sanam asked, "What kind of name is 'Zeline', anyway?"

"What kind of watch is that, anyway?" Quinn asked Sanam, poking at his friend for asking an inappropriate question by asking one of his own. Sanam's watch, another new one, only had words on it, which spelled out the time in English sentences.

Charlie shot Sanam and Quinn a look, but the woman ignored Quinn and answered Sanam's question. She'd clearly heard the question many times before. "My momma was a fan of Celine Dion but she wanted me to have a bit of extra 'flair.' That's what she called it. She was nuts."

Derek raised his voice and said to his unwelcome visitors, "Get out of my house. Now."

"My house, Derek. It's *my* house," Zeline Yearwood said.

"Not anymore, and you know it. You signed the papers of your own free will, ain't that right?" He'd convinced the woman, who had gotten the fully paid-off house when her mother died, to put him on the title. Legally, the house was half his now. Practically speaking, it was his, given how scared she was of him. Stupid bitch.

Charlie looked Zeline directly in the eyes and spoke softly. "Zeline, your friend here is not a nice guy." He could see the "tell me about it" look in her eyes. "We're friends of someone whose life he destroyed over a decade ago. It's taken quite a while, but we've finally tracked him down and intend to make things right, if you understand what I'm saying."

Quinn and Sanam moved to flank Derek, who was now starting to realize just how much trouble he was in.

"He hurts me," Zeline said in practically a whisper. "All the time."

"Listen to me carefully Zeline. You shacked up with a really bad dude. You know that. We're offering you a way out," Charlie said. He nodded to Quinn who tossed him the wads of cash they'd taken from Derek's hiding spot. "Take this. Derek here has been holding out on you. Bury it in that nice flower bed you have in back for a few days until the police fade out of the picture."

Derek, who saw his cash fly across the room, started toward the bedroom, presumably to get a weapon, when Quinn wheeled around and palmed him in the solar plexus. He crumpled to the floor, and Quinn noticed a smile escape from Zeline's makeup-laden face.

Charlie continued, "You are not going to want to be here for what happens next. Go to a friend's house, to a bar, wherever you might normally go. Maybe to the grocery store. Yeah. That's it. Go grocery shopping and take a nice, long time. When the police ask, explain that you hadn't had anything in the house to make your boyfriend for dinner and needed to shop."

Zeline understood what was going to happen, if perhaps not the particulars. These men were going to scare, hurt, or kill Derek, the creep, and were offering her a chance at an alibi. She nodded vigorously. Clutching the bundles of cash, she grabbed a sweater from the coat rack in the corner of the living room and said, "Give me a few minutes to bury this in the back. You'll hear my car when I leave." She leaned in and gave Charlie a peck on the cheek and added, "And... thank you, whoever you are."

By the time the men heard Zeline drive away, they had Derek Johnson unconscious, gagged, and roped down on the kitchen table.

As Derek Johnson, serial rapist, regained his senses, he was terrified to realize he was tied down with the three men standing over him. He was even more terrified to realize that his pants were down around his ankles, and that the older man had a cleaver in his hand. Just before he passed out, the man lifted the cleaver and said, "You won't be needing this anymore." Derek Johnson bled to death soon thereafter.

Quinn, who had drawn the short straw, put the man's privates in a small box, which they would send to the home address of a certain high-ranking legal professional who worked in a fancy building at One First Street, NE, Washington, D.C.: Associate Justice of the Supreme Court, Julian Kingsley.

Chapter Fifty

Senator Royce Carrington lay in his hospital bed, looking down at his distended belly. It was something he did often since that fateful day. As someone who had always been trim, it was a strange feeling to look down and see an enormous stomach protruding from his body. It seemed so... alien. He supposed it was, in a sense.

After fully recovering from the surgery, something that was made more difficult by his decision to call the early vote on the "Sanctity of Life" bill, Carrington had faced a decision. Should he come up with some excuse to hide from the public eye for up to nine months? In the end, the decision was easy.

At first, it was difficult to conduct regular business as a Senator. Once he started "showing," his colleagues and members of the press all wanted to talk to him about it. What did it feel like? How did he feed the baby, given that his "plumbing" was different from a woman's? Did he think he would give birth to a healthy baby? Later, as his belly got even bigger, everyone wanted to touch his stomach. He resented the invasion of personal space when people reached out and rubbed his stomach without asking his permission. For a long time, it made his blood pressure rise every time someone would ask, "When are you due?"

The worst part was having to give up his brandy and cigars.

Carrington was wealthy enough to pay an obstetrician to come to his home. He couldn't stomach the idea of having to go to an OB-GYN office and wait in the waiting room with a bunch of pregnant women. The doctor indicated that it was likely the fetus was fully developed and likely healthy, based on the baby's vital signs.

Now, in his private hospital room, outside of the intrusive eye of the press and the judgmental eye of most of his Senate colleagues, he was ready to "give birth." What a crazy world that that phrase applied to him, he thought.

The surgeon performed a modified Cesarean section. The operation, commonly known as a C-section, while relatively safe, is still major surgery and carries risks. Still, Carrington had hand-picked this doctor. He was more worried about the health of the baby than his own.

When the surgeon removed Hope's artificial womb through Carrington's abdomen, he couldn't help but admire the device. It had served its purpose well: when he removed the baby, he was a healthy six-pound, five-ounce pink little boy with ten fingers and ten toes.

The labor and delivery nurse administered the Apgar test to the baby and announced to the doctor that the score was an eight. The surgeon once again found himself admiring Hope's device. Truly remarkable. The baby's skin color, heart rate, reflexes, muscle tone, and breathing rate were all well into the healthy range. Still, he would recommend to the Senator that the baby undergo frequent checkups for the first few years of its life.

Later, when Carrington came out of the effects of the anesthesia, he was united with his baby. He obviously couldn't breastfeed the infant, but the nurse lay the little guy on his chest and Carrington was beyond ecstatic that the baby dozed peacefully, his little body rising and falling as he breathed. Carrington gently uncurled his son's tiny fingertips and found himself in awe of nature and of human life. He silently praised God. Tears of joy slid down his cheeks.

The nurse, noticing the Senator's emotions, quietly left the room. She came back a half an hour later to tell Carrington she was going to take the baby to the infirmary for a few more tests and to feed him. Carrington gently kissed the baby on his forehead before she took him. She smiled warmly at the man because of his obvious love for the child, surprising herself. She was well aware of the man's politics and history of voting to systematically limit or abolish women's reproductive rights, his recent surprise vote notwithstanding. She silently thanked

Hope Hunter, whoever she was. Maybe now things would change.

The following morning, the doctor stopped by on his rounds. After a quick checkup, he declared the Senator to be in good health.

"You'll need to rest for several days, but you'll be fine."

"Thanks, doc. For everything."

"Well, it was a first for me, I'll say that."

Carrington said nothing.

The doctor took a deep breath and steeled himself for what he had to say next. He needed to get through it with a straight face. "Listen, I have to tell you," he said, "that having a C-section— which is pretty much the procedure you underwent—can raise the risk of having difficulties with future pregnancies, and you may have problems attempting a vaginal birth later." He stopped driving the nail of his thumb into his forefinger.

"What the hell are you telling me that for? Is that your idea of a sick joke? I'll have your medical license—"

"Sir," the doctor said calmly, ignoring Carrington's unfinished threat, "The law clearly states that as your attending physician I must inform you of the possible consequences of having a C-section."

Carrington was still enraged, but if nothing else he respected the law despite the fact he wasn't able to put his finger on the particular statute the doctor was citing.

"If you don't like the law, Senator," the doctor said, "you could change it. After all, it's a provision in the 'Family Values Sex Education' bill you sponsored several years ago. And if I may say, it's one of the *least* offensive provisions in that bill."

With that, the doctor turned and left.

Senator Royce Carrington stewed for a few minutes, stinging from the man's rebuke. As a U.S. Senator, and a powerful one at that, he was in a position to change the law, especially one he himself had had a hand in passing, despite having not read it carefully.

More significantly, though, Carrington was still basking in the warm glow of having brought a baby into the world, however odd the circumstances. Nothing would interfere with his enjoyment of the new life he helped bring into the world.

Chapter Fifty-One

Saturday, December 15 (two weeks later)
George Washington Hospital
Washington, D.C.

Two weeks later
Forty weeks after Reverend Brooks' impregnation

Reverend Porter Brooks was a tired, broken man. He was mad as hell at the crazy woman who put a baby in his body against his will. He was mad as hell at the infernal judge who'd let her off after just six months in prison. He was mad as hell at the world. And he was deeply, deeply embarrassed.

Brooks had spent the past nine months in hiding. At first, he'd needed to recover from the surgery he'd undergone. He was not a young man, and he wasn't in the best of health to begin with. After he fully recovered, he faced the same decision Royce had, but made a different choice: to remain out of the public eye. His phone rang nonstop and social media was flooded with memes about his being pregnant. He had no choice but to stop answering the phone and to stay off of social media. For a man who craved attention and public affection, the months were like purgatory. He'd remained out of the courtroom during Hope Hunter's trial. God, how he hated that woman. And Judge Lorraine Jackson, too.

Reverend Brooks couldn't fathom his friend's decision to maintain his normal life while carrying an unwanted child. The idea seemed unbearable. When Royce gave birth and called him to tell him the news, the Senator was downright giddy. Brooks couldn't understand it, and thought his friend was nuts. Brooks would have had an abortion, if that was even the proper term, but he knew his career as a Reverend would be over in a second if he did. The irony of his views didn't occur to him, despite being someone who claimed that every life was sacred. The best he could do was somehow live through the pregnancy and give the devil child up for adoption.

Carrington graciously allowed Brooks to use the services of his personal physician, who now was focused exclusively on helping the Reverend reach the end of his ordeal. Brooks had struggled for the months of his "pregnancy." Somehow, he experienced more problems with the device, his body fighting fiercely to reject the foreign body within. His stomach had distended to an almost comical extreme, almost as if he was carrying twins. The doctor had told Brooks that everything was fine despite his inability to get clear x-rays due to the stainless steel and titanium mesh Hope had used.

Finally, after forty weeks of hell, Carrington's physician told Brooks it was time to deliver the baby. He explained the procedure he would perform, the same one he'd performed on Carrington.

In the birthing suite at the hospital, Brooks lay sweating and panting in bed. Despite not understanding his friend's apparent happiness given all that had happened, Brooks invited Royce to be present. Carrington thought it was to share in his confrère's joy, but Brooks' real reason was that he needed someone to help him through the ordeal. He was going crazy from the thought that a human being was going to be removed from his body, one that was put there without his permission.

Carrington stood at the side of Brooks' bed, holding his baby, rocking slowly side to side.

"How are you doing?" Carrington asked.

"How the *fuck* do you think I'm doing?"

"Now, now, Reverend. That's no way to talk. Especially in front of a child." He nodded down to his son in his arms. "Isn't he wonderful?"

"Oh, fuck off, Royce. That baby is an abomination and you know it.

The nurse prepped her patient as quietly and invisibly as possible. It was all she could do to hold back her laughter at the Reverend's behavior. Man of God, my ass, she thought. Within a few minutes, her work was done and she slunk away before incurring Brooks' wrath.

The doctor entered the room, fully garbed in surgical scrubs, except for a mask and gloves, which he would don once in the operating room. The nurse returned with him, also in surgical scrubs.

To Brooks he said, "Okay. Here we go." To Carrington he said, "Senator, you can wait in the waiting room."

The nurse wheeled Reverend Brooks down the hall and into one of the surgical bays. The anesthesiologist put the man to sleep. After the man's bloated stomach was rubbed down with Betadine, the doctor ran his scalpel across the Reverend's abdomen and removed the artificial womb from the man's body.

The doctor and nurses could all tell immediately that something was very, very wrong. When the doctor opened the gibbous artificial womb to remove the baby, one of the nurses passed out and another vomited.

Inside the artificial womb was a baby lamb.

Epilogue

Senator Royce Carrington was sitting in the waiting room cooing at his son and admiring the sounds of someone playing piano in the atrium below when the surgeon came out to get him. He could tell immediately that something had gone wrong. He prayed the baby was healthy and that his friend had come through the surgery okay. When the surgeon asked to speak to him in private, Carrington walked, his son in his arms, behind the doctor to the man's private office. It was there that Carrington learned what happened.

The doctor kindly let Carrington sit in his office for as long as it might take for him to process what he'd just been told. Carrington took full advantage, sitting numbly for a half an hour until his son's cries of hunger stirred him from his funk. He took a bottle of formula from his bag and fed the baby, trying to hide his upset from the little guy. Hope Hunter was one cold-blooded warrior, he had to give her that much. And, he realized, she was out of jail. Out there somewhere. He made a mental note not to go anywhere near Faye Young's lab if Hope Hunter went back to work there.

Carrington walked to the recovery area to visit his friend, but Brooks was still out from the anesthesia he'd been given for the surgery. Carrington asked the nurse to tell Brooks that he had stopped by and that he would call him later. For the first time in his life, he had absolutely no idea what he would say.

Senator Royce Carrington's Home
Village of Oyster Bay Cove, Nassau County, New York

Carrington made it home an hour before the monthly Benevolent Overlords Society meeting. Between the sleepless nights of single parenthood and the shock of today's events, Carrington wanted to cancel, but there was simply no way he was going to break nearly two hundred years of tradition. The meeting would go on, no matter what.

At eight, Carrington and Julian Kingsley sat in Carrington's study. Carrington's nanny was with the baby in the upstairs room he had made into a nursery. Carrington nursed a brandy and watched with disgust as Kingsley chugged a beer at the bar, then opened two more and took them to where he was sitting.

"You have a serious problem," Carrington said. The word 'serious' dripped with disdain.

Kingsley said nothing. He sipped on one of the beers.

Reverend Brooks was still recovering at the hospital, so it was just the two of them. Carrington said the standard opening prayer and performed the standard ritual with the card stock. He sloppily wrote 2160 on the new card and tossed it carelessly into his desk drawer.

"What's wrong with you?" Kingsley asked. He had never seen the Senator so agitated.

Carrington explained to Kingsley what had happened at the hospital.

"That's sick! That's perverted!" Kingsley's skin turned red and blotchy, something that happened when he became angry. "I can't believe that judge let that bitch go free. She needs to be—"

Carrington found himself wondering if his son was resting peacefully. The little guy was so adorable. Maybe it was just gas, but it sure seemed like he smiled an awful lot.

"Royce! Royce! Are you listening to me?"

"Sorry, what?"

"Never mind. What are we planning to do about this bitch?"

"Nothing. And that's final. You understand me?"

Kingsley didn't understand, so he changed the topic. "And what are we planning to do about preventing women from getting abortions?"

Carrington had been thinking deeply about what to do about the subject since that fateful day nine months earlier. Did Hope Hunter's stunt with Brooks' baby lamb change things? No, he decided.

"Nothing. It's time to move on to do something on the immigration front. Maybe something to fight against homosexuality, too."

Kingsley was angry. "I did what you asked years ago. I got *Roe* overturned. You wouldn't believe the hate mail I get because of it. And I would have found a way to uphold the 'Sanctity of Life' law too.

I don't know how, but I would have done it. If nothing else, I think I can get a majority to overturn *Vuitch,* so we can probably throw a monkey in the wrench of most of the state abortion laws." He was referring to the 1971 case in which Hugo Black wrote a five-four decision that a Washington D.C. statute prohibiting abortion unless necessary for the preservation for the mother's life or health was unconstitutionally vague.

"I'm not going to argue with you, Julian. I think you blew it when you resorted to a states' rights argument to overturn *Roe.* Maybe you had to, I don't know. But we'll never know because the national anti-abortion legislation is dead. It will never be resurrected, at least as long as I'm a Senator."

"Is this because of what happened to Reverend Brooks?"

"No, you idiot. It's because of what happened to me."

"What do you mean?"

"I was, for all intents and purposes, raped." It was hard for Carrington, a man of power, to admit this. But he wanted Kingsley to understand. "In my case, I wanted to carry the baby to term. I actually believe the things I say and fight for in the Senate." He wanted to say "unlike Porter" after witnessing the Reverend's true nature at the hospital earlier in the day, but didn't. "But I finally see an important point: I might not have wanted to go through with it. Hell, Porter didn't want to. He never told me so, but I could tell. Let's just say I've walked a mile in high heels and now I have a greater appreciation for a woman's perspective."

Kingley didn't know what to say. He needed the Senator as an ally in his efforts to punish the women who'd almost ruined his life.

Carrington read Kingsley's mind. "Julian, you have serious anger issues. This isn't about the women that came forth and testified against you. This is about all women. And, maybe, someday soon, about all men too. Think about that."

If there ever was a man tortured by conflicting thoughts, it was Julian Kingsley. He was horrified at the thought of having what happened to Carrington and Brooks happen to him. Yet, one doesn't just magically let go of years of holding a grudge.

Carrington realized he would never really get Kingsley—or anyone else, in all likelihood—to fully understand what it felt like to be violated like he was. For someone used to a lifetime of power, it had been, until now, inconceivable to him how powerless he'd felt. Kingsley would likely never come to understand. He decided to push the conversation forward.

"Look, this group exists to push a wide-ranging Christian agenda. We are not focussed on a single issue. Let's switch gears. I think we need to find a test case somewhere, probably Arizona, under 8 U.S. Code § 1158."

"Asylum?" Kingsley asked. "What do you have in mind?" Kingsley was the courtroom equivalent of a "gym rat." He memorized the U.S. Code for fun.

"I was re-reading the statute. One of the exceptions under 'Conditions for Granting Asylum' is if the Attorney General determines that there are reasonable grounds for regarding the alien as a danger to the security of the United States."

"Sure. We've used that for years, at least in many cases as we can."

"Right, but I've been thinking... What if widened our definition of what constitutes a dang to the security of the United States?"

Kingsley hated when Carrington tried to use t Socratic method on him. He'd hated it in law scho and wanted no part of it now that he'd risen to position on the nation's highest court.

"Disease. Infection. Pestilence. Contagior Kingsley said. He understood where Carrington w headed. It reminded him of stories from Ellis Islar in the early 1900s.

"Exactly. Use the fact that they haven't bee properly vaccinated and hence pose a grave thre to the security of the United States. All we have do is find one case of bubonic plague or whateve Or just let people think we have."

"I think we can make that work," Kingsley sai excited. "If it gets to us, I'll be able to construct strong legal argument supporting a ban based c this idea. *Jennings v. Rodriguez* from about ten fifteen years ago comes to mind. I'm reluctant count votes, especially since I never know what th chief is going to do, but I think we can make work."

The two men ironed out the details. Carringto was good at this; he'd had decades of practice. H had a clear picture of what he wanted to hav happen. They would find an unattractive, scar looking, illiterate young man from Mexico or Sout America and arrange for him to be denied asylur because he lacked the proper vaccinations. The they would anonymously sponsor his defense by th ACLU or some liberal do-gooders who wouldn realize they were being used. When the case got to court, the poor sap would lose his case, but Carrington would achieve his goal. Along the way, they'd find someone in the press to run with a rumor that the man had some horrific disease. Causing a panic wasn't that bad if it led to the outcome he wanted.

An hour later, the plan had pretty much come into shape. Kingsley was still sore that he wouldn't get to uphold the "Sanctity of Life" law, but he went along. The country was overrun by these disease-infested aliens, and he needed to help put a stop to it.

"Let's see what's going on in the news," Carrington said when they concluded their conversation. He clicked on the television which was already tuned to Fox News.

Much to their displeasure, the lead story was that at least ten states were working on legislation to remove restrictions on abortion. The Senators and Congressmen interviewed, all of whom were men, were clearly spooked. The female reporter who was reporting from the steps of the Ohio state Capitol had a smirk on her face and concluded her remarks by saying, "Perhaps these moves have something to do with the fact that men can now get pregnant. I'm Anna Kissinger from Columbus, Ohio. Back to you Sean."

"I told you—" Kinsley started to say.

"Can it. Hope Hunter won this round. Deal with it. We live to fight another day." He made another mental note to call Faye Young and ensure she was hiring all the researchers and buying all the equipment she needed.

Meanwhile...
A snowy hill
Somewhere in the United States

As the sun set over the horizon, the temperatu
dropped, but the children sledding on the hill we
having too much fun to notice.

A boy wearing a lime green down jacket and
bright orange wool cap took off with a running sta
and went down on his stomach. He whooped an
hollered as he slid down the hill, and almo
crashed into a tree at the bottom. Another we
down in a disc and flew off of it when he went ov
the makeshift ramp he'd made about half wa
down.

A slight, sinewy girl, just a few months shy of h
tenth birthday, climbed the last few feet to the to
and carefully lined herself up for her run. From
very young age, she'd been like this, alwa
carefully planning, always needing to contr
situations as much as possible. After visualizing th
path she would take between the other kid
climbing up the hill and the various tree branche
and other rough patches, she pushed forward wit
both hands. Down she went.

At the bottom of the hill, she lost control of he
sled and crashed into a boy from her class a
school. He saw it coming and was able to avoid th
worst, but still ended up in a pile on top of her.

"Whoa! You okay Isabelle?"

She liked that he was concerned for her, despit
the fact that she'd crashed into him.

She grabbed his mittened hand in hers and said
"Come on! Let's go down together!" And as she an
the boy swung their arms and climbed back up th

hill while holding hands, Isabelle's adoptive parents watched with smiles on their faces.

Afterword

Imagine a technology, like the artificial womb described in this book, that is geared toward saving premature infants. Imagine that it is meant not for transplanting the unwanted fetuses into other people's bodies, but rather into a medically safe environment where they could safely mature until "birth." Aside from the fact that such technology is beyond our current medical capabilities, would such a device be "a good thing?" Should a woman be able to choose to have her fetus transferred out of her body?

Would right-to-life activists approve? After all, such a technology could prevent or reduce abortions as, presumably, some number of women and young girls would choose to undergo this procedure instead of an abortion. Despite the rhetoric from the extreme right, nobody is "pro abortion."

Would pro-choice activists approve? A procedure like this would allow women to shorten their pregnancies without the need for abortion but might actually make it less likely that states with conservative populations and state governments would carve out abortion exceptions for rape and incest. They could argue that, with such an advancement, the burden to the woman is minimal, perhaps only as little as three months.

How many women would choose to undergo such a procedure? How many of them would do it for reasons unrelated to concerns about their health or the health of their unborn babies? Would all or most women carry their pregnancies to term except for these concerns? Would it be morally acceptable for a woman to undergo such a procedure even if there were no health concerns?

For victims of rape or incest, would such a procedure be helpful or hurtful? Most victims likely feel they want the whole experience erased, wiped from their memory, and want it to be as if they were never pregnant in the first place. Would a procedure that might lead to more births of babies conceived by rape or incest be fair to these women? To the babies born?

The ethical questions here are no less complex than those around abortion.

Thank You

Thank you for reading *Children of Hope*. I sincerely hope you enjoyed reading it. As an independently published author, I rely on you, the reader, to spread the word. If you enjoyed the book, please tell your friends and family. And, if you're willing, please leave a brief review on Amazon. Thanks in advance.

I started writing when my first child was born. I wanted to "journal," but that didn't seem to capture his incredible sense of joy. So instead I started writing short stories that chronicled my children's lives. They are the light of my life, and being a father is the single best role I hold. This book is dedicated to them, especially my daughter. I hope she never has to live in a world like the one portrayed in my novel.

—Mike

Visit me on the web at **blackfoxbooks.com** or find me on Twitter at **@michaelcfine**.

Made in the USA
Middletown, DE
28 March 2021

35675596R00210